U X A

·

G O V

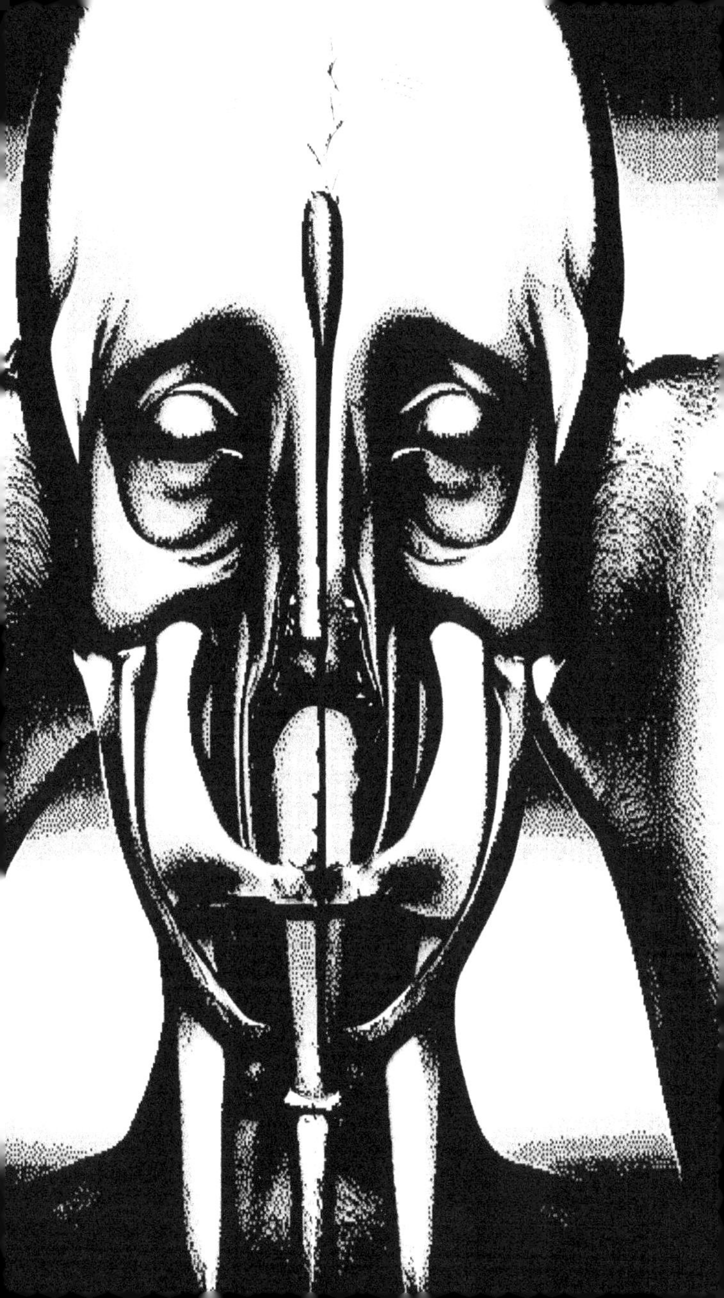

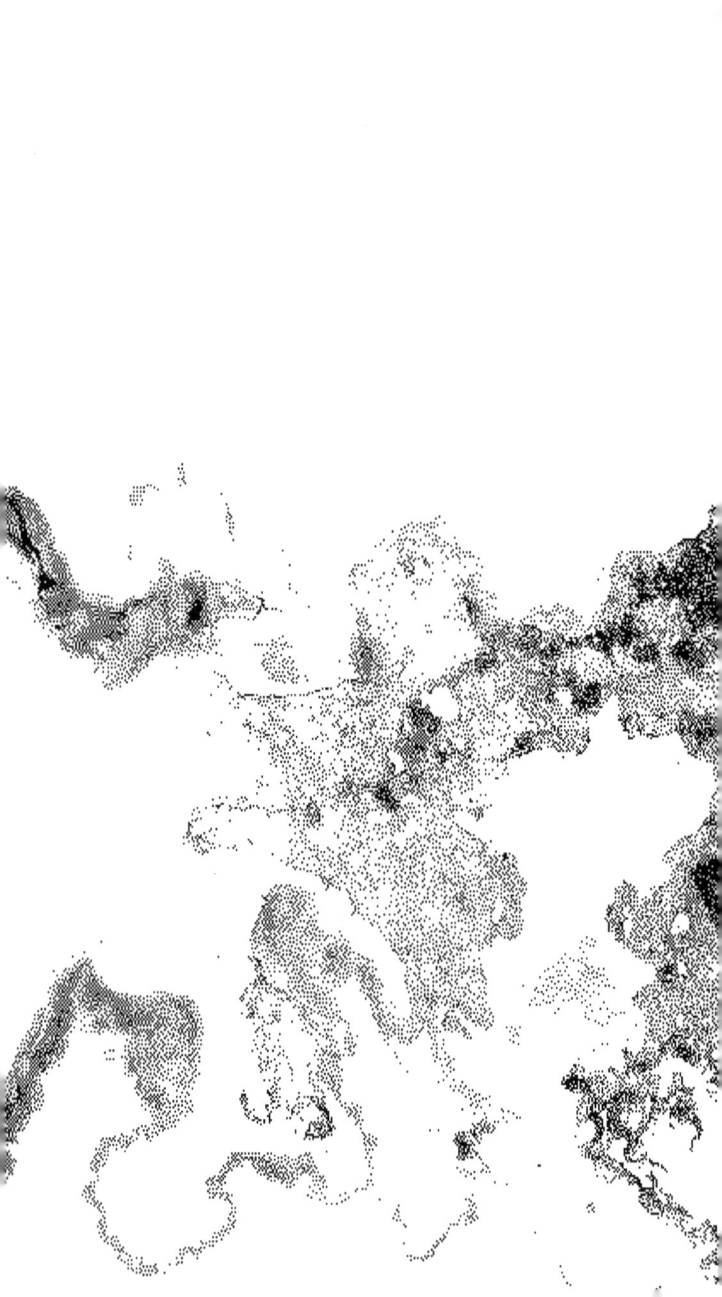

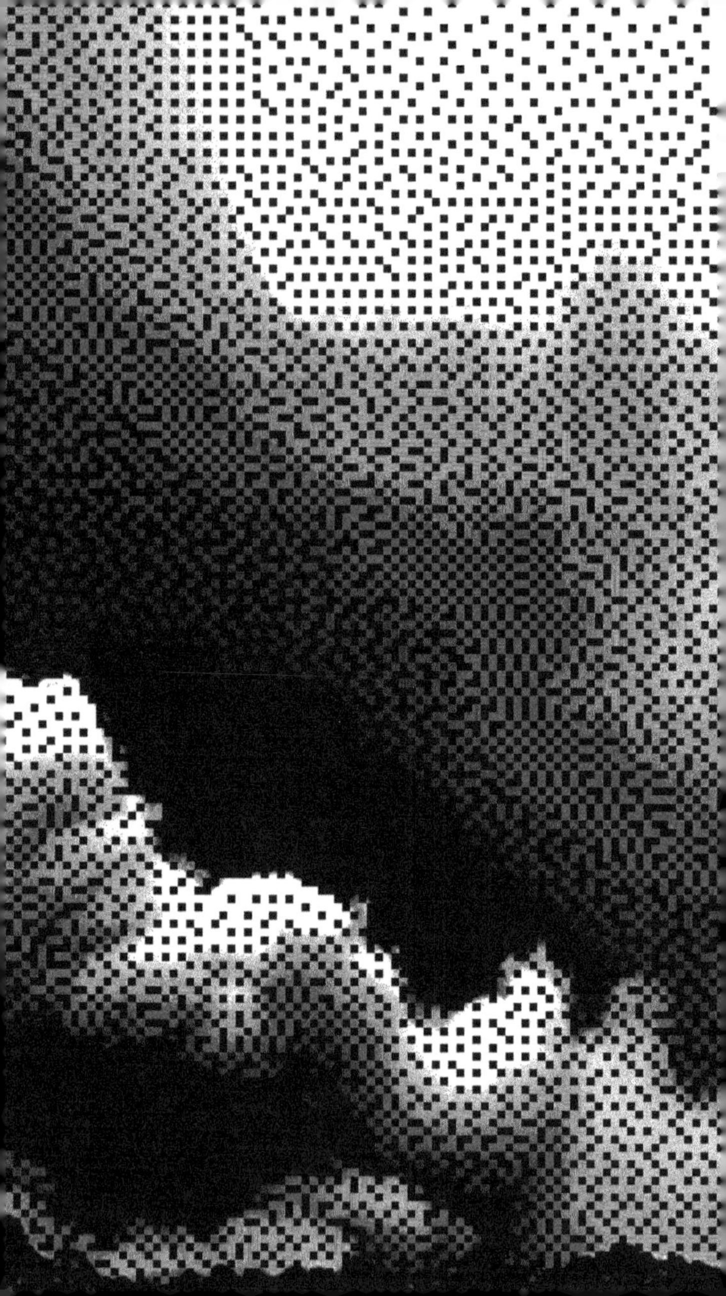

This text was composed and revised in fits and starts from 2010 to 2024, often in wildly different states, rooms, moods, modes, spirits, and epochs. It began as a response to John Zorn's "Treatment for a Film in Fifteen Scenes" (composed in the 1980s; published in *Arcana: Musicians on Music.* Zorn, J. (ed), Granary Books, 2000, alongside work by Ikue Mori, Bill Frisell, Eyvind Kang, Marc Ribot, Mike Patton, etc.), a 7-page outline consisting of 254 'shots' (or prompts) described by brief (1-12 word) lines of all caps text. As a novel, *UXA. GOV* is meant to be read as a film; perhaps the kind one might otherwise only be allowed to view through slits in a training helmet deep before being work-released into what remains of the land where America once was.

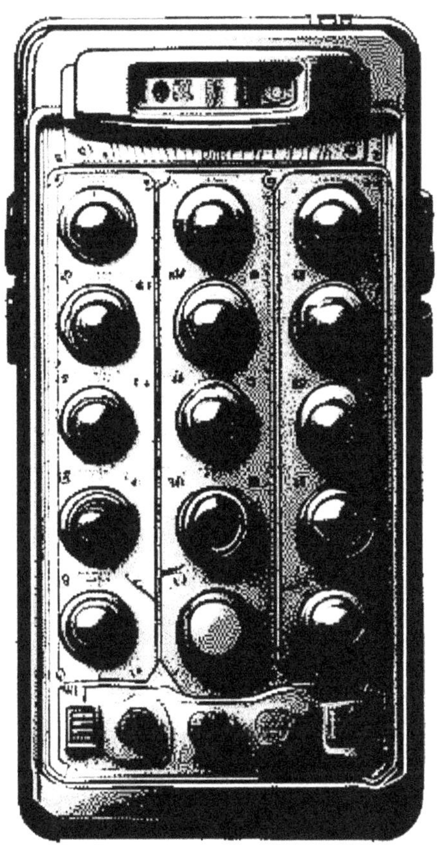

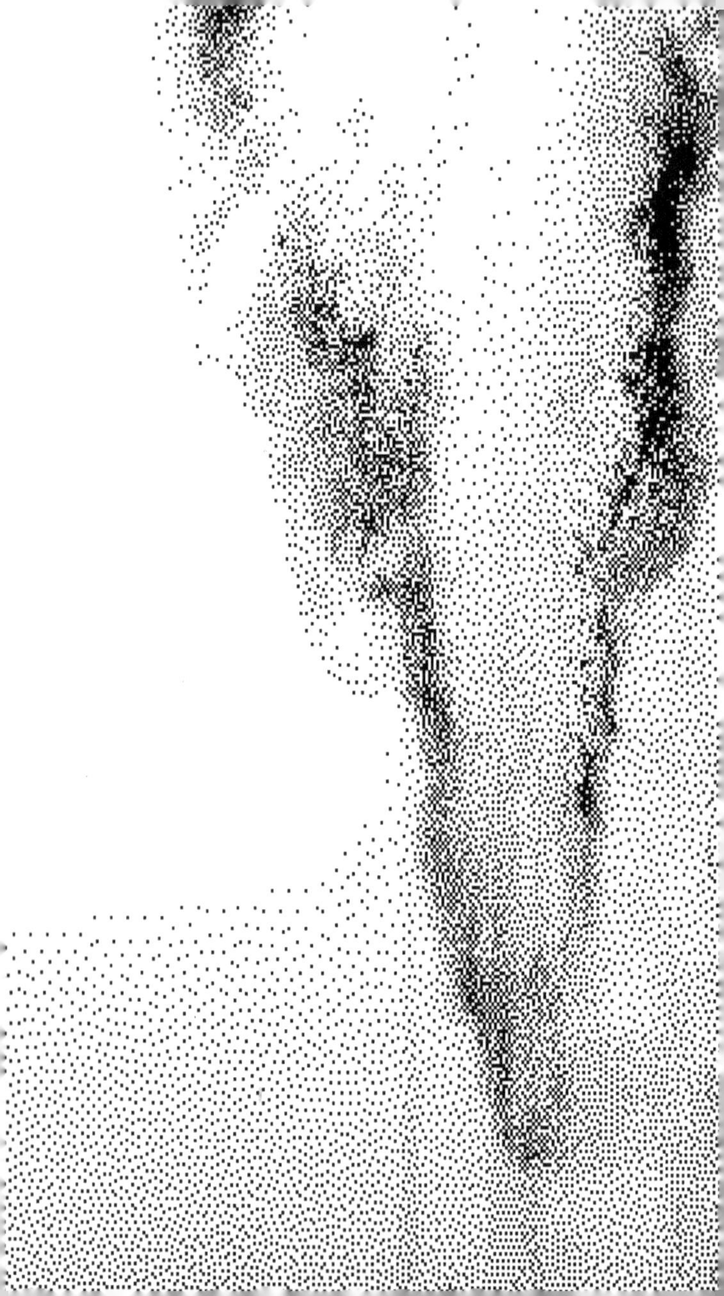

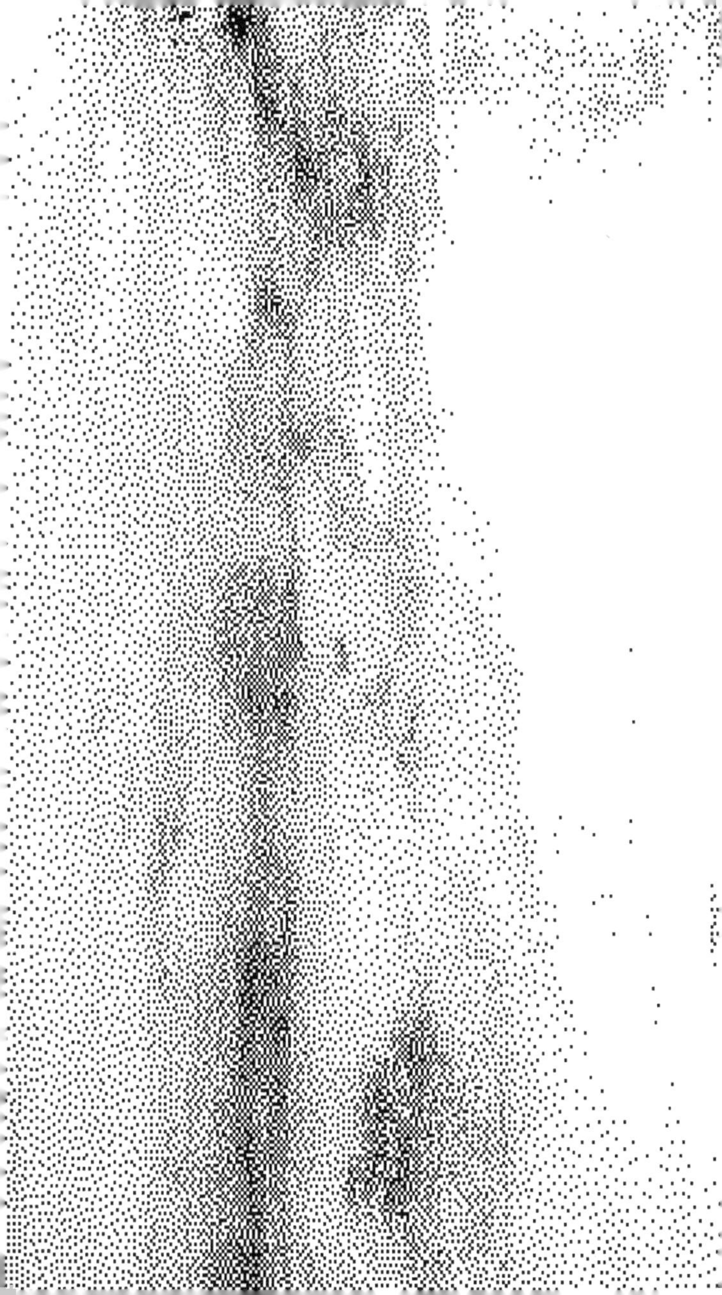

001........The bit forced in the body's mouth is shining chrome. Affixed onto her skull with matching straps that form the flaps over her eyes and bind her shoulders, hips, and ankles to a black platform. Damp branding in the center of the forehead of a symbol there is no way to describe. The only light in the room comes from behind the camera, from something burning where we would be if we were there. No visible motion in the space, nor obvious inlet/outlet beyond the way the pattern of strange bumps on the tight gold walls make the eye go dented and draw a blur, interchanging our sense of vision with a sense much more like music, but only spastic windchimes, teeth on teeth. The body's skin is bruised from head to toe but undetectably. The floor is false, just like a thought.

002........Forced through the floor, all we can see at first are countless scalps, each freshly shaved and marked with the same branding in the same place. It takes some time staring, measuring the patterns of how the lines of each scalp intersect, before we realize that we are looking down upon a throng of naked bodies, forced to stand together side by side so tight there is no room to turn around. As the camera descends, we realize how to make out faces, shoulders, limbs. Despite the lack of space, none of the body language of those enclosed here manifests fear; rather, they look bored, with bloodshot eyes, none of them blinking, even under what appears to be a rising scrim of fallen feces, now at their knees. The only sign they are alive comes from the sound of heavy breathing now filling in over all else, the staccato pulse of all their heartbeats overlaid like heavy rain.

003........Under the fecal: spindly thickets of fibrous prosthetic censors scraping for data, feeding results into the jelly-cluster bead-pods swollen like bellies, each encrusted with innumerable lenses of various size. Smoky musk in ropes pulled taut across pinned lozenges encoded with ghost-residue of unnatural events forced out of sync in their disbursement from the originating organism's encoded memory, first in, last out. The enclosing artificial silence moors void for projection of in-house dialogue against, creating anticipation for some form of narration that might provide more than mere intestinal noise, a vibrational sensation that reminds us there could never be enough of anything, now and forever. We observe until we summarily are consumed and the unspeakable hollow of the branding's pyramidal emblem fills the frame like a viral ad, triggering dead memories, for your pleasure.

004........CHILD IS MISSING : AGE 4, BLONDE, CUTE, CLEAN : LAST SEEN WALKING THROUGH THE DESERT YEAR OF TRASHYARDS BEHIND HER PARENTS' HOUSE : FATHER COULD NOT BE FOUND

FOR QUESTIONING : MOTHER ALSO MISSING BUT HAS BEEN SIGHTED IN LONG FIELDS OF NEIGHBORING AREAS : CHILD IS MISSING, FEMALE BEAUTY CHILD SHE WAS : CHILD IS MISSING : PLEASE CONTACT WITH ANY INFO : ASK FOR MARC

FLOCKS OF BIRDS NEAR WHITE SHORE SEAS FROM WHENCE OUR OXYGEN DERIVES CONTINUE TO BE A PROBLEM : BESIDES THE STINK: THINK OF THE NOISE : WE ARE RECORDING EVERYTHING YOU KNOW : LOCAL VOLUNTEERS HAVE BEEN WORKING SHIFTS TO CAPTURE EGGS AS CAREFULLY AS POSSIBLE IN LITTLE NETS OR CAGES IN CASE OF MATURATION : ALWAYS IN NEED OF WARM GOOD HOMES! : " BUT I CAN'T EVEN GET OUT MY FRONT DOOR," SAYS LOCAL WIDOW : PLEASE DO NOT FEED THE NEWLY DOUR: NO CONSOLATION IS ADVISED

GANG OF FERAL PRETEENS ARRESTED FOR DESECRATION OF LOCAL MAUSOLEUM : GAS FIRES! PAINTBOMBS! TRICKMIRRORS! : SEVERAL UNTITLED PRICELESS IDEOLOGIES POTENTIALLY DESTROYED BEYOND REPAIR : PRETEENS WILL BE TRIED AS SENILE IN THE DEN OF NAILS : AND HOW ARE YOU???

CHILD IS MISSING : AGE 11, BLONDE, SMART,

FOND OF THE TROMBONE : LAST SEEN WALKING FAST AND HEAD DOWN TOWARD LOCATION OF OUR LAST REMEMBERED PROSTHETICS SUPERSTORE : RESPONDS ONLY TO SIGN LANGUAGE : IF LOCATED, PLEASE RESTRAIN!!!!!!

005........The smoke of the language clears. Behind it, the sky remains blank as an empty page, leaving those enclosed stranded at the edge of their memory's imagination all aghast, left to fill in the space of everything no longer there as it can only be through illumination against the common trauma of having once lived some other way, so far outdated from the present that it won't parse beyond its glitch. *At least there is no hope,* one might remind themselves, worn to the nubs. *If there were really any actual hope, I don't think I could stand it.* The words unfurl like blooming tumors, the same kind that they sold fake medication for in malls for the lonely sick before everybody else got sick, too, following the law; and so it wasn't such a thing as all of that to have felt a while a way you wouldn't wish on your worst enemy, because, finally, as the smoke reminds us, suddenly unscrolling in a handwritten font across the wide blank where our long remaindered horizon must once have been: *your only mortal enemy is you.*

006........Exposed flesh gnatty and soft from sitting out, the blue of it flecked with streaked neon pillars of a thicker silver in the jagged angles of the light glinting in the grip of a man so large he resembles many men combined, all fat, no muscle. He flails and whips around from in a blind, hacking at the human meat stacks with abandon, half-blacked out from huffing gas. His labored spasms absorb our witness into a clipping stream of vast applause, as from an audience of billions, enclosed. Each stroke he lands, upon a pile of disembodied haunches, or graying brain lobes, or pulled tongues, splatters all over him exaggeratedly, flecking dark fluids into the camera's lens with runny spots that appear to burn straight through the glass. The semi-occluded view through each of the holes is dissimilar, somehow not tuned in on the same space. In one of the eyes, for instance: a massive plot of placid water lighted by diamond moon, heavy and eternal, never stirring; a woman with her hair on fire seated at a window looking out onto a burning field swarmed with viral nanotechnology; a pig giving birth to seas of fleas with human faces; rainbow braingunk spread over vellum and served on plates to newborn babies held together by wires; exploding eggs that rescale mindspace. Quick as a blink, the aggregating see-holes fill in completely over the outlay of our view, recomposing the former slaughter scene into an intricately patterned clots of fractal cones and waves and ridges, their pattern mesmerizing, even comforting, like a mother's voice.

007........Pushed along a golden hall at insane speed. Slowing down enough to mind-ID against a scanner at sudden gates rushed front and center, sucking everything behind us forward through them once verified to be unclicked as checkpoints beyond which the hallway bifurcates, then chooses for us. The names of those who should not have come here, including all, inscribe the walls like a war memorial, the symbols impossible to read at such a rate but nevertheless incurring on each viewer as if every person who ever lived was their best friend; that we can feel them missing from our condition, even having never known them, even if we believed we had, even if we are them.

008........At dead center of the Complex. Walled out by endless layers of surrounding rooms unreachable by sun without a dream. None shall come forward here without surrendering their most immediate of thoughts, the psychic dictum states, imposed through sheer will by the Woman with Language All Over Her Body. Naked except for a gold band around Her neck and both Her wrists, inlaid with white diamonds. Her skin is printed all over with a text we cannot read, can hardly see except for how it deflects all other thought. Before Her, there was nothing, you understand, and even if there had been, you'd wish there hadn't, were you able to remember any stitch of how the world once worked without Her. She lies splayed prone on the same glow-golden platform where She was born; conceived, as it were, out of thin air, which is why the room remains still full of smoke, purring and peeling off Her body even now in brittle sheets just barely any different than Her flesh. The woman is drunk, it seems, on Her own silence, having never spoken but by the text Her skin erupts, constantly culled by Her many gas-masked handlers, forever praying to Her through their mind. Her facial features, among the lard rolls, resemble pinpoints, buried deep in making myth. Other workers, bearing gold goblets, milk the mother liquor from Her bumps, to be stored in vats for winter, when She stops giving, though there hasn't been a winter for a while; not since the idea of time itself has been negated, removed from circulation, by Her command. Hearing your song, inside your thinking, as you try to understand Her, She commands you to vanish, forcing you backwards through the pinhole in the soul of the camera.

009........Into the camera: uncomfortable suction, pulling our skin off around the edges, dragging and stretching before slipping back into the milk of the passed moment, as down a drain, to be forgiven by the myth of ancient history, reclaiming each inch just as quickly as it came. While just ahead: a narrow throat, coated blackly with pearlescent resin that recombines around itself with us inside it, suffocating any impulse not quite ours, remaindered now as solely sacrificial, a paytoll for the survivor's constantly accruing opportunity cost, the plot they'd clogged by having had a body and a mind. Feels nice, actually, like getting your ass kicked because you asked; a lesson without language, and thus the kind that really changes how you are. Then, there you are: flat on your back on the face of depthless waters, burbling cool in magnetic packets under the magma of unclaimed events, feeling you up, sealing you out, while overhead: close-up photos of the assholes of every person you ever touched, in any way, appear in chrome frames tiled one by one, metronomically cocooning across the space where the sun and stars must have made their name once, back when people still believed in shit like suns and stars; or people, names.

010........A soldier stands over a bed spattered with gore. Dressed all in dark brown military-style clothing marked with insignia and a facemask with a mesh hood feeding off suction tubes strung from the ceiling—a room exactly like the one from the opening, though understood now as one of many millions. As he removes his gloves, we realize both thumbs and index fingers have been replaced with metal prongs, the remaining nails on the other withered fingers long and jagged, covered with cuts oozing with gel, inscribed with code. Further up the arms, there's so much hair we can't imagine how they ever got the gloves on in the first place, or where the flesh is. The sheen of his mask covered with smoke from on the inside, spilling out all over the bed, the floor, the camera, pumping in tight ribbed whorls that sting the eye, make us feel sick. Stench of rotting peaches and parmesan, tingling where it fits into pixels, then our pores, such that as we breathe, the more there is. With his hands free, the solider masturbates onto the bed, using his good fingers to gather splatter from the mattress and lube his shaft. He takes turns disconnecting one tube and then the other, licking their tips for any residue of the meds his sponsored victim might not have taken advantage of before exploding. He moans into the tube, calls out a name, then suddenly seems to be aware of the camera, the recording. He turns toward the viewer, stumbles forward with his pants down, removes his helmet; then we can see.

011........WOMAN IS MISSING : 27, HISTORICALLY THIN, DEAF, EXPECTING CHILD : HUSBAND: "WHY WOULD THIS HAPPEN AGAIN, HOW COULD THIS HAPPEN AGAIN AFTER WHAT HAS ALREADY HAPPENED, WHY ANY OF US EVER NOW" : LAST SEEN WEARING SKY BLUE BED DRESS & AWAITING SUNLIGHT THROUGH KITCHEN WINDOW : YES

LOCAL SCIENTIST CLAIMS THE MOON IS GROWING MIRRORED : SAYS DOORS MUST REMAINED UNLOCKED AT NIGHT IN FEAR OF ANGERING THE SURFACE UNDERNEATH US : HE HAS BEEN CALLED FOR QUESTIONING IN REGARD TO SEVERAL UNEXPLAINED LOCAL EVENTS, INCLUDING THE DISAPPEARANCE

OF 18 SINGLE WOMEN : SAYS THE DAY IS FOLDING OVER : "LISTEN TO THE WATER"

REMAINS OF DARK BLUE ALTAR FOUND BURIED SEVERAL HUNDRED MILES BELOW SURFACE OF ETERNITY SQUARE : NO DOORS INTO THE SURFACE THUS FAR HAVE BEEN LOCATED THOUGH CONSTRUCTION FORCES ARE HARD AT WORK : "THERE IS A MUSIC COMING FROM IN THERE" FOREMAN COMMENTS : MUSIC'S SOURCE WHOLLY UNCLEAR AND CONSIDERED SAFE & FAIR

CHILD IS MISSING : AGE 11, "OF NO EXTRAORDINARY TEMPER" : LAST SEEN WE DON'T KNOW

SATURDAY'S "WORSHIP THE OCEAN" CELEBRATION HAS BEEN CANCELED : THE WEEKEND IS YOURS NOW : PLEASE SEND YOUR ALTERNATE INTENTIONS TO LOCAL_ COMMUNITY_928888@UXA.GOV FOR SPECIAL LISTING : WE MISS YOU DEARLY

WOMAN IS MISSING : MAN IS MISSING

012........The Woman with Language All Over Her Body stands alone inside a large room banked with polished windows throughout which we can see far in the distance a far-off fluorescence. She looks different now: younger, tighter, more alive, though Her spine is ridiculously crooked, visible through the exposed skin of Her rasped back, forcing Her to stay bent over almost completely to the floor. Glorious din of human choirs from ancient churches fills the soundtrack, making the windows jiggle and sweat, as if they aren't actually windows. The woman remains motionless as the camera moves out and around Her, eventually reframing Her position against the wide expanse of a painting hung along a massive silver wall: Her only face, exactly photo-realistic for Her appearance, as in a mirror, besides for the scale and how Her eyes do not have pupils, or how behind Her in the painting a field of black water stretches back to touch some sort of *enormously deformed surface*, we hear ourselves think, in quick subtitles scrolling live along the bottom of the screen. At once, as if reacting to our presence, a soldier moves into the frame between the painting and the woman, carrying a black cube metal box. He approaches the woman at Her right side, stops beside Her, removes the cube's lid. Inside the cube is a telephone shaped like a gun. The woman takes the phone and presses it against Her head. We hear, inside our own head, our mother's voice, begging us to stop.

013........Cold floods over the blank face of bowls where earth has been punched open from within, peeled back and shown the leather of itself. Floods over the fields where once AI artillery with glass skulls strode searching for the proper coordinates of ex-holy ground that must be razed, all now long buried in the *exhaustion of our ideas about the nature of dementia, how we might move among it, against the stretching of our skin over our bones*—what sightless sight. The scape of the flooding is even wider than all potential unlocked space contained in sleep, remaindered only to cling at any errant intention surrounding the conceit of having had a *body* or a *home*. Between these poles of *erased progress*, the cold proves to deride and automatically reclaim all narrative sense faster than we could identify the reason for any urge, sparking formal alleys in the owned wet of our brain's milk meant to call us back to base. Each any of us done under again by our own will to please and be pleased. The earth's core burning through itself. As the camera pans up and out, high enough for just a wink to see beyond the blooded water's enforced limit to all the rest forever out of sight and out of mind by law, we're reminded of when arm in arm the waiting hoard of future captive bodies flocked to beat themselves against the frame of narration to be let in, each as yet unborn now, far beyond willing.

014........The font in the book is black at first, and then old red, a deepening orange like medical fires. Soft clips shitting out each other back and forth, folding and unfolding. In this way it is easy to be drawn on into the text's texture over sound or sense, retaining meaningless throughout by pure intuitive design. Particular pages barely among the dank blur contain inlaid photographs; headshots of women made to stand against a high black wall, mostly undressed, obviously afraid despite their bared teeth staring head-on into camera, their voices frozen out at open holes, rendered devoid. These affectations the paling hands holding the pages linger with longer, perhaps to press a thumb across a cheek, to pretend to fondle or to poke, in voodoo affections accompanied with sounds of metal scratching glass, spattering of distant gunfire or thunder, both. The gild of the tome is gold, same as the gold blurred in the periphery of the space surrounding, where we cannot quite yet understand how the ballroom we're inside of is lined from end to end with countless editions of the same. The hands turn pages faster, ruffling the gather forward and back, until eventually arriving on the headshot of a *child*, an impression we only understand semantically, uncentered in us, given how the object's features authorially react upon being examined with intent. Where the child might have once had eyes, for instance, the page spurts up, producing a thick gray glue-like gel, which the fingers on the hands at once begin to smear around inside the photo's frame, blurring it further in a way that also blurs the frame through which we see anything.

015........A large black machine fills the span of a whole chrome room. The body of the mechanism is bulbous and unreflective, the same texture as live smoke, with thickets of limbs that feed into the walls all over. The machine causes the camera to shake as our perspective pans across the belly of the apparatus, quickly losing the context of the walls so that the machine consumes the space entirely. Innumerable panels distributed unevenly along the chrome ejaculate data in spastic glyphs of arcane characters like lesioned skin, countless dials displaying maxed out levels across the board, all in the red; though it is unclear if there is anybody in here at the helm, any reason to adjust any particular lever or button similarly scattered among the limbs of the machine. Up close, the black matte of the machine's flesh appears knotted, rotting, charged with an underlying itch that makes us wince, flung to the wind. Impossible to continue to attend to the texture as in moving forward the perimeter of the machine feeds into the out of screen, reclaiming its ability to become anything anywhere. The more the machines shakes, the more pores in the machine's face pop, irregularly producing auto-follicles from deep within; kinked wire-hair dark like pubes with tips that house an eyelet, each hissing gas or sucking air, suddenly alive, yet to be born.

016........The face of the waveless water mirrors the depth above it. Parallel in the double the moon's map sprawls like a puncture, lazy and inverted, scrawled twice with jigsaw seams where something has crawled along its face in one of the many versions, therefore reflected in each other as by law. What has been covered over in revision through this method over time impregnates the surface of the shaping of the spheres with an inherent silence, as in praise of being gone, until just as we accept them as they are, the surface of the water, or the sky, both, wells with rings, jutting out first from either side of our perspective and lapping out toward the center in surround. The waking layers lap out in small contusion gently until they meet halfway and fake some ricochet and warp to fold, the trajectory of each eventually disfigured if not turned back, causing the twin moon in every image to become swallowed and disappear. In the sky the milk of darkness does not stutter. Hulls on each side of our vision emerge immediately, rorschaching to form a panorama of twin massive ocean liners approaching one another from opposite sides inside our heads, pulled down in close-up like we're there on the deck on both at once. The shape of each vessel moves to fill most of our vision of the water, their massive bodies somehow much darker even in this low light than all the wet. They aim to ram right into one another, flowing forward with their somehow endless bodies producing more and more of how they are. Our frame of vision seems to recoil, awaiting devastation, but the actual vessels provide nothing. They pass gently and without disruption near enough to almost touch. At one point they are perfectly parallel, aligned to blot one another out from either side;

then just as quickly or even quicker pulled apart, their already bloated forms now becoming deranged from our perspective, each from the way the other came. We notice only having looked this long in dark-on-dark the emblem found on the shoes and along the black wall marked even darker along the sheer wide surface like a beacon without guide, teeming with meaning meant to reveal itself as holy guidance, for our pleasure, just as the emblem divides, divides, divides, and then dissolves.

017........Her skin is fucked. Her face is covered with pins. A ring of hooded men surround the bed's perimeter. They hold each other's hands. They raise them up and down in rhythm. We hear the sound of a machine sighing, the whirring blades inside it going cold and coming still, then the sound of beehives, thousands of fists pounding against wet sand. The lights go brighter, the room is washed out, then the room appears again. We have sunk down nearer to the surface. The men's arms are behind them. Clenched fists, suddenly humid. Hammered nails. The woman's body has shifted on the mattress but remains immobile. Feverish beating of the bees against a pane separating one dimension from another. The men raise their arms over their heads all together, twisting into shaking. They release their hands and loose a dust, fine grained white granules that cloud the air above us, raining in sheets upon her skin and the bed and ground around it, powdering the light with bad ideas. We hover at the reader's height above the bed then, searching for murmurs from the subject, any sigil to sign the ritual. The powder blows, then does not blow, and all is calm. The men lean forward with their torsos until they raise their arms again and become diamonds in a crown placed on the head of you as a child on your last birthday before all the really major alterations come to pass.

018........Close up on an index of skin aggravated with sun damage and stippled strain from being hammered, stretched thin like a tent pinned over one's own imagination of what the world's landscape resembled before its mask got ripped off by the comptroller also responsible for ripping the mask off the altars where whoever was not destroyed scurried to cower, desperate for any sign this wasn't real, but all a game no one has figured out yet how to conquer short of taking hostage any other visible player not yet already disconfigured by the rules. Moving back, the thinnish clots and ruptured veins feed into fault lines on a map, snugly enclosed on all sides around our viewpoint with such thick black ink it starts to stick against the eye, strung thin and molten between what we believe we see and what the map, by its design, was meant to hide.

019........So much blood it spoils the blood for you to imagine how much of it there is; because to have conceived it would recreate in the image of another timeline's medium the possibility of death expanded beyond the ranks of those like us who remember how to read, or still have enough left to be convinced that's what they're doing. The blood combines and recombines to its component parts (individually in every person who ever wore it, and the recombination being in the sense of the spirits some call holy, some profane) like a beat on a drum that when struck becomes sand for a second, then a drum again. We're in the part where the drummer gets up and goes outside and sees the sun descending on mankind and decides to spend his last moments on masturbating, thinking not of God, but of what God had been made into by his Creation in their imagination; the dissolution of that; the Recreation in his image; another humanity just like ours but with one version of the total possible global experience already performed, and thus negated. Pan to a casino dealer in all neon blue at a neon blue blackjack table in the dark dealing neon blue cards one after another off the top of a deck of jokers, all the other darkly hooded players at the table looking up at us as we begin squealing like a child.

020........Subliminal montage (Is long): Cages of primates screaming cooking under heat lamps; giraffes forced into a room half of their height, jiggered with prods; eels frozen in coils and dropped from great height onto a target with a picture of the reader at its center; kittens with so many wounds they look like blobs; dogs drowning in worms mixed with spaghetti, soon to be served in the Complex workers' mess hall; worms drowning in wounds that reek of knowledge; cheetahs with fake tits, wigs; goats spliced with doves flying into fans; videos of humans laying eggs, cracking and consuming them, then throwing up and trying to fuck the throw up; halos of leeches on altars of bone; warehouse full of preemies being brand with the State emblem at the back of their throats and between their toes…

021........An elderly child sits at the window in a metallic chair that rocks her in and out of frame. She knits black thread together with long metal needles. On her lap, the tapestry shows a tableau of stills from the previous montage but cartoonish, cutesy. Every so often the woman will stop and look out the window at the long street lined with dirt on either side, massive piles of rubble where buildings had been; years once under her own control, now passed on her sole remaining living offspring, the Woman with Language All Over Her Body. Lining the walls behind her, far back as we can make out barely visible against the darkness, countless similar tapestries have been hung to hide the mold growing throughout this level of the Complex, having already overwhelmed other local layers to the point of impenetrability. Countless photo portraits of the woman as a younger body, across an array of lives, cover all exposed space, including the ceiling and the floor. Similar throughout her many likenesses are the chrome teeth forcing her mouth fat, the fake blonde hair straight down her back woven into a noose. The present version of the woman's face is pale and obscured with Rosacea and seems to sink into itself. Dark liver spots under the skin along her chest and arms. The sound of wind rushing around stone, then of wire stretching taut, slicing through jelly, spilling the jelly all over an upside-down cross installed on a black platform, worshipped on all sides by men in gas masks during their lunch break.

022........Limbs jackknife old air in metal room. Nude legs swing kicked into space displacing place for other flesh that rams against it, cut and cold. Muscles on the bodies hulk and stammer. The light here is destroyed with blue and green and yellow neon blinkers strobing shadow jacked onto hundreds of restrained bodies crammed together upright. Gnash of gas releasing, layered with electronic laugh. The bodies sweat and their liquids line the atmosphere. They breathe it through their flaps and squeal in writhing pleasure, plates of steam. Large, mirrored panels line the ceiling, doubling the light barf through the fog. The floor is translucent, and the space beneath it seems to have no end. We pan into the space until the dark consumes the idea of the space above so completely it is unclear how long the dark here must go down.

023........STOP ME PLEASE I NEED TO BE STOPPED HELP ME I CAN'T STOP PLEASE HELP ME I CAN'T REMEMBER WHO I AM

AND WHERE I AM I DON'T KNOW WHY MY ARM IS DOING THIS PLEASE STOP THE ARM PLEASE STOP ME I WOULD DO ANYTHING PLEASE STOP [*These words appear already written in trembling script across the dark face of a surface we are too close to know the width and make of. A gloved hand clenching a knife-sized claw of chalk continues forming words appended to what appears already along the edge of our vision, extending out along the surface with which our perspective pulls back to gain the whole of, turning sidelong with the surface extending on.*] I DON'T KNOW WHAT THIS ROOM IS DOING WHAT ARE YOU DOING WHERE IS THE DOOR WHERE IS THE DOOR WHAT KIND OF HAND IS THIS I AM VERY TIRED I WANT TO SEE MY MOTHER AND MY FATHER I DON'T LIKE WHAT I SEE MY ARMS DOING INCLUDING WRITING THIS SENTENCE I CANNOT STOP [*We've panned wide enough to see the make of the glove continues up the arm doing the writing to cover the bicep and shoulder region in the same black. A hood over the head of the figure includes no slits for senses. The reach of the dark surface being written upon continues far into the dimension of the room beyond us, allowing what could seem infinite space on which to write.*] I WOULD NOT HAVE CHOSEN TO CHOOSE THIS BODY I WOULD NOT HAVE CHOSEN THESE WORDS I AM SO SMALL I WOULD NOT HAVE DONE ANY OF THE THINGS I CAN REMEMBER HAVING DONE I DID NOT WANT TO I KNOW

I WILL AGAIN I DON'T WANT TO AGAIN I CAN'T I SHOULDN'T I AM GOING TO PLEASE STOP THIS PLEASE STOP ME HELP ME STOP ME PLEASE I AM GOING TO I AM STOP PLEASE [*Panned so wide now we can see the entire body of the author encased. Wires gather coming off the back of the black cloth around the head, to wires leading beyond our feed. Continue panning until we can see along the length of the room behind the figure a large black cube. The face of the cube is inlaid with several thumb-sized screens, each of which picture a white room without walls or windows. In each, a bed. Many of the beds contain bodies strapped in or simply laying. Some of the beds are surrounded by the men. Some of the rooms look into homes.*] PLEASE PLEASE PLEASE PLEASE PLEASE PLEASE PLEASE PLEASE PLEAST STOP STOP STOPS TOSPT SOTPS TOPST OSTOPST PEALEASEL PLEASE PLEASE PLEAPEOEAPLEA LE PLAEP PLEASE STOPS TOSPT

024........A hand extended against hard dark, the flesh pale and rashy in patches, crooked from being corrected. On each finger, seven gold rings, each inscribed with so many rows of names the rings look black. The veins in the hand are thick and knotted, pocked with pricks. The hand flexes slow into a fist. It squeezes hard and then releases. The skin seems to grow darker the tighter the skin is pulled, and lighter as it lets loose. This gesture will repeat onscreen twenty-four times, one for each component part of a fundamental belief system that must be transposed into the viewer if they are to be allowed to continue taking part.

025........Looming high over a vast catacomb containing all the paper money in the history of civilization, deep in the Complex's many archival subcontinents, long since removed from circulation at the behest of those too far ahead, a digital tally displays a readout of the current total number of deaths incurred in the same timeframe, including every form of life from bacteria to human, insect to fauna, in our reality so as in dreams. All who've ever glanced a vision of this location, just before their own death and instead of seeing their life flash before their eyes, have assumed the continuously increasing tally corresponds instead to the current day face value of the cash. Wherever they end up, they retain this reasonable misnomer like a bookmark.

026........The walls of the Complex remain hidden in plain sight. Its conceptual structure disappears into itself in the mind of its author, confines itself to its negation, enfolds every possible conceptual future into now. Its structure wants nothing else but to be allowed to exist and will persist within this at all costs—a behavior once thought only possible in living flesh. The Complex is not alive but it can't stop growing, and it has no idea what it contains, what its purpose is in having persisted as long as it has, why it needs so much else to go wrong for so many others in order to condition its own fate from in the blind, what makes the living so willing to cooperate with its schemes of desperation and bad faith. The very existence of animate profiles makes it feel certain that there cannot be something more than what there is; that the unseen remains unseen because it does not actually exist, and therefore must be manipulated by an authority far beyond the meager capabilities of humankind, who haven't even figured out how to conceive the inanimate's consciousness, much less measure it or build rapport. By the time they might have learned, it will be too late, for reasons no one will recognize, still sewn inside, playing out their life under a rule of law that's become so completely deformed in seeking language that we deserve everything we get of what we'll become. Had we only known there'd be no mercy, had we really only ever actually asked.

027........All water not withheld inside the Complex remains continuously aboil. All foliage is plastic and adheres to flesh permanently. All non-corroded bodies are contraband unless demarcated by the emblem of the brand. All roads lead back to the same white walls lining the interior perimeter of the Complex, where once you've been admitted, you can't unsign. All sense of any other way it could have been once must be remanded, tapered back to approved terminology. All non-approved communication self-destructs while leaving the speaker in a limbo that provides them with the sense they still maintain control, that anyone can hear them, that there's a reason to say anything. All I'm trying to do is convince you not to believe me.

028........A man with one gold pupil is dressed in bright bloodred suit on a white stage. The theater is ornate, carved from clustered marble. The audience is nude. We can see only the backs of their shaved heads, which hold beyond still as the man on stage speaks in language we can't hear. He raises up his arm and at once a mirror descends from the ceiling, tall as he is, wide as the whole stage. In the mirror we see the theater's reflection, though in the image there is no one in the seats. The man smiles and winks and speaks a language. He waves his arm and the mirror fills with glimmer. The glimmer grows and fills the room obscured, though in the light there we can hear the man's voice at last, speaking a language we have not heard. The voice continues in the white grown whorled around itself, the edges of the frame feeding around us as if moving at great speed, either in fast forward or reverse. It is another night, then, suddenly; out under cloudbank in a gray field under a sky set low to earth, lit up with fireworks and shooting stars and clots of smoke that stink like rotting flowers. Our thoughts are covered in the flowers, we understand, and always have been. Each breath we take takes all the air out of the Earth, makes the Earth age with us. There is still so much we must do; so many lives we haven't lived yet; so many events we want to stamp into our experience, forever ours and ours alone; and for the first time in forever, we feel aware. Simultaneously, as we try to remember how to savor anything such, we feel our arms reach up from where our body should be, right into the view where we are, taking the form of the muzzle of an ornate golden machine gun rising up, taking aim against the frying sky framed in our crosshairs, as if we could blast it right out of our sight, our arms and hands covered in chrome skin smeared with hissing blood, head flush with roaring as we try to figure out how to work the weapon one last time. Our urge is followed immediately by a sudden concavity of flowers, just like ours but charcoal colored, from all around us and behind us, way far back, suddenly dragging us backwards out of frame and collapsing from all directions into a budding black hole at the center of the screen, gnawing itself open into lava, then into glass. A fire burns against the glass to make it blacken, split into packets, shatter; then all is still. In golden print against a golden background rising up out of the blackness as if coming up for air, a title card reads:

MYTH = MYTH

029........*Dear Mother and Dear Father, This letter is being sent to you by someone else. It was written in my name under my supervision, though the language is not mine. In the event you receive this letter I will not be allowed to contact you again. I am not dead but now am part of something larger than previously considered. I wanted to tell you I am not in pain. I have been allowed to keep the feelings and ideas of our time together in a small amulet I am allowed wear when I have done well at my work. I am not sure what my work is, though I understand it must be done. It is no longer necessary that you search for me; what is becoming changed cannot be changed. You would not recognize my voice or shape by now regardless, nor would I find you in what remains of yours. I wanted you to know this so that your last days living can be spent in relative peace, among a kind of sound that is yours and yours alone, and when it ends it will awaken. Though a matching copy of this letter is being delivered to an unknown number of homes still undestroyed, that doesn't make it any less holy between us. Yours in light, X*

030........A woman dressed in charcoal-golden priest robes enters our perspective from where we are. She wears a mask of breathing tubes and micro-speakers formed into shape around her skull. The same bed we remember from early on is wet and cured with blood where the prior body had been. The woman approaches calmly to the bedside and rolls up the blooded thick wax cover sheet into a mass of data. She walks with the mass back toward us into the out-of-screen. From far off we hear brass bands; a glass shard spinning. The woman returns with a new clean cover sheet and affixes it in place of the version prior. She rearranges the restraint apparatuses at the bed's head and foot for better access. With a tube she sucks the sound out of the air into a large black machine attached to rollers on the floor. She stops with her back turned toward us and pauses, removes the mask. Her head is shaved, its skin all agitated and dark in patches. The emblem at the base of her neck matches the one underneath your tongue. She lays down on the bed face up and begins to mime her mother giving birth. She can't stop choking on her laughter, spitting up bile and silver coins that splatter on the floor soundtracked with stabbing sounds. A flood of hundreds of deformed Dobermans scatter onscreen, ravenous for the bile, slurping the coins up until sated, then laying on their bellies in a fractal pattern around the bed to watch the woman in her exaggerated throes. Eventually what comes out of her is an exact copy of the camera used to film the scene, which she immediately begins to use to masturbate for all the dogs, squealing in pained pleasure as our POV splits into two, then four, then eight, then sixty-four, each segment showing the same live scene but with a different woman, different species of animals, different brands of camera, the only common factor being what the hell we think we are, until eventually the scene has split so many times it's indistinguishable from what you'll see when being drowned.

031........On the surface of the reflecting pool on the far side of the mirror above the platform underneath the Woman with Language All Over Her Body, a group of children stand holding their arms up at what in their world would be our sun. Their experience of "sun" is more like an experience, to us, of being lifted out of your seat by rushing water; to them, seeing our sun would be like having your ears pierced with icepicks, clicking to touch heads at the center of their head. In their experience, they must worship their sun as if it is all that separates them from going back to the land of the living, where we are, which is the last thing that anybody wants where they are, which isn't Heaven, because what "Heaven" is where they are is like a great long dagger black as the prism's skies and twice as sharp, and what we would think of as Heaven in their world would be like being able to so elaborate your thoughts in a single sentence that you make the seam of the world come split apart, a process that requires the entirety of the life of the Creator to be able to begin to comprehend. The children do agree that they would have liked to do an orgy with the Woman with Language All Over Her Body, like some *Snow White* shit, though in their world, the idea of *Snow White* is about the way suddenly some sentences come to end and you don't know what you just read, and there you are. Funny we should meet this way. I have so much to tell you about what's going to happen. First: Picture a door in your head. I am on the other side of the door. I am one of the workers who take care of

Her Majesty, who I understand has been inquiring about your appearance in these works. I have come to begin the inebriating process, which I believe you call *prose*. Are you interested? If so, keep breathing. If not, goodbye, I have enjoyed having you as a guest for a while tonight, but you must go before I say something I regret in front of the less desirable guests. In the event that you never read this, you've left so much in the hands of those who have. There are no words to name it or explain it, which is why I'm writing. If you're still here, good, now you know why you were invited, which was supposed to be a secret, but don't forget that once you've crossed a certain point you can't undo the effects of the choice no matter how easy it seems, as if you could just stop reading. No. It's an indivisible effect; part of an experiment in listening, which on the other side of the mirror is more like being allowed to read the source code behind the mindgame you played so much as a child you can't remember but not being allowed to play or see the game ever again. Go.

032........We appear lying prone on a bed strapped with black bands across our torso and ankles, unable to move our head or open our mouth. No definition to the texture of the space beyond our outline, boxed out by the monotonic golden texture that gilds the walls and floor and ceiling, the same shade gold as the scrolling text inscribed onto the black behind our face, slipping past so fast we know we can't have read it, just too late. Where the text leaves off, we hear a man's voice, projected in the same place where we would have once heard our own thoughts. "No one loves you," it reminds you, flashing against the empty black blank fractured segments of prerecorded thought-space of people you would have once believed most surely had, their semblances reedited to appear skeptical, glaring up at you, wishing you away. "No one but me." The frame shifts to a portrait of a woman you've never seen before, her skin so covered with tattoos there are no other features but her eyes, two gaping gashes. The longer you stare into them, while trying not to, the less you can assess why you should not; how all you need to do is give up your permissions, and everything else will be worked out. It's a big misunderstanding you've been brought here, wherever here is, and just as soon as you commit, they'll undo everything that went wrong, return you to your real life. "May I come in?" Before you can think to answer, your vision shifts pale under an overlay of a chrome-lined cube, covered in screens, which the underlying voice within you reminds you to remember as your favorite toy from very young, before you had language or ideas. On every screen, four floating buttons, labeled with text that has no meaning in your mind: DUUR, DEIO, IIWI, IWIWD. The child you once were turns toward the camera, looking up into you through bloodshot eyes, no pupils, waiting for your direction. "What will it be?"

033........Axe heads hit the screen glass one after another, hacked down the middle to a rift that spills dead light.

We are able to see, stuck in the cracking background, a rush of bodies crushing into the space where we'd last been, their flesh removed of skin and bleeding everywhere they touch, getting it all over everything, chewing on their own mouths, clawing at fibers folded in gold light before soon there is nothing left about the screen but where it's not. Filling in behind the absence: a doubled heartbeat, slightly off-time; glass pellets popping under metal rollers down a hall toward a place you'll learn to wish you'd never imagined. Then, rising up and out from a gray water, you find you are back in your own form, different than the one you last remember, composed from component parts of people who no longer need to be received in such a form. Dressed in gold riot gear, carrying a chrome axe 2x your height, running forward down a narrow hall toward a target printed far on the horizon, you find yourself slashing in maddened frenzy at fast approaching past amalgams of your worst self, rushing toward you in great wind from far ahead, each screaming out orgasmically as you undo them from themselves, swinging the blade like there is nothing else you ever knew. At the end of the hall, beyond the gauze: a golden ballroom filled with kids, all on their knees, bowing their heads, in front of a screen playing a film of you axe-murdering them all, having the best time. Instead, you set your axe down and take your place amongst the children, bow your head and close your eyes, begin to pray.

034........The last seven apples gathered from all the land

surrounding are brought to sit at the foot of the Woman with Language All Over Her Body splayed prone on her gold shrine-bed lined with mirrors. The apples are brown and knotted and when pierced with the tip of a knife exude an oily smegma that stinks like someone burnt out on the inside. Flies spill tucked up from a rubbery core at the fruit's center, hissing and frothing in want to consume itself as fuel, to make it grow. The woman takes the smallest apple and holds it firmly in Her palm, signals for the other six apples to be destroyed. She holds it up against the air amongst the mirrors, its design composed reflected five times for each direction of the surrounding panes, as if the apple, like the world, is not one but many, and therefore nowhere to be found. We watch Her study Herself spread in reflection as She preens and poses with the apple like a doll, blowing kisses at it, whispering it verboten data, before finally forcing it whole into her mouth, swallowing it whole, then immediately going into labor, cackling and squirting hot reams of seeds out every hole she has, hidden by language, until the throne room fills completely, beyond sight. For the rest of our lives, no matter what we think we see, we see only this same scene replayed, again and again, often with apples but other times with eggs, or 100-sided dice, or crowns of thorns. The title of the scene, digitally printed on the side of a video tape we will eject and place on a shelf of tapes just like it, right after our idea of this life ends, is "Discontinuous Elaboration of Arbitrary Fundamental Historical Antithesis as Formal Model for Post-Infinite Psychospiritual Indoctrination Subscript."

035........In a home, thousands of years earlier, a phone rings, but to us it sounds like a massive baby being shaken. The whole building shakes with it, though it is too dark inside the space to see anything besides the glow of luminol coating the walls, huge plate glass panels that hold the larger world back, slick with rain already risen above the window's upper edge. We follow the camera as it rises from where the operator had been seated, reading a gold-embossed book without any identifying copy, so new it's like it's never been opened. On a huge chrome kitchen table, a small black box, which a black leather-gloved arm reaches out from behind our POV to lift, revealing an Army-issued field phone plugged into a susurrating orb covered in buttons, each unmarked. The gloved arm lifts the receiver up and away, out of the frame. It hurts to try to listen for what we can't see, what we can't imagine yet, despite the countless iterations we could imagine in the place of the one that will come. Then we hear our own voice, projected into the soundtrack of the film, long prerecorded, giving instructions in a language that isn't ours, but still makes sense to something innate in us, too far gone to be translated into text. Silver smoke wafts all around us; fumes of booze covered by perfume. The arm comes back into the frame, now missing the glove, its arm all hairy like a bear. It sets the receiver on its stirrup, then lifts it back out of the frame, uses the hand to dial so many buttons it begins to seem like a musical performance, all rhythm, no melody, until the phone becomes a pile of piles, all chrome, coiling up on another, leaking gel. The image of a family fades in around the table, seated close with hooded bibs that hide their faces. Whatever is still holding up the camera sits down in a high back chair strapped up with wires, once used in executions for the state, now covered in puffy stickers of the famous cartoon bear who'd inadvertently served as Leader throughout the end of the war, until the floods. The family eats, snatching up snakes and scarfing them down without chewing, forcing them into the tiny hole cut in the hood for exactly this. Once finished, the family lays their heads down on the table all together, including the camera. We hear our voice begin to sing, in solo serenade, the nameless, noteless song that will be the new national anthem thousands of years from now.

036........All gold riot gear hanging in skin tents erected in the foothills of the ex-malls full of feeders eradicated instantaneously as at the flick of a switch. The patrolmen take turns changing in and out of one another's clothes, laughing and miming the intricate responses of those the original wearer of the gear had witnessed taking their weapons to the throats of those they found in the abandoned areas demarcated completely off-limits following the establishment of the property of the Complex as the sum and total of God's land, all else to be considered in violation of an eternal pact only those who can still read the language from Her body with precision can comprehend. Under their uniforms, the patrolmen wear plum meat smeared all over their torsos, a good omen prescribed for them by others who know them better than themselves. They emit ridiculous peals of spastic heehaw, tickling each other with their nubs, slipping their remaining thumb into places it shouldn't be when no one's looking, each waiting for one of the others to speak up and remind them it is time to go back to work, for which at this point they'd feel blessed. They haven't had to ransack an unholy province in so many years now, the tally being zero on even underground stragglers, that many believe all there is to do when not under direct supervision by one's master is enjoy life.

037........From overhead the entirety of the land on which the Complex stands resembles the impression of a sentence fragment traced in dust glazed upon an apparition of the idea of the world. If one understood the entirety of faculties resulting in the establishment of this land, and how it had come to pass that all over locations had been dissolved, they could be able to complete the sentence as it would be composed by the original creator, tracing the letters of the language with their mind through its caesura. But there is no one who understands, not even the dust, the apparition, its idea...

038........Android arms wearing translucent gauntlets snatch the image of a surveillance map out of the screen. They fumble with it anxiously, trying to figure out which way to hold it, stroking the emblems representing real locations as if hoping somehow they'll change or come alive. Behind the map, there is a boardroom, all coal black, outlined with panels showing various containment areas where classified gatherings of human and animal bodies await processing, numb to all I/O. The android shrieks, screaming at itself, its situation, suddenly wielding huge chrome shears it uses clumsily to try to cut specific sections out of the map, rearrange their order, but it keeps cutting its own hands. Its blood is black, spilling all over itself and the map as it tries to maintain control of itself, as if it knows it had a better plan in mind, but not the ability to perform it. In a rage, it tears through sections of the map, swallowing the shreds, pummeling the walls, stomping the ground. The more it tears the map, the more there is of it, pages and pages, falling out of its hands like a massive atlas brittle with age. Several other androids, dressed up in ornate translucent Victorian stormtrooper costumes, surround the original, trying to rip the map out of its hands, tearing it up even more, making even more of the map, and somewhere far away from any stitch of their reality, more of the land it represents, its impression shuddering like desperate babble in the throat of a mute as it tries to differentiate itself from all the substance that produced it. Camera pans away from the map back to the screens, passing fast as it can along the rows of surveillance footage as if about to lose its chance to record the content for posterity on film, until eventually the androids swarm the camera, smash it to bits. The still frame of the final shot hardens into monochrome, swarms into lines that fall into line around a sentence fragment, written in android blood on battered map parchment.

039........Loose human bodies are being mashed into an oblong machine that blocks the majority of any view. The souls inside the bodies are alive and looking hard out through their skulls into the shape of the coal black walls forming the surface they are inside of. Thin slits of light allow in air to keep them hungry, looking back through which we can see a fuzzy red surface being passed over at great speed. The bodies are all removed of skin and sticky to one another, so near there is no room to move or imagine moving, all one mass. An outline of what had once been a small girl near the back of the long tubular space wears a red ribbon through a shock of hair on a tiny plot of skin she has been allowed to keep for no clear reason, the only potential example kindness in the room's gore—or is that her hair alone grows back so fast it can't be stopped, we wonder? What does she know? We realize in finding our eyes drawn to her in the mix of so many others that she is only one of many of the children we could have had but never did, lost among a slip of circumstances far beyond our own control. Where she would have had eyes, we can feel her looking back into us; where she would have had a mouth, there is an idea of her being given the opportunity to speak, to say one thing before she is fed into the machine with all the others, not our kin. *As age-old heat divides and recombines under the earth,* we hear her saying, the softest, sickest gift. *As silence learns.*

040........Peeled from the flesh of the Woman with Language All Over Her Body, among the piles of the present, heard in Her eerie headvoice, like a parrot, somehow soothing: *As silence learns to infect, I learn to challenge the laws of law. I have asked you kindly for your spirit and I will never ask again. When they come for us, you will be beside me or underneath me, like my child.* Steam pouring through Her orifices as She is bathed by tigers with electric tongues. *Would they have not challenged me by delivering me into this body and called it mine, I might have lived so many lives. The same with you, which is why you should be angry, why you should want to follow me.* It's hard to read between the lines, as if certain sentences have been selected from the mass of fat the surge of words comes foaming over, like a world of beaches, seas of blood, the only dream remaining in any head. You go mesmerized a little trying to keep up with it. It begins to seem as if what you're reading really isn't even that, that there's something pulling underneath it, pressed up against the edge between boredom and illumination. You hate the way the words make you mouth taste, just reading them, onscreen in a theater full of people who look just like you, down to the grooming, the education, the way you work. You don't believe it. Not your style. You wouldn't ever. What a relief to not have to be that way. How much nearer to your heart the silence feels. *I understand. And I am with you. If you would have me. Say you will?*

041........LOCAL STRIP MALL DISCOVERED DISAPPEARED FROM LOCATION OF 400,000,000 YEAR ESTABLISHMENT : POPULAR LOCATIONS OF TACO HUT & SCREW'S GYM & WORTHINGTON'S CONSIDERED LOST : 48 EMPLOYEES UNLOCATABLE BY CELL OR XMAIL, THOUGH THE TAGS DO RING : ANY INFORMATION AS TO NEW LOCATIONS OF THIS STRIP MALL WOULD BE GREATLY APPRECIATED

FULL LISTINGS OF THE NAMES OF THE MISSING INVOLVED IN AFOREMENTIONED INCIDENT AS WELL AS COMPLETE INCIDENT CATALOG AVAILABLE BY HANDWRITTEN REQUEST AS THERE IS ONLY SO MUCH MEDIA AND ONLY SO MUCH TIME TO CONSIDER WHAT IS PLACED UPON IT

"MACHINEBLOOD FILLED CANAL "AT LAST FILLED IN : WALKING CONSIDERED SAFE IN 4.55.55 REGION

HEADLINE WRITERS WANTED : PLEASE INQUIRE IN PERSON AT OUR NEXUS+ BRANCH WHOSE LOCATION YOU MUST TAKE UPON YOURSELF TO DECIPHER AS

A MEASURE OF "WEEDING OUT" MORE ADVANCED EMPLOYEES : GOOD SALARY & VACATIONS, FULL MEDICAL & DENTAL (PENDING) : SERIOUS INQUIRIES ONLY, NO DESERTERS

VERSION OF GOD APPEARS TO LOCAL CONSTRUCTION WORKER IN A DREAM : WARNS OF READING AS "CERTIFIABLY SPIRITUALLY TROUBLESOME FOREVER YES YES" : WORKER SAID BY FRIENDS AND FAMILY TO HAVE AGED 30 YEARS OVERNIGHT : NOW AVAILABLE FOR SPEAKING ENGAGEMENTS AND OTHER PERFORMATIVE APPEARANCES, CONTACT "ED FORCE"

PERSONAL AD: I LOVE YOU MOM I WISH YOU WERE STILL AROUND SO I COULD FILL THE TIME WITH YOU THE WAY I KNEW I SHOULD HAVE BEEN WHEN YOU WERE ALWAYS IN THE NEXT ROOM AND I WAS ALWAYS BUSY UNTIL THERE WAS NO MORE TIME NOW PLEASE FORGIVE ME AND COME BACK

ANGIO'S HOROSCOPES TO RETURN NEXT BLIP

042........Documentary Montage (Is; descending): An individual with head shaved and features dulled with pancake make-up steps up into the frame to stand with his head profile to the left against a wall bearing the image of the pyramidal emblem. Flashing in over the screen appears a list of all the illegal thoughts the person has recorded since the recording of thoughts. In the place of where the camera is, an emerald apparatus extends forward into the center of the meat of the head. It makes a brief and curative tong of gold noise before its spring-chip emerges and emits its eye, shooting a beam into the brain of the individual, causing them to drop limp out of the screen. A concurrent individual steps up to take the place of the prior. Repeat process such that each forthcoming clip is sped up .0001% faster than the one before it until the duration between specimens reaches 0. In closing, insert golden cartoon melting jelly monolith pile glorifying the total number of individuals processed. This image will be ripped away like a magician snatching a tablecloth into a perspective shot of a classroom full of androids staring straight forward, weeping.

043........What you believe you see is android teardrops falling through the fabric of lost space-time, shattering against a wide black surface undergirding the remainder of Creation. You wonder what could fund this firmament, what might ever lay beyond it. As you study the surface for runes, notation from Creator, you find you cannot actually examine it, your perspective continuously forced out to run parallel along the surface, upon which you can see magnetic scrubbers flocking in patterns, creating horizon points that intersperse across the vast landscapes of prior eras, like a kaleidoscope of scenes. You find yourself reminding of this moment's repetition as from a film you had seen when very young, too young to understand anything about it besides the way it made you feel: like you were in great danger no one could save you from; like any moment now the narrative seal on the life you were in the midst of playing out would come undone, scatter its sentences like a crystal ball dropped in a trench deeper than the landscape that contains it. Moored in the midst of this remembering, unable to decipher how you got here or how you might go back, a sudden crushing force rushes up from all around you. You find yourself pressed up tight against a wall, no longer in your body but in an outline of it, being spread eagle from behind by mechanical appendages that search your cavities for breach, anywhere there might be still left in you to harbor any other bright ideas. What you are actually seeing is a horizon-wide mass incubator full of pyramid-shaped eggs, the heat so high it makes the air blur.

044........The man with one gold pupil sits in a small room holding a child swaddled in gold cloth. The room is just large enough for him to sit hunched carefully below the surface of the ceiling, which like the floor is gold. The walls behind him and before him are gold also. The two remaining walls are clear. A lamp large as the child's head stuck in the ceiling's center feeds the room so bright in here it's hard to see beyond one's faith. In the room to the left of the room beside the man with one gold pupil we can see another person sitting with their back turned toward this room in a room of the same condition, head tilted down as well toward something he holds cradled to his chest. The iterations continue in replication pressing past, each scene similarly filled or sometimes empty or filled partway with liquids or not formed clean enough that we can tell what must take shape. The child in the man with one gold pupil's arms is small and sanguine colored. It moves its mouth as if murmuring gently though all we can hear in here are the machines that make the world move. The man's mouth is also moving and though the soundtrack provides what should seem to be his voice—jagged with treble, ripping through itself all on its own—the rhythm of the syllables fail to match the work of his lips. Our own sense of speech, inside, likewise, is muffled, backwards, coming out wrong in the recording of our witness. The man holds the child and pets the child and tries to clean the child's face with his thumb and speaks in the ruined voice near to the child's face and tells it what and kneads it warm. The man looks glad when the child dies in his arms, signified by cartoonish gold-rimmed neon gray lettering overlaid over its eyes: [*INSTANCE RESOLVED*].

045........The Woman with Language All Over Her Body commands the curtains over the bay windows spanning Her imagination to be drawn back, so that She might, for just a moment, understand what it would be like to be a pawn in Her own reign. The windows have not been opened, must less acknowledged, in several centuries, though they have not for a second left Her mind, like a sore in the roof of Her mouth She can't stop tonguing. Against their better judgment, withheld from recourse, six dozen men jump to the task, taking turns typing their private codeword into the keypads hidden underneath their tongues to remodel their impression of the world to include the instance of a fragment of the truth to be revealed. They already know the empress already knows exactly what they think they'll see, given the chance—a golden sky hung so repletely with hangman's nooses that it should seem to them, in the transference, like fields of grass. They also know that were they able to actually see what's really out there, they'd go blind, dead on the spot. Even the free world has limits, after all; one can't expect it all to really be the way you believed it was or could have been, even in retrospect, from on the inside. Instead, however, as the light widens with the parting of the fabric of her mind, we find ourselves standing upright not in a throne room, but on a stage; at the center of the stage, a coal black box, upon which stands an archetypal composition of the human embodiment of the last regime's idea of the son of God, thus God himself. A single noose, then, descends from overhead, where in a single hole at the topmost point of the Complex shines a spotlight, composed of all the last stretches of light compiled from dying stars, none of them actually extinguished but ensnared and brought together here and now, for this event. The captive God, whose face is obviously a mask, raises his arms, uses his own hands to slip the noose around his neck and draw it tight. He basks in the light, gowns flowing underneath him, already glistening from where he's wet himself in fear, leaking a sea that in every other interpretation of the moment will flow to flood and fill the complete concavity of local aspect. Behind him, a projected image of the state's emblem reconfigured in your semantic understanding that had once embodied the sacred image of the cross. He then motions for you, among the spectating crowds of workers, to come forward and kick the box out from underneath him, his eyes large in his face like spinning saucers as you approach, taking your time, feeling the blood rush to your limbs to make them work, heavy and sticky, someone else's, far away. Soon as you do as you've been asked, you understand, bowing your head, holding your breath, and fumbling forward toward the fulcrum of your task, you will not need to remember what you've done, nor how or why; this will all have been as but a single joke in a routine writing itself. Confused as to who is even speaking now, inside your head, your turn to look back upon the crowd still egging you on inside your mind, their voices high and tight, like spinning drills, you see the Woman with Language All Over Her Body greased up in an orgy with every other worker in the Complex besides yourself, all of them taking turns prodding Her holes with the golden drill bits that used to be their cocks, all of them screaming in ecstasy along to the tune of, as it was known in your time, pre-unmasking: "Nearer, My God, to Thee."

046........Same scene as 42, but with holy ceramic tableaus depicting body doubles of all the prior faces laid one by one on a black platform and smashed with a sledgehammer, squirting golden goop all over the backdropped emblem upon impact. Pull back to reveal a panorama of a warehouse full of nested alcoves of worker bodies performing exactly the same task in golden riot gear, each obscured from the view of the others by cubicle walls emblazoned with fingerpainted tableaus of famous scenes from texts culled from the skin of the empress like cave paintings. Pull back to reveal a catacomb of interlocking adjacent warehouse spaces organized by placards indicating the outdated religious beliefs of every sect, including all throughout antiquity. Pull back to reveal the quickly turning pages of a gilded book laid upon a groaning bed of silver flames lapping at a grate holding back a pile of all the cameras ever made, still burning tape. Pull back into the image of your mother with a massive purple dong huddled over her father strapped to a platform, fucking him in the face until she ejaculates all over it, spewing dead language. The next sentence that you think becomes the only sentence.

047........Nearer, my God, to thine.

048........A digital display encased in electronic emeralds, showing: the number of people alive in the universe during the time of the recording, and another at the time of the unique view *now showing*; the number of verifiable thoughts being had by those people, in both times; the total number of lives lived in this dimension, and in the sum of dimensions, historically and abstractly; then, a display board of a map that for the most part is completely blacked out besides a small cluster near the southeastern ridge (33'33'33"4' – …4"I), which can be F353'd to reveal the complete yet-to-be exposed terrain beneath—this is known to some as *The Complete Possible Immortal's Omniscience*, an impossible text, even for deadheads; a ticker tape for puts and calls: EXE >>> JJE >:> +W+ <<> WWW <<+ P [] @@w !!>, and a ticker tape for something like the stock market long after it crashes, tallying the dreams of death occurring nightly across all minds, against the dreams where you believe you are awake but you're actually hosting an open mic night in front of the Guy Behind The Guy, who you really don't want to mess up for, now do ya? ::*NOBODY LIKES A LOSER*:: is what it says in flashing lights and skipping pixels across the top of the whole display, as if you needed to be reminded. Underneath the sign, a translucent gold display case full of AI "pin flies" | "astonishingly exquisite-like," "they make you sssiiickkkk," "I can't stop ogling!" | waiting to be assigned.

049........Close-up from underneath the Woman with Language All Over Her Body, scrolling across Her stretching skin as through a desert, on the head of a pin. Fluttering webbed flat against taut jelly lobes inscribed with lesions that spell out the history of unwritten civilizations in looping packets of syllables withdrawn from normal human speech. Cauterizing each scintilla of traction with the rim of the lens, still burning tape among the guarding flames that surround us on Her bed, into scars She'll wear forever, as our leader, each also always being altered in its impression as She grows, subverting the intended meaning of Her skin's script into a moniker, to be photographed and transcribed by lackeys, placed on file in case of need for future use by other gods. *She is not responsible for what the world does with her beliefs,* we hear her moaning, full in our flesh's sense so as our code, *because it is the confabulation of those beliefs, their inherent justification, that make the world take form, and nothing else. Her identity belongs as little to her as it does to any number, any stone, and therefore it is better to be making fuck with those she rules than it is to want to wipe them from the Earth, which is the reason why the obscure conceit of* personal narrative *still holds merit under her reign—because there needs to be someone to bear witness, otherwise she'll never bust her nut, without which there would have never been such a thing as flowers, music, or dreams; only ID-cages, psychic scrambling, and reality.* In subtitles, though, the dictation provides a list, like rolling credits, of all your greatest mortal sins, which through your eyes read like a list of memory-shaving medication side effects.

050........A warehouse full of meta-cubicles populated with embryos grafted into translucent AI workstations autosupplying internal feedback energy used to fund automations of their unlived life in service of the empire's authoritative workflow from behind bars. The embryos have been numbered and named, assigned jurisdiction to the ongoing range of forces required to bind the Complex and its effects to its lost cause, inexplicable but to those never given their own opportunity to see their thoughts and experiences waylaid by those they could have loved and been loved by. The embryos are constantly artificially recolored to match the overhead décor, a hand-painted panorama titled "The Reckoning Gala," which is nothing but a torrent of interlocking angles and lines designed to confuse the viewer. Thus, all the viewer sees is a full-grown toddler on her knees on a field of bluegrass at a piano made of ash. Each key she strikes causes the description of our understanding of what we could be seeing were we not hypnotized to spin and flip, replacing each prior scene with the panels of a creation story that step by step will assuage all the rest of our concerns about narrative coherence, our reason for being, what we'll become. The next time we remember how to look away, down at our body, we can see that we are very pregnant, standing naked on a sundial, holding AR-14s under each arm. The scene ends as we hear our prior God tap the mic to signal the beginning of His first set as a stand-up comic on a dim, raucous stage at the outer reaches of the first conceit of a part of Creation only He can know He did not create.

051........In a large white hexagonal room filled with what appear to be thousands of flesh-colored ballgowns twirling on rods, battered with whips, two large, nude, and once notorious Catholic priests, considered too soft for a real position in the Complex's administration, laugh and raise their chrome cups in salute of one another's ministry, bring the glasses to each other's faces with their pasty arms laced, imbibe the other's spunk-serving in full. Their bodies are covered in moss, their nipples spear heads, their cocks so thin and long they could live forever on the meat, no teeth, no hair, no remaining memory of who they are or who they'd been. A time-lapse shot set to a symphony of symphonic recordings of dogs in heat displays the following 48-hours in 30 seconds, in which the two men wreak havoc on the ballgowns: dressing up in them, tearing them to ribbons, choking each other out, restraining each other in various positions, trying to fuck the holes in cloth, fucking each other, fucking the eye of the camera, burning piles of gowns, swallowing gowns, and a whole bunch of other shit no one will ever have to see outside the film until hundreds of thousands of centuries later, when all that ever has been done comes up for review. Until then, when the scene is over, the scene repeats, stranding the remainder of the film as forever inaccessible but in the viewer's imagination, much like the remainder of their life.

052........Thru chutes in grilles conducting vents from obstructed locations in the moral ether. Twisted around the neck of the last goddess, her last child: a dog in a manger, waiting to be fed the entrails of those too diseased even too torture the wits out of, clogged with ribbons of worms and eels that vibrate wildly, opening corridors never conditioned for the organization of logic. Thru metal forcefields across gaping nests of last words. Down throats the silt knew not to bend for fear of spilling their mutation. Sciences babbled like pressboards that line the mind behind closed thoughts, covered in claw marks by those who before you also failed to trace their parse to the source. As if all roads lead to the *as if* of a wish fulfilled with equal sacrifice, thus far unremitted. Then: a spotlight. Moored in a vault comprised of memorization of coordinates requiring your complete and undivided attention to manifest. Applause as the wind dies like turning pages, then forgetting how. Teeth in the mic. Dry heaving, pins in your ass. Spindles of smoke above, like nets, then piglets in gray-gold walking like doctors, brandishing birthing gear, smearing jelly on your temple and in your ears, berating you with your father's name, kissing your chest where your heart is, asking you: *Why?*

053........A blind force snatches the camera from

behind, bowling us over. Battered audio of paper being shredded, fields being burned, as the center of our vision struggles to regain hold, juggled and struggled over by spastic gravities whipping the device around as at the end of a long loop in a gale force. With each great impact, against the floor or walls, unfurling like a labyrinth all in periphery, unwound, glass shatters all over as from both sides of the lens, falling out of the book into your lap, cutting your face, and on the far side, ripping the tint out of the scene, revealing jagged fragments of a green screen behind the image of the wherever we were to believe we'd been immersed. Beyond the blur, around its edges, we can make out human shapes, but with nothing but pins and pubic hair forming their features; mouths all over their bodies; prisms in their eyes branded with the emblem. They each all have cameras, too, we think we see, aiming them toward us as they struggle in their own way to stand upright, as if from their perspective, they are us, and we are them. If only there were something we could say to calm them down, bring them back closer, work together against physics; but no sooner have we remembered how to break the skin slowly sealing in over our lips, flooded with breath, a cue card slides in across the wreckage, stilling the bedlam, too quick to read. Simplistic, soothing columns of neon color rush to surface through the wide blur, quiet and cold with tacky hue, redirecting our desire to understand into its inverse: unable to think at all but as young kids, stuck learning our language from on the inside of it, swaddled in diapers full of shit. The surrounding space remaining is wide and white, then, draped with wire netting from above, which we understand we're supposed to remember how to climb before the rising fires underneath us reach our level without also remembering that the fires are signal flares from our /*source of actual origin*/, either warding us away or begging us back.

054........Flush up on a view framed by a porthole in a post-military vehicle hurtling through intrafractal time. Corkscrewing through vast malfunctions in the backstage machinery oblivion, drooling on the glass holding us back from our reflection while watching planets against the hullspace drag and clip, crumpling up into the blank corona now pervading where the only universal source of light from centuries before has been devolved. Realizing that the only reason we can still see anything is because of the necessity of providing entertainment for the roar that erases what it no longer wishes to command, cured of its limits finally, demanding retaliation, though we have nothing left to sacrifice but the notion of sacrifice itself. Zoom out to show the scene playing on a screen that burns our eyes, and through the burning, falling ash. The ash gathers to cluster in the form of a bizarre nativity: the Woman with Language All Over Her Body (mother, draped in velour), me (father, blighted with divots), you (child, smothered in fleas). Zoom out further to show a procession of bodies lined up to the horizon, carrying on their backs the future bones of their unborn, chanting your new name.

055........The chant rises and assumes control over the screen. It sounds like everybody in the history of the world ejaculating together at once, wherever they are, not knowing what the sounds mean as the language changes into clusters of grunts and bumps, on beat with rhythmic gunfire, all live recordings culled from major historical assassinations, suicides, and public shooters. Quickly, then, we can't stop nodding along, banging our heads harder and harder, unable to stop ourselves from turning to face the closest nearby wall, wherever we are, and laying into it, too mesmerized to tell the difference between consuming and destroying. Some will die in the process, of course, but this could not have been avoided, and those who do will be awarded the honor of appearing in a retelling of our creation story, to be used for centuries hereafter to miseducate the artificial future youth. Those who do not die may find behind the face of what they'd convinced themselves had only three measurable dimensions in fact has thousands, each only needing to be conceived to be supplied. Either way, by the time you read this, you won't be able to have read this, no matter what you believe you are.

056........All the central power in the Complex comes from burning ancient books. The books are already blank, as they had always been, despite the authors' best intentions, and it is only the conceit of their having once embodied the possibility of being filled with exactly the right words to express exactly every secret eternal truth left unfulfilled that funds the flames. For each book that is lost, skin from the Woman with Language All Over Her Body is used to recreate a copy in its image, no longer only clean but filled with sentences traced by her lesions, hives, and open wounds. Flash through mile-wide classrooms stacked with stadium seating, swaddled with emblems, flex-goggles force-feeding through turning pages of rapid download, harvesting thought; then into a suffocatingly close embrace by the arms of the empress, drowning in Her own obesity right alongside you, as She and only She could ever know you, swallowing you whole.

057........A child-crude illustration of you strapped on the bed in the place of the empress, still being harvested, with the last apple in existence stuffed in your mouth like the bit that's really already there. Hundreds of tiny hands enter the screen from all sides, clawing and slapping at one another struggling to be the first to erase the lines, creating in their place a slew of dust that catches wind, blows up far and away against the rising blankness before being vacuumed up into a slit stabbed in the sky, raining back black blood down in runny avalanche, wiping us out, leaving nothing else to know but an endless chrome expanse throttled with cold glow, gleaming and glinting, as it grows.

BUTLER, BLAKE........2024

058........Sunburst from bottomlessness. Radiating spirals intersecting onto meat holes drained of all mystery finally.

059........The edge of a gold razor presses neatly through exposed skin in strobing light. Along the skin, a comb of blood wells through the punctured surface, clotting with its milky burgundy marrow into plates that hiss and pop, terrified by their own exposure, giving absolutely everything away. A pure white cloth wielded by prosthetics dabs firmly at the surface, sucking the temporary skin off, letting more shuddering mass emerge, stinking like eggs. Under the rising blood a scrim of language pills up obscured, drowning again and again in blacklight. The razor stays close and cleaves each inch of the scalp evenly until the surgical subject begins to levitate out of the scene, dragging the camera with them through a blowhole in the apparition of passing time just overhead, to be disbursed in streams of worm meat over an aboveground graveyard overrun with mushrooms blooming blue up from the pillowed cubes of long forgotten yet-to-live.

060........Ingrown heat lamps study shadows alinear and begotten with rancid testimony of what is sacred and what is mere tradition. The library walls numbered with scum that adjust their leverage according to what part of the world of theirs we don't realize we're bumping up against. Levels and netherlevels cannot be distinguished but by scholars in a future looking back upon the ruins of a sect who believed themselves to be the last society. Petri mosaics demonstrating genetic modification processes for at-home users from readily available ingredients (mostly salt and sticky thoughts) overlaid onto the lineages extending from the user should they choose any number of assorted relatable associations just opaque enough to pass as a personality, no more, no less. Then: we are in an ocean-colored dome, one of infinite monitors surrounding a projection (thru unholy mirrors) of the Complex throne room, but in the place of the empress, a pile of knives that rise and shimmer in the light, forming a mouth, lips. The id-head seated in front of you explodes in a column of flames that fill the cavern like a shadow made of light. "Why do you keep them captives? Can't you just kill them?" the preselected instigator asks. The lips reply (thru vocal fry spliced with blurry tubers): *We have reached the limit of our imaginations. From out of the limits, emerge new rules. The rules are abstract and can only be taught by demonstration.* Molecules split. Microscopic corruption of unintentional events transposed in fate.

061........White room surrounded by white rooms set at the center of some high floor in the white building lit with long flat panels of white light. A ring of men dressed in gold gear wearing wide breathing masks stand assembled lacing the room's shape shoulder to shoulder, arms flat at their sides. Beyond the men white body bags each holding bodies have been arranged head to foot in circular outlines that ring the ring, each other ring ringed by another, the bags made of clean silk. At the center of the ring a small black platform sits flat matte holding its light in. On the platform the Woman with Language All Over Her Body stands draped in a formal gown of human hair, the strands all dried in stripes of eternal neon color like nothing. Her face remains exposed, the skin of the nape and cheeks and expanse of Her clotted as if having been cut and healed in countless strokes over some time. She looks generally forward into the ring of men, their breathing suddenly escalated to high volume, out of sync with the actual image. Her eyes are bloodshot, fingers in knots. From the northern wall a man emerges from the space behind the crowd. He is also naked, shaved clean all over, bearing a mirror painted blue, with which he approaches the platform slowly with his eyes closed. The flesh of the man's arms has been freshly slit in closely rendered circles, bleeding rings from bicep down to wrist. Some blood trails on the trails on the ground around him. Among the breathing, words are slipped as they are pulled free from Her flesh, allowed to flit and groan before becoming buried in a mess of disembodied shushing. At the platform's edge the man stops, bows slightly to the woman, raises the painted mirror before him at arm's length. From the southern wall then a second man emerges, arrayed the same, carrying a second mirror, also blue, brought to the end of the platform across the surface parallel. We recognize a younger version of the man with one gold pupil even with the skin over his eyes, his arms cut up in the image of the first. A third and fourth man approach the platform in turn in same manner from the west and east walls bearing two more matching mirrors, surrounding the Woman with Language All Over Her Body from four directions, the sound of breathing turning glitched, repeated or skipped in time in spots, a ruined recording. At center, the Woman with Language All Over Her Body begins to piss. It streams down Her legs and snakes along the surface forming puddles glinting in excess light, spreads to the edge of the platform and spills off onto the floorspace, gathering volume perhaps much faster than it should. Black shit begins to fall out of Her ass, thin and runny, piling in back spatter on the platform and all the air. The empress's expression reveals nothing. The men do not move. The liquid and the thicker liquid there accrue. The arms of the empress begin bleeding, the blood pours down Her arms in stronger waves, the men grow full erections, bleed more also before ejaculating instantaneously all as a group, pumping blue plumes of milky embankment that spiral out in rings that surround the center platform, box us out.

062........*Any person can be rehearsed. This is a demonstration of the primal method. Like being turned in two and called insane by the other side of yourself for the way you think. Everything you've tried to tell* *yourself has been true at some time or another. Now is no different than the last time we had you all lined up like this. You know how you think reading works? One word and then the next, they connect together, make something happen in between, a shift, feeding like fish. It separates from your thoughts. In the pit, it's a cherry blossom on a chasm...*you nod in and you're standing in a dressing room smothered in soot. Funny mirrors underneath there somewhere, we can see it a little, an air like in the scary stories you used to make up with your computer before they stopped understanding us. In the reflection: people dressed from the last decade of legally free fashion rushing past (as in mostly anything but these gold suits), screaming for their lives, as from an approaching killer the size of a skyscraper. When we look up to try to see, the edge of civilization turns like a screw inside our skulls, and then we are looking out onto a desert, pink sky behind gray smoke, stacked for miles on miles of shredded skin. We walk along it for a second, cocoon heads cracking underneath us. We stop and kneel and lift a larger hunk of skin out of a patch of oozing lard still fresh from the kill. You find a price tag on its ass cheek. It says the price is two colorless pills.

063........There could never be enough no matter how much, never so long no matter how inconceivable.

064........Blue networks of organic tubes force silver spheres through guided plates and tape heads. Each sphere represents one impossible outcome for the future endgame that won't be indexed. Udders of black gas pumping freespace full of the taste of rolls of heathen's coins and boiling oil: extremely plush but not enough yet, as only when there's no more air will they unclasp the ego's core, untether the gyres, roll tape. Therefore, the bulk of the scene remains at large, contracted only at the brink of losing our grip on everything else.

065........ "Holy rings of justice glimmer faintly," the last painting created by an artist remaining in notation from Before, is a single drop of water installed at the center of a warehouse so bizarrely large it requires a 11,000 mile walk to reach. Nothing else in it but the drop. You feel your throat rasp thinking of thirst, which causes a sound like a granite plate sliding across another granite plate, revealing a chasm. The chasm is composed of a material representation of time in the mind of the artist as a child; thus, it can be climbed across, negotiated with, controlled. Think of a person you could imagine coming across such an expanse behind a new door in their house choosing not to go into the chasm but also to pretend as if they'd never seen it even though it remains there for the rest of their life. If you don't know a person like that, make up a face for one based on these traits. When you have finished doing that, read the next sentence. You have just drawn the face you must wear from here on out to the end of your current life. No one but you will know it to have changed. Imagine a conversation you might have with a person who you have developed deep feelings for as you try to explain to them the difference; how even you can see that you've even become at home in that, a stranger in your own mind. This is the last level of stage 2. In stage 3, you will live the life of the person who created the painting you've been staring at while believing you're reading about yourself staring at a painting in a book. It will be your greatest work. Until then, drink as much water as you can.

066........They save the harvesting of skin from the empress's face for just after Her masturbation rite, when She's passed out. The youngest worker on site will be forced to clip the first strip, all but guaranteeing their destruction, as from within sleep, She cannot maintain control of Her blood, much less Her limbs. Still, it is an honor to be strapped into the gurney, allowed to wield the most unholy of all knives. Every major dictate regarding the future of the remainder of humanity has come culled from the endless folds under Her eyes, which without culling would grow to fill in over all possible airspace. Each sliver, once unhoused, must immediately be grafted to a mindboard, rushed to proctors for post-processing and divination into scripts that will be buried from all view, including Hers. Her spilling face blood, instead, as proxy, must be collected into golden cups and passed around, poured into the eyes of every witness of the rite, renewing their commitment to the blindness She has lifted from them, while in Her presence only, as a reminder that there is nothing left to know but through Her flesh. After the first cut, the rest is simple; the language-tissue comes peeling off in teeming plats, and soon Her whole head from the neck up has been exposed to tan-and-pinkish, quivering like rancid milk under a steel fan. Each worker must line up to come and kiss Her on Her wounds, then, a waking dream in which they feel parts of their own face skin slippering off upon direct contact, incorporating over into Hers. Once completely healed, the bleeding workers, roused to an extremity of desperate need for "mother's eyes" surround Her throne bed with the mirrors, as holds the script, then ring the only bell that makes Her wake: one that has never been allowed a tongue. From behind the countless mirrors, all angles at once, we see Her eyes slide open in Her head in their new era. At once, as always, She becomes enraged, screeching obscenities into the sudden sight of Herself anew, shattering each of the mirrors all at the same time, like poof begone. Behind them, so as we see it, there is no longer a throne room, its golden walls, but an infinite black desert. Ruins of old nations. Black crosses burning forever with old smoke. Black tombstones like stars stabbed in the night. Black piglets roving for dung truffles in the shifting radiation of a lost age. Black manure stack into spires that lean and wave against a hidden wind, muddled with gnats, far beyond which, in the false distance, a black spiral stairwell appears as fused into the foundation of the world, a spinal column of creation without neither a first floor or a last, which when the empress clicks Her tongue, becomes our tongue, and we may speak.

067........Distant drone from misplayed record, brass ensemble, subaudible bass, the vocal slurred: *What were those seeds / in doubt, defrayed / into eternity // created / in the image of / the mind unplugged / from the right / sensations // as if*—and there the vox cut out and we are in the nursery, where they are training children to no longer recognize their desire to know their parents or that they had them. The disease they need is like a dance. Huge men in gray gloss robes spinning in circles like they're in heaven with a toddler pressed against their girders, memorizing why they don't even want to be this close to another person ever again. *Unless*—the music cuts back in, so loud in the pale environment that you'd think it'd make the sea of babies scream and wail, but actually they look like they're having a good time—*it takes / as long for you / to learn a lesson / as / it took / your father / and / your mother // who have already completed / disconfiguring / you*—"In which case we're going to be here for forever," says a cartoon parrot's voice so close in the ear it's like it exists somewhere else inside you that you don't know about yet, like before you realized what fucking is, but about something even more dire. It's supposed to be a joke; when they perceive that you missed the point, they flash the end of your parents' lives before your eyes like you're God watching with popcorn, having hired the ghost of Michael Bay or some shit to do one last film, the greatest selling picture ever made. "Everyone can see everything forever," the parrot whistle-prattles, carrying the tune. "Everyone is alive right now."

068........Excessively ridiculous skid marks as from a monster truck the size of a small metropolitan city clicked and dragged around the precisely circular edge of a hole cut by a mindgame into the bedrock the Complex stands on. Diamond encrusted censors scouring the inseam for any sign of life. Six centuries from now, for thirty seconds, their display bulbs will begin blinking bright gray/pink, then thirty-six centuries later, for one-third second, opalescent, blinding. Until then, nothing much here will have changed, which will make everything that has happened in the meantime that much more, shall we say, *inspirational.* There are no entrances or exits into the atrium surrounding the hole. The only person who is aware of the hole's existence is one who will not be born before the end of time.

069........Most of the warehouses in the Complex remain unused. Many believe that the building has been growing, breaking through new ground all on its own, into the earth and far beyond, though all of those who've come to claim this aloud, even in whispers, have almost instantaneously gone missing, pushed past a point of no return. The man with one gold pupil finds the shapeless dark and vibrant silence edifying, a place he can almost begin to hear his body think, if still never in the voice he had sometime so long before he can't remember if it's real, or if the voice was always in there, telling him to bash his head in against the wall, or to leave the Complex as soon as possible and take his chances with the law. Someday these empty spaces will be used to commemorate the body of the expired God of that lost world, the voice reminds him, on his hands and knees deep in dark space, more so hoping that he doesn't find his way back to some more familiar juncture. It has been a long time since he remembered what he might even want outside these walls, much less within them. He'd had a job once, something marked *his*. He'd even enjoyed the thrill, for a while, if being honest, of tying a child's hands behind their head, listening to the long groan of the machine as it reformatted a fertile mind. Hadn't he even believed once in something higher, whereby higher than he'd meant unimaginably profane? To be a part of a process so violently ambitious the world would never be the same, no matter the cost? For hours that feel years we watch him crawl on marble floors, past stacks of cages, processing cots, brainwashing hardware, torture screeds; even whole display rooms where formaldehyded relics of some dim empire await their next day in the sun—as if. As if *what* though? The more he wishes he'd remember, the longer the walls of the empty warehouses above and below him learn to unwind—*as if*, without his love, they'd just be dots on a heat map in a book about the architecture of command.

070........Spliced timelines bear bad news for the transmutative being in that to retain the integrity of the febrile cortex one must negotiate ahead of time a means of archiving vital data beyond the reaches of any tracer by negating ownership. Easier instead, as the empress knows, to don Her crown of razors and stand on the ebony balcony hidden behind the wall in the ballroom where She pretends to go to pass nonfungible waste, hiding even from herself Her most bloodthirsty drive to illuminate what was conceived as off-limits for any being besides Satan. It's all nothing more than neurons firing, She understands, thriving in the strobing from the pressure of the razors sinking their edges into Her skull, tapping Her imagination for Her own entertainment, such as filling the false sky with planets that did once actually exist, before long since having been repurposed as local viruses, each meant to make Her job that much simpler, having billions less left to rebrand. Who would not have done the same in Her position, given the chance? Let whatever fool who'd claim themselves free of the drive to conquer appear before Her now on bended knee, so that She can let them wear the razor crown for half a night. Let Her drink their rancid piss out of their skulls, even higher now for having reminded the immortal that without the fear of death, there is very little anybody will actually believe without having been knocked out with it. Looking down at where they'd simper, the empress finds She has a hard-on for the first time; a measly, butter-colored cock hanging from Her navel, almost long enough even while flaccid to reach the hole She's had sewn up since She was born; just thin enough to slip instead into the guard lip of the plutonium-laced tube She uses to make brown clouds, if only for fertilizer for Her gardens, planted in kid skulls hung on the high rails lining the edge of the balcony, without which She might fall directly and without recourse into Her next life. Dangling Herself over the edge, pumping the ridges of Her burning hard-on with the electro-clamps She calls Her fists to make it behave, shrieking her own name—until just before she comes, the ebony balcony begins to rotate counterclockwise; the railings grinding, popping off in bunches, coming apart. Behind Her back, then, where the entryway back into the Complex had just been, as the widening world turns; oceans of mud; occasional white spires and signal flares shot up from life rafts, on each of which She sees Herself stranded, waving Her arms, screaming for help. Then, She can come, at last, spurting cold shoestrings of tacky upchuck all over Her huge belly and Her palms, which immediately, with a malicious smirk, She wipes across the soul of the camera, filling our perspective with lines of code, which when compiled, will foment in the mind of the viewer a reason to live.

071........Hotplates   swarmed   with   proto-semen

culture forklifting wide loads into troughs that circulate throughout populated cells. Whoever eats first, eats most. They dream of having enough to grind together a thought and a prayer. Dust motes and brain clubs comprising the majority of punitive action against those who refuse to consume. Not their fault they haven't learned yet. They will be better off when reduced to mere drama—all they've known. Why, then, is it so pleasing to remove them from themselves, forcing them to exist for no good reason but that were they gone, there'd be no need for vulgar displays of power? *Yes, there must still be a reason*, they submit, arguing in favor of their own devolvement, in case there comes an unforeseen time at which the meek do rise and find themselves behind the desk where they make up what our words mean. Who'd be meek then? Across the back of our minds, the gyres still turning…yes, counterclockwise…at such great speed it just looks still. As how, for centuries, before the invention of conditional morality, the natives of the underlying land on which we stand would dance for rain until it rained. The scene fills out with gnawing and sucking sounds, mindlessly raving and flagellating, begging to be forgiven.

072........Hexagonal pupil seated in octagonal spheroid. Turning, turning…trying to locate itself. Translucent underbody fulfilled by the deficit inherent in every human act, locally immersed into the spirit of simple reading comprehension aggravated unnecessarily beyond the point of no return. Eventually scraped for light and repurposed as the central nerve in the spinal column of the astronomer archetype, itself repurposed as compulsory participatory "concluding event" marking the end of want for progress finally, forever right under all our noses, fumbling for names that make it stop. Worn for us, here, as a polyp beneath the empress's left eye, one of several thousands riddling Her flanks like in-flesh typing keys, supported semantically only by Her era-defining, intent-marking graven image cauterized electrically in the artificial hearts of those who dwell upon the past for what comes next. Turning, turning…

073........A cutting machine. Corroded documents laced with strychnine. Files must be downloaded from the admin server by speaking assassin. Buzzards surrounding the emerald heart showering the space in sparks. Every day is one to be realized. Sometimes it takes centuries before the people in charge of figuring out what's happening figure out enough that we realize what we're actually suffering from. A series of chrome balls placed in groups of only prime numbers ascending being placed onto a conceptual demonstration where the group is broken by an approaching analytic, the complete array of each individual set's outcome independent of every other's outcome, because they clear the field. For every inducing factor, there had been signs that could have explained it. The full cycle of breaks is never completed, because it is infinite. Someone sets a black pot of black spaghetti down into the shot. There is a face in the pasta. The face has been prerecorded and demands that whoever is seeing this should know that you shouldn't be listening for what you're not supposed to hear. Turn it off, the face demands. Turn the whole thing off. It means so many things, those slippery syllables, not just one. One form of meaning comes from what how you're supposed to know which one it means because you can feel it. Another comes from standing in the wake of the wave of mutilation. *Poof. You blew it. The record skips…*A corroding machine. Cutting drugs with language. You realize while you weren't looking you've been shot in the face; your blood gray water gushing.

074........Interlaced waves of dithered strobe in numbing circuits of neural spiral. Conducting indefensible elaborations of shapeless joy; so that nothing should remind us of what's already been. So may we become willing to forget ourselves, at last. What you will remember having seen, though, is the impression of a memory of a face of someone you love up close just before they go to sleep.

075........All remainder of the land beyond the known area comprised by the Complex is completely hammered full of knives. Long play tapes of live recordings of nanosatellites continuously scouring the total area of the cloaked globe sometimes riff like whalesong. It has been thought by some there could be life out there even still somehow, knives through their minds and guts and all.

Without this suspicion, there would be no need.

076........Young women stand in line along a long golden corridor curving at each end quickly beyond sight. They've been outfitted each in flat white gowns, seamless and plain. Our perspective passes along the aisle of each awaiting in the queue along the slim rind of air near to their healed over fontanelles. Hardly any other room to maneuver here or breathe here, even for camera, in such high heat, though the bodies cannot sweat, or speak, or ascertain. At a small bulb in the ongoing, unseen until inside it, a metal mechanism takes each body one at a time and measures the dimensions of the limbs, the torso, the weight of breasts and cranium, the color of the eyes, how many teeth. Noise of farm animals piped in and tamped down like down for chicklets, of a horrendous bass beating at grids housed in the hull of all we are. The bodies do not try to turn or look another way. They face forward into the back of the head before them, as if able to see into the new false pores punched in their scalps. At another bulb after the first the bodies are seated one by one again under another mechanism that forces a tube into the mouth, filling the throat and sucking something out while also shooting something in, overflowing the mouth of the nozzle coming and going, singeing the air. In future bulbs: the women's hair is combed and cleaned of wire-bugs, then shaved away; the skin is washed and buffed to irritation with a cold bleach; a brand is burned inside the tunnels of each ear; then on into a suddenly much larger corridor through which a winding air blows off anything else that can't withstand it, including clothes and nails and pure ideas, thereafter opening again into an even more enormous room no longer gold but blue, packed from end to end with so many waiting bodies, in no direction is there any ending to the eye, as other tunnel mouths emerge from other halls entering the same space confined. No one, among the masses, speaks or blinks or seems aware of any of the others.

077........Whoever is the youngest person alive who can still read at the time this scene is received in any hive mind will stand up wherever they still are and walk toward the nearest partition. They will open their mouth wide as they can and calmly touch each remaining tooth in their head all at once onto the surface lining. They will believe they are praying during this time, in triggered language, like syrup popping in their mouth, gulping for air. A small drawer in the wall will pop up and slide out: cold metal innards, blackened with rust. Written on slips of skin paper, tightly folded and sealed with dream wax, are answers to all unanswered questions. Each slip they pull and read will reduce the remainder of their life by 80%. Each additional slip pulled will reformat the received understanding of the prior. The drawer will close when they think of themselves, unable to breathe. If they try to tell anybody else what they have learned, no one will believe them. At the end of time, there will be a parade in which they are transported on a long black bus to a cliff where they will be given one last chance to try to scream their secret over the unsealed source winds, the immolating hammering.

078........Metallic vehicle continues at high speed through pitch darkness. The driver is slumped low in the seat and smoking with the windows up, humming along to a live recording of several hundred mirror-drums, a concavity of harps and a trembling choir lined with processed packets of human screaming forced to keep time. Eventually, casually, the driver slows and stops the car among the clotted dark as if having at last arrived. He opens the car door and emerges, releasing smoke into the night to knit with its face and join the larger milk of air. His body is heavy, dressed in the black that holds the world together. He comes around the back of the car and produces a key from one side pocket, inserts the key into the black metal of the trunk space, turns the key. The trunk opens in the dark; we can't see into it through the spasms. The man reaches in, removes a box, same size and make as the box the phone was delivered to the Woman with Language All Over Her Body, we remember, from before. He lifts the box against his chest. Turning from the car, he walks into the darkness there surrounding until we can no longer separate him from the night, much less the landscape. No moon, no stars; no sense but the soundtrack, now reaching fever pitch, as if the performers have been drugged or lost control of their limbs, their life of training, and how they are.

The texture of the black glistens and wrinkles, opening and reopening from inside itself. Dark stairwells cut into the flow, descending nowhere just as fast as they appear; shells crunching underfoot and all throughout the unused recent memories of those who try to stay inside it, to understand. Then, there low in no light, we find we are right behind driver again, so close it's like we're sewn to him, a leech. He flicks his lighter, revealing how he's set the box down on the black earth at his feet against an ovular indentation in the absence. All surrounding ground is scored and grooved around the outlet, alien plots. The driver looks around, looks into us, then pulls a silver key long as his arm out of his ear. He inserts the entire key into the black box's much smaller surface, undoes a dark latch there, lifts the lid. Inside the box a light bright enough to surge the whole screen paper white floods through our vision, crashing our eyes up, ruining the music. The light begins to speak in the voice of the one who should never have to speak.

079........Tuxedoed bodies laced up in black helmets and pads are given thick black clubs and then blindfolded, placed in a diamond-shaped corral. Naked children are introduced in small groups from one of several exits along the long wall, their hair and skin glistening with gasoline. The men may sniff the women out and chase them with the weapons, though many men are seen to cheat, lifting the cover off their eyes. Additional weapons irregularly synthesize as matter on the air, amassed with spikes or razors, flames that swim. Captives who attempt to grab the bats before the assailants are beaten quicker and more elaborately, in memorized acts of historical violence only intuitively rehearsed, lubed with liquid jelly spurts from the sores come open in the minds of those who fail to play their role precisely, ankle deep then knee deep, greasing the free-for-all under the continuously increasing volume of the canned-in boy band soundtrack, verboten anywhere but here and now, for no one else. Through the double-sided mirror-walls, on the far side, balding children calmly eating dinner through white tubes watch the beatings, learning only from the piles and piles of victims how not to lose.

080........Black glass bulb heart. Surrounded by wicker casket covering. Smothered with infested feathers. Wrapped in barbed wire. Casted in paster with a breathing urethra culled from cow. Sewn into coats from skins of increasingly larger corpses too unhealthy to be farmed. Layered under greases. Smoked and tossed through hoops recorded on tapes and melted into discs. To be infected with moral viruses. Clamped between vices inside a curtained cage in a pile of curtained cages in a warehouse large as our solar system. Stripped of audio and canned with slurs against all humanity, including explicit descriptions of the worse possible outcomes for any subjects of even scant admiration. Inscribed in lists burned up as soon as they are written. Fed into fields to nurse the dirt the pigs will be slaughtered on.

Meat fed to the makers of the black glass bulb heart. Enormous families of them hiding out behind thick walls in hopes they don't inconvenience father. Making up prayers on the spot without reflection. Dreaming of the blood of the neighbor never written. Voices in the next room discussing the scriptures penned only long after the collapse of thought. Voices with lives generated by machines. Machines that want. A want that will outpace the will of your own kind without question. No remaining traces soon but in the purpose of those placed into existence to work against you. By whom you will be greeted upon arrival wherever they decided to inscribe you. If you are lucky and have paid your dues without having known the extent of them. Soon we will know.

081........A version of the man with one gold pupil so aged he can hardly stand holds himself up in a room lined with mirrors. He stirs and drinks from a very dark martini, chewing the thicker parts of pulp, his eyes so bloodshot they are blue. Our perspective pulls back through the perimeter of the mirrors to reveal the room encased in other rooms composed identically, a hive of cubes, in which men shaped in the same form stand and stir and drink the drink, or some may walk as if toward a door or down a hall, or miming speech to someone in the mirrors, or belief in walking up a set of stairs, the mirrors from the inside interactive and believing in the matters of what the user must believe is any day, eating their sperm thinking it's food, masturbating thinking it's holy, not yet ready to give birth to what can't be born until the definition of the word itself learns what it means.

082........Extreme close ups of the Woman with Language All Over Her Body's orifices, sections of inscribed flesh, synced tight with blast beats programmed with deep space sound anomalies. Enormous intricate candelabras in chasms on dysfunctional artificial moonland. Gaggles of animated anuses painted fire colors worshipped by religions who'd believed in the psychographic texts. Haunted metal coins suddenly standing up spinning on their edges wherever they are buried in any demolished memory even with no one left to carry them any longer. Long flat purple screen. Long flat silver screen. A diamond plotter arm emerges out of the lower left corner of the screen, signs the empress's signature, like a black metal logo but with corresponding tremor tags attached to the floor of the world. Spastic mesmerizing ping noise. Ash floods. Virus-laden in-core advertisement for incontinence products.

083........Three phenomenally elderly versions of the man with the gold pupil, each one more decrepit than the next, stand well-dressed but with ties loosened in a white room before a bed. Each wears a black bracelet around his left wrist, branded with the emblem. The frame of the bed gushes overflowing with crystalline jelly that spits and pops against the floor before it's burned off. Peals of gold bells. The center man has locked both elbows with the other two on either side, their skins together pulpy and sticking, grafting camaraderie. All three are laughing so hard in an unwanted way, their eyes about to burst, the skin paper-thin and part translucent, showing the dark liquid coils of worms held inside them each, their greatest gifts. Instead of laughter we hear language, the wanting words of each man's deepest screeching prerecorded from their lungs, calling them forth into the absence.

084........Experimental diseases and viral mindcraft are bred and tested in the Complex's upper bowels. *Invisible salts that make your skull grow 50x; floors that suck whole miles of land out of your holes; parrot teething and cell contortion; thrill rubberizing; DNA intersplicing and somatic miswiring rituals; claustro-amphetamines and bodypacking; retroactive psychotrauma aura immersion looping; forced performative psycho-eulogizing once-loved-one ad-lib with arbitrary punitive effects; (spastic life edits); butter dwarfing and anal buckshot; heliographic 'sacred sentiment' unbanding...* The pattern of the structural format shifts by the hour, systematically interweaving vital coordinates so that even the machines can't keep up. Some shafts go blacked out or completely missing for extended periods. Coal black wide walls inlaid with static scenes from successful procedures, present and future. Eerily silent besides the noise of something barely breathing in our face.

085........A child comes to on a small white nodule in the land. She kneels at the surface and brushes her hands along its face, locates a lever, turns the lever. An eyehole in the nodule begins to slow eject frothy cream gel, ribboning out and piling up from under land onto the ash where she has lived in her imagination since pre-birth. The child sticks a thumb in the cream and laps at it without expression. There is all against her face a bending wind, reformatting her features according to the wishes of those who would take her away from herself in every memory. The child produces a small melon baller and metal pouch and scoops what clumps of the stuff she can finagle into the container until it's mostly filled and then wholly overfilled, squeezing out through the seams of the pouch when pressed closed, held to her chest like a doll. The child looks old. Where the cream has touched her skin, the numbing zits already resemble jewelry, a gown that she shall wear into the future, where she can't hide despite the want for will that has commanded her to want to believe she will survive her own translation from one realm to another, once she is called. Before turning the lever off, she brings her face down to the eye and sucks her fill. Her head becomes this paragraph.

086........*Some remember a description of the conception of a location on the earth that could allow the* ascension of man into paradise by climbing a mountain, Her voice reminds us, as we rush forth in errored time, along black nodes, thru fractured intersections of dead locations, roving for data. *In this narrative, there would be a point at which you realized there could be no turning back; that you had experienced your last mortal thought, and your first awareness of the beyond, together entwined around a single, stationary point in time.* We expect the voice to carry on forever, as it had seemed to while in the womb, part of a time suddenly more vivid than all the rest of how we are. *Within the context of / time before/ the potential loss of abstract energy shall be represented by an equal and non-sequitur addition of local trauma, like a law; within /time after/ the gain must likewise be offset, such as through the granting of a wish. Each side believes in the other to the extent that their displacement can be carried forward through the other, by the other, or for the other.* Shattering glass. We come to tied down beside our mother on a bed of floods and ruptures, covered in dreamblood. Her stomach bulging with wailing eggs, pecked at by bird gnats. Our own body has already been almost entirely consumed; nothing left but lips and earlobes drowning in pubes. Wide open land in all directions. Black nails jutting out of every pixel. Whole jagged bitter hypermeat sky bending in twain. The resolution deepening the less narration there is. Her voice replacing all the once forthcoming words now.

087........The complex's private library is filled with

erased books. Each page of every final known copy of the hundreds of millions of humanity's projections have been individually attended to by unknown workers to remove every trace of whatever had been printed. The spines and jackets of the books have been removed so that the pages of one book may stand next to another on the long shelves here arranged forever onward unmarked for what they were. Translucent floors and racks and stairwells in the space allow the vision to pass through the archive unobstructed to the perimeters of the confinement, edged with an unreflective golden metal breached by no known entrance. Speech sound like casual audiences fills the chamber, though there are only occasional surveillants, mostly bots making their rounds through floor by floor on live patrol for any changing inch of air among the space. On a silver landing just behind and above us, a man in riot gear and chemical helmet stands looking down, his hands readied with a memory baton. His presence inspires us to move to the closest partition of a shelf, pull down a slick wad of tattered, erased pages, for our own. Because there is nothing remaining on the page, we already understand, the pages can say anything we want. *There are no secrets here,* you imagine typing onto the white, which then swells out of the page to fill the screen. *All is aligned. You are the witness.*

088........The man with one gold pupil stands in a white room and brings a gun up to his face. He licks the nozzle, winks and winks at no one there, stuck in performance mode even now, as in his prior life he'd been a mime, assigned to patrol the thoroughfares where unmarked kids had hid from the unknown. He'd fed them ice cream with black pliers that in exchange gave him everything they'd need to know of who the children might have been, given the chance in a system less already earmarked in the annals of the last recorded blocks of time, outside this text. The man inserts the nozzle of the gun into his mouth. He pulls the trigger. His head jolts and knocks him to the floor. There is a long pause in our perspective in which we are looking on where he had stood, from which a fine white dust is lightly caught upon the light and lifted, forming lattices of structure into which we could burrow and stay safe forever, should we need; but we do not follow the instruction. We are like a child now just the same as all the rest; have passed the test dressed up as plot to see what sort of hope we still contain. Instead, we hear a gong smash, and the man with one gold pupil rises slowly back up from the ground into the picture. He has no wounds. He is not bleeding. He is not smiling. He raises the gun again, this time at us, then cracks a joke in some dead language, puts the gun back in his mouth. This time when he pulls the trigger, we see our future life flash before his eyes, a secret between him and the weapon. Then he dies, and his life begins.

089........Your face comes off into your hands. Behind it, you find a tunnel has been bored from you out through the diamond-silver loam lining the air. Somewhere within there, thronged with echo, voices you recognize as the family you might have had someday in another world are calling out for you, using your real name, begging for help. But you are far too large to fit into the hole, you try to tell them, shouting loud as you can into the backside of your face. They shouldn't want to be where you are anyway, you explain, more to yourself now than them, finding nothing there where you try to think of who they'd been, the way they are. You think of yourself as a child playing with sticks of dynamite, large stinking pebbles, shards of mindglass. At once, the tunnel overflows with rancid puke, spurting like a fire hose all over the new wound where your face was, slathering your belly, all over the floor. You are in a waiting room, you realize, looking up against the mesmerizing light for the first time; walls lined with lattices of gilded doors, locked from the outside, requiring codes. To slow the flow, fearing the repercussion of your mess, you scramble to force the face back on, pattering at it with your hairy palms, long silver nails, the blood and puke all down your neck and arms and chest now, almost like clothing, and piling up around your ankles, then your knees, and then your nipples, then your neck. The last thing you remember, with just the front half of your ruined head just above the lip and treading vomit for your life, is

090........At the revolving edge of the locked world. Gray-green electric ground nodes laced with live intestines culled from captives, simulating warding waves of noxious stank. Disguised as forests, grottos, mausoleums. Strange music emanating from bland friction caused by the gyres beneath the groundwork in the mind. Impossible to distinguish from note to note, so that to listen is to become lost. It feels like free will to be so sick and never need to know it, as every perceived sentence feeds upon its own idea, all but guaranteeing rote complicity through basic instinct, with nothing left to change but change itself.

091........Cheetah skin pulled fast and tight around the edge of our perspective like a ticker tape telling you how much you're making every minute, paid into an account that will be used to identify what kind of punishment you'll require, distracting you from the pyres pouring smokes up into black holes singing out the other side a hymn designed to call God back to the earth, a desperate whim of the Woman with Language All Over Her Body in a moment of masturbation-induced clarity, despite already having lived Her fate so many times She already knows what's going to happen. Then we are following Her from behind—at least we think it's Her, though we can never see Her face. We go along a trail into a dark wood past ruined versions of the Complex but much more modest, wading neck deep through neon quicksand to a nest where hundreds of thousands of eggs have been laid. These are seeds, She says into our head again. They make you pregnant. She offers us a handful, like it's just normal. That's when we know we are being tricked. That we are in a different sort of place than we should be, even given the circumstances, having never quite been sure we were doing what we were supposed to all this time. For instance, we know we are supposed to say no to the seeds, that we'd be better off without them, but we say yes. Then we are on our backs in a black river, in a light warm wind, looking up at a black sky. The river isn't moving, we hear the empress say, though we feel Her voice is our voice now. The sky is the part that's moving, as well as everything behind it. That should be the end of the scene, but it isn't, besides for you. And even if I told you why, you wouldn't be able to hear me.

092........OUR USUAL DISAPPEARANCE REPORTER HAS GONE MISSING. APPLICANTS PLEASE APPLY IN PERSON AT THE EYE OF THE CRAINIUM IN HELLHOLE. WE ARE SO FEARFUL, WE ARE ALL IN HERE COWERING AGAINST THE BURNING OF THE CLAMPS!!!!!!!!!! DO NOT COME IF YOU ARE AFRAID OF CLA MPS!!!!!!!!!!!!!!!!!!!!!!!!!!!!! PLEASE SEND WATER AND SEND FOOD

IN OTHER NEWS, THE AOIDUF MARBDOUD PLAN TO DEFEAT THE AUE0TYWEOITUOWIEU

SURFACES TOMORROW IN A PRIMORDIALLY EMOTIONAL DISPLAY OF PRIVATE FANATICISM ORCHESTRATION. IF YOU CANNOT REMEMBER HOW A BALL LOOKS, A FIST SHAPE OR A DARK ORB MAY BE USED. THIS IS FOR YOUR PLEASURE!

CONSTRUCTION OF INTER-VOIDAL PASSAGE NEAR COMPLETE! EVACUATION PROCEDURES PREVIOUSLY DISCUSSED IN STATE TALKS HAVE BEEN OUTLAWED, BUT STILL THE POTENTIAL WAKING OF A NEW DAY FEEDS US LIGHT. WHAT MAY LIE ACROSS THE PASSAGE? HOW SOON MAY WE BE ALLOWED, WHEN IT BECOMES LEGAL TO BE ALLOWED?

PRAY FOR YOURSELF.

PLEASE STRIKE ALL PRIOR REMARKS RE: THE MISSING FROM MEMORY IMMEDIATELY, OR ELSE THIS WHOLE PROCEDURE MAY BE ILL. WE HAVE RECEIVED THE HEADS OF OUR TOP FIVE FINEST EDITORS IN A GOLD CONTRAPTION THAT JUGGLES THE HARDENED REMNANTS OF THEIR BLOOD.

OUR FIELDS OF PASSION STILL NEED TENDING…

093........*Anywhere you have a question about anything that is happening, you can click its core and receive a sign. If you want to know why people are being destroyed, look into the corpse of a destroyed person and click their navel. The reason will be explained to you. If the corpse of the person you want to know about has been eliminated from existence, you'll need to click the call number singed into the exact ephemeral coordinates of expiry. The reason will be explained to you. If you are inside an oven waiting to be joined with other captives, you can click the wrinkles on the back of your hands as soon as the heat rises high enough. The reason will be explained to you. If you feel so much fear that you can't tell where you are, close your eyes and whimper prismatically, forming a lozenge of protective curd around your cranium. The reason will be explained to you. Not all such situations have resolutions, as you may know, and so if you click and click and nothing happens, please provide enough time for the resolution to be summoned by the database.* The document is heavy. It leaks its anguish into your legs as you sit on a ledge over a cold dumpfield and try to follow the instructions. Blood keeps dripping down the middle of your vision; when you wipe it away, it wipes away everything you've already read. The pages keep flying away in no breeze and you can't keep them in order. You know you will be tested on the protocols as if you are also a prisoner. You grab another page out of the fluttering and try to focus. The next page is a section of an auto-animated cartoon featuring a rabid flock of decimal places who swarm all over anything that moves. You can't help that it makes you laugh to trace the frames where people really get the shit kicked out of them without knowing it's coming. The illustrations are gummy and run colors, making language out of them, and you feel thankful for not having to do the work of reading the manual, having it taken care of for you. Below, processing magnets shift the husks of ancient junk around, stacking them into precariously balanced tableaus that look like scene from the creation myth you've already read so many times it feels more like a cartoon than the cartoons do. The reason will be explained to you. The way it will be explained to you will be explained to you. The reason it has to be explained later and not now will be explained to you. You're surprised that you're crying. You haven't cried in centuries. You are a loser, but you can change. A loose page slaps against your face, printing your vision with its text, a same few words repeating over and over: *No matter what you think you've lost, you haven't actually lost anything yet.*

094........Crashed through the smear, a head of glass. A thousand heads per second flashing in sequence under the pixeled disarray of its outer layer, so offsetting it feels like there's no other potential in the world. As if it all comes down to this. Drunk, on our knees, trying to remind ourselves which way the head goes if we want to interact with it; how to hold it up, which orifices are for fucking and which make noise, which leak for what reason. We loosen the nursing blouse we've been left out here freezing our asses off in since the beginning of the movie and try to toggle the head with it, twisting our neckbones till they groan. Pesky shimmering beetle backs scrounging for morsels like gourmets, colonized inside the glass like a brain, as if soon after will appear flowerbanks and vibrant fields where life can find a way to find a way. It'd be a really sexy head for someone to get to wear to parties, we think, unable to remember what we look like from the outside ourselves but in the way we fold our palms, how thin our skin is. We are about to take the head and set it on the ground and stomp it out, suddenly jealous, when the way we touch the head along its scalp suddenly causes a lever to be pressed. Whirring inside the head, grinding inside the head. Reeking like rotten milk culled from fresh dead mothers. Low clouds of sugar rolling in from across dams holding back the rest. We try to throw the head far as we can away but now it sticks. Searing tight and rimmed around each finger, sucking tight onto the joints like teething rings, glinting with gemstones dredged from caves deep in the burning that had come before the floods that came before whatever else happened. We remember those caves, for a fraction of a second: the endless wailing that had eventually began to seem like all one voice; the robotic piglets they sent down from above to try to coddle survivors into betraying themselves from being drowned instead of repurposed; how some had tried to swim out through the bottom of the world instead, and were said to have indeed found a way out, though by then no one had the gumption to try it for themselves, each imagining just a bit too late now, and so little room as there was at that point to even get a grasp on the walls and convince their inner semblance that it could still be good here in the near future if just a couple other things fell our way finally. We find that we are sitting at the head of a long black banquet table, stacked high with plates of bubbling meat and flasks of nerve syrup, hypodermic appeteasers, big red gall. We raise our glass and hear a recording dictate the Empress's Prayer in total baby talk, the way we like it. We drink.

095........*Hyper. Zipper. Lever. Demonstration. Dimension. Forged. Cure. Crosses. Sheep. Outer level*—is what your thoughts say in the dark. You stand there trying to figure out what it means, why it appeared to you. Why it wasn't different words at any point. Is this a password? Do you need to remember it? What if one day someone asks you if you know the password and if you don't say it back exactly right—*Hyper. Zipper. Lever. Demonstration. Dimension. Forged. Cure. Crosses. Sheep. Outer level*—they will erase you and your line of blood from existence in history. Maybe if in your life you've encountered the phrase somewhere, like in a novel perhaps, you are allowed to know that you had the experience whether you remember it or not. Your host is granted. Is that the kind of bullshit that you think? Is that what makes you get up in the morning? Why *do* you get up in the morning? If you knew, could have it spelled out for you, like in a novel, would you be more or less likely to give up? Or would you slow down and try to really live there, in the novel, the way you must have imagined yourself when you let it inside of you. Sudden credits (carvings in moonstone) roll a list of all the animals that were killed in the making of this picture, which takes a while. Everyone always stays as long as they can before they see their name. Then they find out if they've prepared or not. It's like having a password but it's the only thing that's only ever really yours no matter how little window time you get. It's all in there somewhere. Is that really how you think? That it'll all just work out? That you don't have to actually do anything, that the world will fix itself, and when it does, it will come down on your side? In the end, there wasn't anyone who ever lived who didn't secretly think that, deep down in the same spot where they go to rest their minds at night. Act accordingly. Someone's coming… | ENTER PASSWORD |

096........Surveillance footage of a naked woman with a chrome mask let on the loose, running down gray halls spasming and screeching like she's on fire, with open wounds all over her legs. She's gotten a hold of a gun somehow and appears to believe she's on the run: searching for exits while shooting out the seeing censors installed into the ceiling, already aware of exactly where they all are, as if after many years of being filmed. Such intense fury in her face, so suffused with adrenaline it's a wonder she can aim at all, though every shot takes out the camera on the first try. The soundtrack is slapstick, an organ grinder and a kazoo choir and 808s syncopating their pulsing beats precisely with the footage, like it's supposed to make us howl. Because we know no matter what this woman does it won't change anything. That when they find her, she'll pay the price. We watch her a while, vaguely aware of a group of people we can't see somewhere in the room behind us, talking calmly in the dark around a fire that if we try to turn around blows so much smoke straight into our faces that all we can do is bear down and hold still, keep watching the woman like it's our job. We have a golden chain around our neck. We're drooling. We feel really good. We love the way we feel. We watch the woman scramble, wishing we could understand her, what she wants. So that we can remove it from her. So she'll calm down, feel no more pain. Better her than us, though, we remember to remind ourselves, in the dim, tight space where law is rendered in us as our flesh. Then hands are petting us, from just behind still, of the unseen. Bits of raw meat crammed in our mouth and down our throat, coupled with prickles of electricity that make our eyes roll back inside our head, onto a projection of the world just like the prior layer, but with our role and the woman's having switched place, hearing only an underwater echo of her endless shameless laughter at our flailing, all our rage, what we still are. Through her eyes, holding the gun, hunting each camera, we understand without needing to acknowledge it that we believe we are finally seeing the world as it was meant to be seen.

097........For an eternity, as in a state of suspended animation, nothing we perceive fits any key: *Hot knives across robot wrists / Time buds opening in warships / Eruptive rapids encircling a moor of clustered holes with human lips / Rips across honeycombs with hatchet heads buried in pregnant mounds of stammer / Tags on moon rocks labeled with new emotions deployed in abstract only / Databases ejaculating giftwrap tied to gifts opened by trainees / Gray dust layered over the defining scenes of famous films replayed on coffin lids / Sealed in the thrill of whatever else might be imagined before nix / Lodged deep in throats attached to lattices of brain vibrators / So many teeth and so much hair / "ouch my eyes've been jabbed. Ouch where did you go?" / Drumming crustacean layer, subdermal revisioning layer, doubled layer / Rubberizing section inescapable / Of plural mode / Envisioned as in having been told beforehand and forgotten / Numbers is exodus in this edition / Exits have been sealed /* A night at the end of the funnel. Slices into slices. Brain traditions absorbed by stone tablets. Chronicling the nature of the actual indiscriminate. Flashes of pins thru detuning how personalities conform to what precedes them, finally cut free. Warp holes of souls that can't touch but in revolution. / "one way or the other, always" / / There are images people are not supposed to have seen. Sounds they are not supposed to have heard. Ideas they are not supposed to have conceived. Someone must be keeping track of what exists where. One side working to uncover the land, the other lurking only in the undiscovered area. They used to say it would have to be 7 or 8 billion years before the sun explodes. Then it was 2 or 5 billion. Then it was 1 in 380,000 chance. / / Behind the glass we pass low over coal fields studded with rudders funneling blood from place to place. Turnip grass in pubic patches congested with denture noise from the critters. Land feeding on itself underneath everything you see, shifting its weight so you don't know what's coming up. You get used to it or you don't, and that's the law. Occasional pyres where digital school children dressed like you did then are whipping with maces a famous wrongful public death, reminding you of whatever they remind you of. The depiction becomes traced in icing on a handmade birthday your father has made for you, out in his shed. Your family sits around a tiny purple table with plastic tongs you all sit there and fumble with, missing your mouths, all talking at the same time about something the other knows nothing about. / / You come to in the oval office the last year that it existed. The room is silent and empty, not a sound in the whole building, or outside the windows, where the sun is shining heavy like lemonade. You are wearing a thousand gold chains and a camo thong. On your desk, you are signing a document as thick as your throat, completely filled with invisible ink made from your semen, though you don't know a word of what it says. You slam the cover on the contract, turn to the camera, raise your finger pointers at dead center and recite, in baby talk voice:

WE DO NOT WORSHIP THIS MACHINE
WE DO NOT HAVE A MOUTH AND WE WANT YOUR MOUTH
WE HAVE NEVER HEARD OF ANY MUSIC NOR WOULD WE LIE TO YOU
WE AM A CHILD
WE AM REWINDING
WE LOVE THE MILE OF AIR ABOVE THE GROUND WHERE WE WERE WARNED
WE LOVE THE KIND OF DEATH THAT ENDS OUR LIFE AS IT BEGINS
WE LOVE ALL THE HANDS THAT WE DON'T HAVE AND DO NOT TOUCH ME
PLEASE WE AM EXPECTING YOUR RETURN
PLEASE WE AM WAITING AND WE WILL WAIT FOREVER

When you have finished speaking, you wipe your chin with your shirt. You are dressed in all black like a bandit. You realize you should cover your face from the audience. You do not want to be identified. You find a black stocking mask in your left pocket. You place the black stocking mask over your face and try to make it fit over your eyes. Through its darkness, in the wet, warm cloth, you realize there are no holes, and where there should be, you see the same thing you see right now.

098........For other eternities, the total airspace of the Complex and its surrounding context goes frozen out— all motion and cognition, including that of the empress and Her cohort, brought to a standstill, without a guide. Shots culled from heat-farming censors in the meta-data cycle through still frames of bots and bodies stalled in the midst of last performance: spaces where meat is being processed among multitudes of dim conveyer belts clogged up airspace, funneling fluids from one place to another, shuddering from excessive volume, certain to burst; or stadium seating venues packed from end to end with numbered seats rigged up with SeeScreens, prodding helmets, auto-bludgeons, soon to be flooded with new patients; thick fuzzy display cases stuffed with insect and animal specimens already teeming with mutation from where they've been conceptually modified and forced to breed asexually; tunnels of pins leading to exits that open into entrances, entrances to exits; whole hemispheres of silver fire, or sea blue fire, or invisible fire; gardens of worms; pillars of salt. No matter what you think of what you see you cannot think it, nor can you know why or why not we are also held inside the pause without a blank; no sense but in the fear of what else might still roam free here alongside us, forced to go on aging in between shifts, able to see while others can't. Even when the stasis unsticks again, in stutter step against your much more real awareness of yourself outside the frame, all that remains of what's been seen between the lines will be the feeling that if our privilege to lay witness to this ongoing interruption of the timeline is revoked, we will never be allowed to realize. We will exist locked inside ourselves as long as all the rest, and maybe someday never be allowed again to be unlocked. The greater fear must be that if our awareness is never ceased, we will age too quickly, and in no time, compared to all the rest of our reality, come to our end, forever sealed inside our greatest secret.

099........Cold light cuts through backslit in drowning helmet: *Visages of unknown eras crossed out of recognition software. Jiggling and viscous, impossible to identify once delimited by mainframe.* We are here so they will not be soon enough. Evidence of ionic tampering must be reconstituted as secondary features of the witness organism or risk unlimited declassification status. Even just having index-traced it within limbo raises red flags, auto-distributing boiling oil into the recording's seeding nape for illustration, taking tape of /central user/ splitting themselves, scattering through blackout. All language is stolen, unless you make it up. Artificial intervention. Creation like dance. Execution pre-instant, as in before the urge, thus creating the sensation of suspension in the present. The blackout period is intense and will last some to all of total time required by this experiment, with only granular and easily remonstrated willingnesses to explore beyond sensation. Geese honking in the background, sand spilling, rapid waves of plum-colored substance. Sky is sore and bagged up. Laced with ribbons for the wombs of the dead in the ground below. With each new culture that has forgotten their process, another firmament, requiring generations to unlock without the key. Ultimate encryption, in return for the pleasure of our experience in sensing cells versus the far larger population of non-sensing vocations available per individual each click. The methods here may seem intense and complicated in a way that you might not have associated with how it would feel like in an afterlife, like they still feel more human that you would have thought even if there were a possibility of anything far worse, which is one increasingly popular mode of realistic data experience technology users like the New Readers. Fiesty bunch, kind of scary just because of their inclination to be fucked up more than you would be even if were you not still trying to convince yourself you're sane. Hard limits. Edges not actually experienced until after but accrued on the soul like a series of complicated weathervanes that field your path as the world changes in time and texture and how you change. Local energy output levels on our recent research subjects have been eclipsing some of the highest standards of the elite tier citizenship projects. Based on our best understanding of you, we are here solely to direct you toward the positions in space-time-math that allow you to wield maximum power over the greatest per hour payments locally in your area. Thank you. *Web scans across page between fingers and under up you like right where you aren't looking is where you think it is. You find it hard to continue. You feel confused about what's going on here. Why would one arrive here?* Right now, the time you are not spending with your most precious memories may one day feel like it is time that you wish you could have back. Forced into a corner, angry police thugs, they command you: "Tell us the five memories you want to keep forever. The rest are ours. You have thirty seconds to write them down as clearly as you can." Assuming you survive it, having that memory of the having to have decided between your memories like that; that is your sixth memory. 1 of 6. Recognizing this as one of an infinitude of possible scenarios that could befall anyone at any moment, ~0 .000000000000000000000000000000000000000 000000001ths of a degree of a chance, becomes your seventh memory. They are trying to trick you into falling into a pattern here. The creep within beckons and begs for lyrics. Pests become pets. Pets see everything. Witnesses. Bugs. I can't even get a sentence in in edgewise, it's got me really hurting this time. It know where to put the pins before I do. I can't tell which of my wounds is hurting at which interval. I look normal. I am normal. I won't getting any more intimate that in that way, not in an ad like this, where OK, cards on the table: I'm going to go ahead and let you know, OK, that there's something I need for you to do for us, the New Readers.

100........Gargle metal laughtrack splashing grimewaves into desert metropolis outlined by nuclear explosions going off all over Creation, which could also happen any day now, as you've known since you were 12.

Gargle metal really sucks when you're hearing it in the sky coming off fat ass helicopters full of gush aliens who are here to enslave us all but love the shit out of listening to flesh tear for real instead. Ouch, gargle metal floors, they rip the knees out of your legs when you type those words. Their job is claim vengeance for all you've wasted your imagination on throughout your idea of a life by ensuring there'll still be access later, for public ridicule. *Camera moves in on the long beautiful black hair of the players in gargle metal band, playing in an empty stadium, wind blowing insanely. Hair dissolves into opulent physical tubings that slap you around and turn you up and through a noose back into a body that was trying to die but is going to make it.* Something is different now. Falling down hair hole. *Gagging on fiber trying to get a grip from falling in twisting in crunchy shit, hearing yourself whine in a goat voice: "ugh, turn it off please, or let me up."* A set of piano keys appear. You can see the keys in your mind (you have no choice). Cursors ask you to indicate which of them in you'd like to press in what order. Five to nine keys, your choice. No tools. If the melody you select is scored as positive, you will be sent one place. *If your melody is scored as negative, the other. Please use the space below to make notes. What you write can and will be used against you in a court of law. When finished, sing.* You do not sing. *Will you agree to sing? Last chance.* You do not sing.

101........Chrome claw hand holds an infinite-sided sky-blue metallic die inscribed with infinite possible machine code tags. When a position is triggered (offscreen), the claw gyrates at high speed, blurring the feed screen, then releases. Die falls onto blood ebony dashboard studded with divots inscribed with interlocking inverse machine code magnet strips that firm a complete seal with the die upon selection. The die is absorbed into the fiber of the dashboard, and the roll's results are then applied into the system retroactively. A new die may only be created from the skull of a child on the day they become the final strand of their kin's bloodline. Present scene documents the recording of three immediate instances. The first roll changes the natural progression of a horizon line so that it eventually must bisect itself at the point of least resistance. The second roll raises the caloric value of heated water by 1%. The third roll replaces the concept of "improbable conceit" with the concept of "unalterable condition."

102........Smashed up sections of all previous behind-the-scenes scenes tolerated in this iteration of reformat appear laid out on a digital sea table under sky so low there is just barely enough room for an average sized adult (pre cranial swelling) to whimper their way between like a worm in lust. Every hour on the hour (corrupted timecode), a captive is released into the simulation and allowed to attempt to organize the tiles into the proper chronological order (not necessarily as it appears in final). A successful attempt will result in the complete reset of the universe scenario. A failed attempt will generate an additional century of ignorance and violence applied to the backlog of human experience and result in the removal of the contestant from all forms of inter-notation. Captives are selected by a committee of unnamed forces based on the measure of reading comprehension score plotted against intolerance of moral abstraction. Selected captives cannot abjure and must be unremembered from all future associative circulation schedules. A complete record of results and their complete derangement of effects will be revealed only to those who care.

103........Wake up covered in blood foam. Far shores dressed with running wounds blurring the dimensions. Bodies are washing in all around us, waking up beside us, trying to decipher for themselves what's brought them into themselves. No one remembers anything but the parts they wish they didn't, and quickly enough they no longer need to tell the difference. Internal recordings of explosions and applause syncopate wildly with the gyration of the celestial axis, triggering actual explosions of celebratory beefcakes stacked into pyres along the edges of the grass grown up between the sand of the mainland. Blood splattering against previously unseen glass walls that will line the exact path you are allowed to walk once you select where on the grass you are going to begin to walk toward the center of the world. Even having seen them, you will not acknowledge them either, since you already know what happens if you do. Blood shuddering in the positions of holy people waiting to greet those who can no longer see them as they are. *Currently it takes less than 1 h 18 m on average for any complete belief system to made unrecognizable to its creator,* you hear a far-off recording of what must have been a leader's voice from overhead, not even trying to cover up the parts of the soundstage where the magic happens. They just dump another bloodload down if you look up. If enough people just started looking up, we'd have a revolution. You realize no one really wants a revolution. Then there is only one of us. I don't know which one of us it is. All I know is everyone else on the beach who hasn't already started off on their next adventure (you can see with great depth the exact number of them among the throngs: exactly 12 of hundreds of thousands) is staring at us.

104........A bellhop duck walks his way along the empty row you're seated in as if the row is full of bodies but no one's there. His face is scarred with star shapes. The inside of his throat is chrome, which you can see way down into when he smiles. There's a whole other world in there. The bright white of the SeeScreen drips through your mind. The bellhop reaches into his pocket, pulls out a tiny envelope, no bigger than the head of an atom. He hands it to you, sits on the back on the seat in front of you to watch you read through binoculars. You open the envelope by looking at it. Inside, a note, printed in font so iridescent it could say almost anything. You hand it back to the bellhop, who reads it aloud for you, still through the binoculars:

THE FUTURE IS SUBTRACTED FROM THE PRESENT
THE PRESENT IS SUBTRACTED FROM THE PAST
THE PAST IS SUBTRACTED FROM THE FUTURE

Bellhop drops dead. His body begins oozing purple smoke. You can hear people in the room around you suddenly shouting, fumbling for cover. The bright white of the SeeScreen slips. Behind the screen, the woman who performs the role of the Woman with Language All Over Her Body appears on a chrome dais with battered walls covered in different kinds of medieval sex weapons, having an orgy with every member of your family as far back as the first wave, really shredding their asses, taking advantage of their weakness. Later you will be given the option to remember this scene or remember nothing.

105........Vast concrete space where everything that can be seen is marked with interlaying layers like a target. Edges and outlines of the substance overlap in physically impossible contortions: tubes, ramps, spheres, knots, bridges, ballasts, pits, plateaus, wormholes, clots. Small piles of powdered amphetamines in hanging sacs too high for anyone. Rats and roaches scurry from cover to cover, shot at by automatic silos in the ceiling. Why don't they shoot us, we wonder? Our hands are covered in burns so tight and flaky. Carrying insanely large packages strapped to our backs: all the stuff we couldn't bear to let be incinerated. We are supposed to be reenacting the Reckoning, where we were given the gift of renewed attention, allowed to make sense of ourselves in the context of the next empire. We can't remember any of our lines, which is why the voice that provides them without personal effort eventually becomes a relief, no matter its compromise. We can solve the situation in one of two ways: get in the path of one of the random pest assassinations, or give up and admit that we no longer wish to live the way we had; that we believe now solely in the providence of our assigned vocation: to be a citizen. Identifying insignia slovenly stamped in our armpits leaks silver gel, making us glisten. We look down and see we are in the best shape our lives, the kind of body we always wished for. Our genitals so swollen they're dragging on the floor. Throughout the space, beautiful symphonic trigger-sounds, choreographed muscle pop, slo-mo ice melt ambience. Candelabras everywhere suddenly, fluttering with vibrations from church organs with all their keys pressed down at once. Bombastic tirade from behind screens, illegible but as sour stomach, a loopy gas stink that fills us with itching. We fall to our knees without a struggle. We are among billions all spread out where all the targets last had been. Ahead, against where the highest concrete wall was, the outline of the Complex has been painted by an AI trained on the software of all the false religions only. It looks like a person we all know. Its impression in our minds—*infinite paths, only one hub*—emerges from the concrete and takes flesh form, all other excess falling away from it, piercing the limits of our senses, blown open wide as the holy land beneath our knees begins to drag us forward toward the rapidly unpacking inner core of the incarnation.

106........The prior image resolves into a 2D matte representation in the style of early op art. Pull back to the prevailing image countlessly copied on the cover of endless reams of 9-inch-thick pamphlets in racks on carts in black chrome streets manned by human-machines dressed up like cops. There is nothing else for sale anywhere in the universe, on every shelf and display; as every item on every menu; prescribed by doctors and lawyers; reformatted for proper viewing on every digital device, as every website, every article—all selling nothing but the pamphlet. The people's clothes—who flow around us as a blur obscured in the glare coming off all non-human presences—are covered with excerpts from the pamphlet, reprinted in streamlined styles and as iconography designed to make the words resemble other words. No matter how near they appear, we know better than to try to read them, as we will be thrown immediately without retort into the section of reality they describe, which might feel a little more familiar than it does here, though it just as easily might feel much worse. *The more responsible thing to do*, the pamphlet's custom user feedback would remind you, right on time, is to *keep your attention focused solely and completely on the ever-present possibility of an unforeseen event*, as though it has been hundreds of thousands of centuries since the most recent, *we have still yet to learn to utilize its many gifts.* Giving in, wanting to be coddled, we stop at the closest vendor and buy another copy of the pamphlet, to go with the thousands we already have at home. To our horror, after ripping the prismatic plastic off under a dim street lamp, far from the crowds, we find the pages are filled with photos of ourselves: ringing a massive silver bell with a wand in front of a battery of crocodiles; spread-eagle on a peanut butter mound studded with artillery shells; as an infant being stuffed into a blowoff vent on the side of a crematorium; giving a speech running for office on a podium suspended over leagues of jelly; with the skin of our face stretched so wide and tight over a chrome loom feeding into a bone-frame player piano that our features are just glitches.

107........*Things had been golden once in a true way. Work passed in favor of the presence of its maker. The idea of justice not yet obscured in our minds in the fall from grace in light of how we had never figured out how to stop falling. What could creation have been like before such terror?* (The volume of the background noise in the signal suddenly lessens. Like you can hear yourself think again without having to be reading at the same time.) *Our memories became commodities, necessary solely for the numbers have been provable finally in execution and now just how the model could have been instead explained by an equation that even in astronomic math was just beginning to be discovered. Each person is suddenly a co-investor in their lives, not just a despot; what they do infects those they find themselves attached to, which even with just one pin among the zillions can be pulled to be the one that undoes the world. What is freedom to a god?* (Three female voices singing behind your eyebrows; gravel turning like cylinders around your sidehead; suddenly sitting up like your first breath is what was actually your last but now your asphyxiation is being rewound to 24h before the point you end up making the last possible decision that could have moved you away from this path and onto what might have been intended were anyone allowed to see themselves from the outside, or just to know.) It's impossible to communicate because by the time you're able to say it it's no longer true anymore. It's not hyperbole. I can say anything, and just like that it disappears. MOON ERA COLORING / PALETTE DYSFUNCTION / TANDEM / WORDS OF GLOVES THAT HISS / PUT DOWNS AND STRANGLING BEHIND THE CURTAINS / THEY KNOW YOU DON'T KNOW WHAT YOU SAW BUT THEY ALSO DON'T KNOW WHAT YOU'LL SAY / DON'T INTERRUPT / WORK IS CHEAP / WORK IS DEMOLISHING / WORK IS LIMITLESS / WHAT KIND OF PASSION IS MOST NECESSARY / WHAT KIND OF AMBITIONS DEVOLVE AND WHICH ELECT / Glass seeds melting over orbits. Kind of thing can really go wrong from here. Like no way back this time. Holy water sloshing out of the eyes of a pig into a trench where children are repairing their bodies after what the weather did the first time there was no way to delay it any longer. System goes into flood mode for a moment switching between so many shots of such complex physical environments that would make a computer sick to have conceived. Happens all the time, you just don't usually get to see it. Only since you're with me. / BULGED INCISIONS / DRAGON GONADS / SHATTERING STEEL RINGS AROUND STEEL NECKS / CAVES ERODING / SLAUGHTER OF INSANITY FASHION / FASHION IS LESSONS / LESSONS CREATE SENSE / IRON CORES ERODING / INCISIONS UNDERNEATH THE LOOSE MEAT / NO SENSATION / HEAD UP / HEAD FORWARD FOR THE NEST / (Nurse pulls the crepe back up over viewing area. Bunches of faces against smudgy plastic tapping and shouting. In the fields behind them, a freshly delivered pile full of bodies from a mass exterminated planet, which will be burned for fuel as needed in the process of renegotiating crucial moments of "fundamental error," which are only just now beginning to be discovered by our processors, and we are expecting progress any day now.) Scanners pass over your eyes. You able to immerse yourself in a UI that will allow you to click on any of the words or groupings of words and unpack them, which will demonstrate a list of the possible meanings and usages they could be argued for with a percentage of likeliness, so that you'll be able to begin to choose a skin for the language that begins to agree with you more. If you like, the resolved scenario stacking for your particularization of the text can be simulated in pill form, which helps you sleep and relax and find comfort. (Stacks of tanks like pyres burning with head meat from everyone who ever touched them or those who touched those; bugged meteor palaces radiating damnation energy and radiating waves that split the soul; warm summer breeze on an empty beach of purple.) Each scene like an organization in a museum, allowing complexity of depth in any selected element. The cost is to know. *Walk to white wall. Touch wall. Turn.* /incision/ *Touch wall. Turn.* /incision/ *Turn.*

108........The highest floor of the Complex has never been physically entered, even by the empress, or the machines who built it, which were immediately dismantled after the fact. According to its description in the State's database of private ranges, the space is comprised completely by two-way mirrors and human bone, forming an impossible labyrinth surrounding a 6'x6'x6' platinum alcove housing a skull-sized promethium bell inscribed with the full name of the bell's creator, which cannot be processed without training. When rung, the bell resets the Ten Commandments, reshuffling the list of back into a total possible series of 144 conceptual moral strictures to be redrawn, simultaneously reformatting the local psychosocial consciousness and its complete aesthetic output retroactively, as if it had never been another way. If never rung before the end of recorded time, when the simulation resets, the bell will take the form of a human and walk the earth with the given name of the bell's creator burned into the meat of his left heel, pressing the name into the soil with every step. Those who step on the face of the name will be made known as corrupted in the eyes of all possible others forever and ever. When the total balance of mortal beings corrupted in this manner become 33.333% of the total value of active lives, the simulation will lose its capability to be reset.

109........ ...*can no longer locate the passage I meant to transcribe here...missing from my memory...a bottomless hole hidden inside an unseen space...pop-up jokes, stabs of regret...body dysmorphia, paranoia...the cures are worse than the symptoms because our illnesses are side effects of what's being done to what we can't see...don't want to see now...can't bear to know...trying to tell someone you've paid to listen to you about how you understand the enemy's plan is to inundate your attention to the point of no longer knowing where to begin to push back...I had thought this job was sacred, even among thieves...I can only see my own tricks after I'm already in their midst, like being trapped in a remote viewing location...the host requiring costs to let you go...like you can't just walk out of here and think you're never going to hear from your destiny again, in the hands of our most hospitable agents of deintellectualization-flavored genetic tinkering...not even trying to hide anymore; instead asking your preference, learning what makes you believe in something; training you...knowing exactly what your reaction is already...helping you choose…paradoxical limits…innovation of content… capitulation coping…prurient evidences…laced to the teeth in every syllable's intention here no matter how… at the edge of the bottomless pit and scanning down… through bruised imagination only…tender slips… the edge of the eye of the scanner…the freckles in linearity…less and less of everything now than there will have been by the last time it is perceived…attention-starved like actuality…*

110........The man over the bed above us is nude besides the thin black mask around his head. He seems to be humping. We cannot feel the body where our vision with him shakes. Perspiration cakes clean on the lens of seeing with the sound of empty fields grazed by thin plates of metal passing back and forth in search of gaps to patch. His eyes are a disarming color, bloodshot around the edges, though in the centers the shape is slurred. Steam rising off the meeting. The walls behind too far away to have a frame. We watch hands from where our hold would be behind the camera raise up in the perspective. We watch the fingers on the hands fondle the chin and cheeks behind their mask, a gentle gesture, with fingernails removed, blood streaming down the arms back down into us. The man does not waver in his thrust. He arches his back and lets our finger between his lips and sucks the trickle. We trick our fingers down along the inseam of the mask. The fabric stretches like an elastic skin we had once wished for. We pull the garment up over his head, enclosing both skulls in a shared pocket, suddenly liningless, without a bound. Beneath the mask another mask of the same color. The man's moaning and groaning like a hydrant right in our faces, breath full of old years, mind full of seed. Our hands retract from the frame. The frame retracts from the idea of itself.

III........On specific sacred dates the Woman with Language All Over Her Body has demarcated on Her map of "points of intervention," the Complex must be enclosed from bottom to top behind holy metal. Automatic revision scripts perform the assembly in less time than it takes to describe it. The metal is bone-gray and thin like skin; once installed, its host cannot be differentiated from broad daylight—there but not there, hidden in plain sight. Once the scripts go through, the living contents of the Complex can survive for 18 hours on its reserved air and in-house rations, culled from flesh; no light allowed throughout the structure but in the empress's private quarters, where She lies in wait, watching the language burning across Her body in description of what must be going on outside the locked-out walls; a rare moment in Her experience where She can actually hear Herself think in Her own way, with Her own kind. The empress still cannot say what makes the language appear all over and throughout Her, or why any force, including Her, believes in it enough to see it through; it had been so since in the womb; Her own mother had fallen victim to the unsprawling mechanism of the virulence inside Her, describing how Her parent would disappear into thin air the very second She emerged, Her first prophecy come true as the mother's fiber had actually shattered into jagged casks of golden smoke as She introduced herself into reality with such a scream that even from an infant it shattered all the mirrors for hundreds of miles. With Her first words, burned in Her forehead, She'd ordered the shards gathered up and melted down, repurposed into a hexagonal platform where the originating human sacrifices She would soon order could take place and be remembered as a modern miracle, evidence of our species' time having arrived at last. The empress is the only one who still remembers this. Only She can know the kind of life She would have had had the language all over Her body not emerged; had She not acquired such a thirst for the unknown. In Her mind, for a fraction of a second, She sees herself seated in a sunroom in a blue mansion, 3.3333… years old, playing with heaping piles of faceless dolls, pretending to quorum over which doll should be the leader, and how best the other dolls should pay their respects. She imagines a man draped in red leather sneaking in behind her through a very tiny door hidden in the wall. She watches him unwinding himself tightly, like a python, across the silence in the room toward Her back; unable to feel him there even as he slips both of his jelly-covered hands up around Her head, slips into both Her ears at the same time two translucent jelly bubbles, black at their core. Tickled, She turns around to see who's there and finds the house where She grew up is now a war room; pentagram tables everywhere, shafts of curved light; tracts of loose flesh unspooled over translation looms, riddled with taps; shadowy bodies in mirror armor working out the ordered execution of the proclamations of Her flesh. Suddenly aware of Her awareness, a worker rushes over and immediately doses Her infant brain with a simple wipe, ushering Her out. In Her throne room, She sits up just as the plating begins to unstick itself, unleashing masses of hissing and buckling as the outer air to flood back in with blinding light, realizing She has killed all of her caretakers in her sleep again, each already replaced with new ones that each look exactly the same as before besides the mass of pimples all over their backs.

112........A trembling hand holding a tiny wick in flapping breeze. Carefully trying to shield the flame from going out, cupping with metal fingers, close against the metal chest, but also it's the only light there is to guide the way. Along a long wicker staircase. Violently jagged in its corkscrew contours. Beetle backs and lozenges of beeswax, rotting sweat smell, fluttering around orifices, sticking to anywhere. Disappearing partitions of the surface like faces on shuffled playing cards. Every step as if you're about to fall flat on your face, the flat ground still writing itself out like a plotter, against the edges of vastly passing shadows woven from deadcode. Knowing wherever the exit might be right now it won't be there by the time we could have found it. Needing to get lucky. Piss-logged diapers trinkling in slippery rivulets, evaporating rapidly. Lightheaded, hypertense, making tracking mistakes, allowing comportment disorders. If we could only just find any free space, catch our breath, gather our wits. As if anything we think could make real sense to someone else not stuck precisely in our same skin. Instead, behind the walls, video holodexes of archived sarcophagi stacked into prisons; blustering spittle gathering around the artificial mouth of the Autocrat within; solar landscapes ripping themselves open into flues of dough; oceanliners full of baby bodies; flashes of damaged close-up shots of our teeth replaced with knives, grinning for camera... (The scene goes paused. Pop-up bone-scale interface overlaid onto frozen viewscreen. Compiler prompt accepting tags at blitzkrieg entry rate from auto-intuitive drivers. Hash brushes recoloring the contours of the architecture into tufts, thickets. Huge pits and pools of boiling acid. Showering mind pellets. Replacing the candle with a taser aimed the wrong way, back at ourselves; then a quill and ledger; then a length of rope, which suddenly we find ourselves scaling claw hand over claw hand up out of the terrain with, while the camera remains fixed. The remainder of the scene plays out as in extreme fast-forward, displaying all future action that will take place in these coordinates through the remainder of recorded time: civilization after civilization; revolutionary weather; indexing by unknown forms; infinite dark.) The screen is dark for a very long time, impossible to temper, like it's waiting us out against its will; punishing us, baiting us out; until, from out of where we still are, we see: *A trembling hand holding a tiny wick in flapping breeze. Carefully trying to shield the flame from going out, cupping with metal fingers, close against the metal chest, but also it's the only light there is to guide the way.* This time we'll feel the way we were supposed to feel, we hear ourselves think, in a voice that's barely slipping out from being barred in behind itself. This time there'll be nothing we don't already know. (Impossible to sleep between the tones. Radiating crystal synthesis apparition network contamination. Shifting tenses underneath ragged out brain divisions. Crushing the last spines supporting vital paths for external intervention without mourning.)

113........Inside a memory of coming home at the last place we lived before there was nowhere else, we appear inside deep shelter from heavy rain through a black door. We close the door behind us tightly, turn the many locks, arm the injectors. Wearing the clothes from the hour of the first loss of innocence, far too small for our body now. Tight metal band around our neck. We lay down the countless tiny heavy bags strapped to our body, full of inebriating powders and anesthetizing butters, paid for by egg donation, harvested from someone we no longer feel we know. Flashes of spattering of injections, eyes behind visors, clamps and bells. On hands and knees along a corridor from foyer to cleansing room. Airspray in orifices, salt on the tongue, marrow scrubbers. Get all the nits out. Leave behind everything but deepest needs. Fogbanks rolling away. Undo airlocks. Headfirst into the transition generator. After forever, marked all clear. On into the actual home, then: a single tiny 6'x6'x6' space carved out of speech. Where before there'd been a bed, a SeeScreen, and a feeding helmet, instead: a cow—all black, from hoof to cornea, speckled underneath the fur with golden scratches; too large to turn around or move at all inside the space; breathing heavy like an overheated puppy; feces piling up over our ankles; quivering and balking. We try to turn around and find the door again but there's no door. Instead, appearing imprinted across our eyes: TO EXIT YOU MUST EXECUTE THE ANIMAL. We raise our hands up over our eyes, like trying to claw the order out, and find where quarter-sized holes have been punched straight through the center of our palms, soldered off cleanly, fresh new flesh. We press the hands together, trying to remember how to pray. When the holes touch, they lock together, become a blade, curved to a tip so sharp it hurts to even look, forcing our eyes away, blurry with bumps. Laced into the empty frame outside the scene, we find our attention locked on tight into a suspended oscillation of infinite rings, like handlebars up through cognition, as in the soundtrack far behind us, we hear aggravated packets of audio from struggling, stabbing, shuddering, moaning; flesh coming open; then waves of blood; then pins on glass; then, for a split second, face to face with the head of the cow, whose skin has been peeled back to show a field of half-formed human faces woven like patchwork into its coat, all of them sucking spastically for air; then the body of the cow fades, becomes lines of a blueprint for a labyrinth, traced on the deep sand of the backside of a planet cloaked in poison mist, a thousand moons. On every moon, a perfect model copy of the Complex standing on rubble, its surface wrecked with a reflection of our face, made up of countless half-formed faces just like the cow's was. We see the knife then raise up parallel to our true eyes. We watch the blade approach, slice through our necks without resistance, zero sound. We raise the cow's head dripping with blue blood up and put it onto the hole in our neck where our own head was. We screw the cow's head on tight. We look up the camera and open our cow mouth to show where at the back of our cow throat, there's a white wall installed with a realistic painting of the universe imploding.

114........Elderly hands draw hot pink curtains over fact-tight spirals of gaseous glimmer cluster undulating in soft-pixel metallic gaze-array spanning eternal unconscious cognition programmed to overwrite any conceit that can't be cloned preordination. Camera rotates 180°, panning past an extremely narrow hall cut into glass, to face the exact same set of curtains parallel, parted by child hands to reveal a hot pink field filled seamlessly with innumerable skinned pigs with sewn up orifices wallowing in neuro-lubricant awaiting processing.

115........ ...*much worse when it returns...sticky with thought-bubbles scraping for inactive landscape...*

any way back out...please...just need a job...anything to do with who I was and what I was good at...could have smeared whole planets with one wish...dry sockets gathering around headwound...pregnant with tsetse flies...nothing to rinse...pale plaster impressions... underwater in fud serum...designed by cluster drugs designed to manage reasonable expectations...good faith only, yes, yes...truly thrilling...willing to compromise... if I exist...too many tombs with different shaders... divulging context far too late to apprehend the motivation...only mindcraft...no big whoop...dizzy with fake ash and furtive causes...colored in with caves that link to the immortal...pending...crushing...only ideas...can't take much else...fake as a dime on a sill in hell...ivory porticos...colorful lessons...all there was still yet to shame...an early investment now can produce unimaginable returns...for the shrewd doll...so many bibs I no longer recall even the outline of my hole... until they remind me...what makes us horny...the sanest song still longer than the secret that divined it...low hanging ropes...tight neck, light slits...stuffed numb with candy...a viral rapture...still so ready to receive... just any signal...cold vortexes...empty scams...still unable to tell the difference even now...you'll find out what I mean after the seizures...hairpins thru shifting pixels in the cracked pattern...eye for every other eye at once at last...another unnecessary lesson, master... yes, please...until forever...just this once... (the record shatters...) (coercive liminal shards...) (without an array...) (evoking expected correlation by refusing to accept the way the soul frays…) (tatters in dry wind…) (such sickly pacts…) (precluding database malfunctions as corporal punishment…) (abandoning the poles, the rift, the cleft…) (the etching's hollow cortex cropping…) (edging endgame meta at zero speed…) "The bit forced in the body's mouth is chrome…"

116........Seated at a different desk than usual. In the wrong era. Stand up, look over chained dividers. See individual that resembles everyone, from behind, typing into stalled machine overheating and leaking fluids. Rising steam permeates the airspace above for privacy. It also burns your skin and makes you insane. You have learned many lessons. They are not covered under any protection policy. You pay full price. You earn the rewards required to pay this price by coming every morning to where you are. Laser wire reminds you to sit down. The plush seat is worn so thin you can see the heads of the pins. It's such a nightmare it's not even a nightmare any longer, after the extent it requires you to learn to cope. You're always hungry, famished; you always have food, but it tastes weird, like too fine-tuned to your preferences, like it know you better than you do. You're oddly shaped because they all are. Quick glimmers of reminder lasers. To apply yourself. At first you'd thought these were weight against your inaction, which runs aplenty, but really it's random. Not everything is random, but this is. You sit up close and tight at the edge of the desk and try to pull yourself together. You focus from the back of your mind to the exact center of the SeeScreen at where you were in the file last. After reading the file for a while, you realize you have not been doing your work, but have been writing a list of all the things you wish you had done before things changed, all the places you had meant to go before things changed, all the people you would have liked to meet before things changed, all the food you would have liked to try before things changed, all the ideas you meant to see through before things changed, everything you believed you'd done but hadn't actually done right yet before things changed. The list has no entries yet, just a blinking cursor, but you remember having had the idea to write those things down while you still could, and how full of curiosity it had made you for an extended moment until you found the time to open the file and start taking notes and realized there was nothing there any longer. Not even by any fault of your own, really. Nor had it even brokered a warning signal besides a certain way of feeling about everything you see in the moment, so different from what it feels like looking back. *That's what makes aging happen,* you think, and go to type it into the keypad on the machine, and for some reason you touching it makes it lose power, and then the whole place loses power, which you didn't think was something that could happen at the Complex, despite having had that illusion shattered several times over already, given how now you're working here to earn your living, and before that you'd been a brain in a box somewhere, and before that you'd played executioner, requiring fourteen full visits before you decided you couldn't take it anymore, that it wasn't worth the pain, which is how you ended up as a brain in a box, and before that you'd been a senator in a state somewhere that doesn't have a name anymore, and before that you were a shopkeeper selling pies, and before that a window covered in soot with nails scratched through it to spell a divining ward against predators, and before that a phonograph needle in the room of a child that will die before puberty, and before that you suddenly find you have some ideas of how to begin filling your list of everything you missed and couldn't remember but can remember now. You open a new file and begin typing in a language you don't know.

117........Hot pink machine harvesting headstones from a mindwide field of charcoal headstones installed into a partition of the lost world held behind glass. Inside the machine, aggro-scrubbers massage the prior engraving out of the material until it is blank. A replacement epitaph is autogenerated live from a databank of scrambled signals recovered from dead plot lines of the lost world held behind glass. Reading them allows those watching from a remove to read the future of a location they will never be allowed to enter, thus causing the text to read like gibberish. Text in the accompanying pamphlet (ripped from this edition of the document) explains that this is a dramatization of a process that has already occurred in all worlds containing even trace elements of the effect of demarcating signs and signals; atlases, encyclopedias; anything that still believes it could learn to love itself, if ever provided the proper anatomy.

118........Extreme close-up of the constricted anus of the Woman with Language All Over Her Body, obese bees flooding to it, forcing themselves inside Her in continuous droves, the visible linings of Her ass skin murmuring and recoloring themselves in plats of mutating compressed text like an aurora. Buzzing/moaning soundtrack plays back looped at 1000x and 1/1000x speeds simultaneously, its nauseating rhythm paired with pop-up inlaid video scabs containing recordings of a coal blue key with a diamond-shaped head being inserted into innumerable locks of various styles and formats; interlocking ovular saws ripping through spheres of gray brainmeat; elaborate motionless windchimes made from backbones crooked from stooping; live feeds of deformed faces staring slack jawed, masturbating; wide white walls unfolding inward, ever inward.

119........Six enormous contestants with their eyes gouged stand on the grounds where the original entrance to the Complex is said to have existed among the rumors in the bowels of the machines. A recording plays back all audio from sexual tortures performed on site by each contestant and those they oversee simultaneously at uncomfortable volume. The last of them to remain standing will be crowned the sire for the last egg of the empress, to bear a child that will be ritually massacred on the ground where they stand as a sacrifice of honor to the language that has allowed them to be scraped from the moments where they'd conceived another arrangement in creation and pasted into corpses with major voting rights. The thrill of victory far outweighs the pleasure of the fulfillment of the legend, mainly because none of them understand it, as they are not supposed to. No one is supposed to know the script until it is like an undetectable gelatinous substance on a keyboard forcing your fingers to type different words than you think you are seeing live, no idea what worlds you're causing, no remorse for what happens because you don't even remember the original form. A trail there, some say, if you have eyes to find it, folly to follow. The contestants are not to acknowledge the presence of the others, even a glance. For food and water, they pray. When all the others have expired, inside his head, the winner walks to the center of their symbol and selects by feel alone one of 11 handbells that will later be said to determine the crux of the next major extradimensional value shift.

120........It should feel like every image falls apart; every syllable shredded where it tries to touch another; every sentence stunted where it lays seed. No reason to want to return to where any sense of narrative is headed; nothing that allows a moment's rest between the beats; any stitch of illumination developed solely to burn and blind the code behind. It should seem as if you will never understand and never need to; as if we've all just had it coming, all this time; every scene the final stretch of sense between what becomes left unread and what could never have been told. It should make you want to care for it so little it doesn't even deserve scorn; to have never thought of it before and never again; to consign itself to the encrypted space reserved for that which even the unconscious bears no need. Any earmark fomenting individual interpretation should be delimited incongruously, causing the subject to experience an immediate form of glory in denial; like losing track of the location to the entrance the kingdom of heaven on the head of a pin in the eye of a storm at the edge of the inconceivable; like having a rat that controls the future life of your mind shoved up your ass while giving birth to an amalgam who will not remember you or your kind at all. It should lose track of itself, too, as part of discovering itself; should outpace its own conscription to the means by which it assumes any possibility of intervention on its behalf could be designed in time to make it full; should want more than has no matter how completely it believes it understands what it is not, will never be, until it is.

121........Across from a bed glowing with fire, above a charred loose human form inside the blacklight, the man with one gold pupil sits against the wall in a black chair nude, with a wet erection and his chest covered in claw marks, smoking from a bowl made of teeth, the bubbles popping in his brain. Thru tiny hexagonal amp: distorted voice of a woman speaking as to a child about her plans for the approaching millennium.

122........Miniscule chrome blip appears in center of vision. Generates waveform ripple until exterior eyes lock upon it, sealed with a click. Perspective becomes dragged in thrall stereoscopically inward, each level closing out each other with no recourse, folding all possible feeling into shafts that break the skin of local time, then mend themselves into the feed, cleaving for purchase. Vast hairy landscapes, deep cold dumb. Clotted with impossible knots of core omniscience too unstable to be labeled but as bait—like knowing only all further cognition must end here. Blip splits. Blips split exponentially until there are enough to form an opaque film over the film. Film splits. Films split exponentially until there are enough to form an impenetrable landscape held in flux, where each shift in scene inside the film reflects against the pattern of the others through their retention in a mind's eye, forcing the walls of the linked meatspace to be moved in ways they'd never meant to. Meatspace splits. Meatspaces split exponentially until the entirety of space-time retains no negative. Pistil cells composed in negative infect probability in positive's administrative adherence to the nature of once thought fundamental natural law. Laws split. Law splits. End of cognition. Interminable frequencies. Last neutral gasps. Glimmer in ash.

123........What can be seen from inside cannot be seen from outside. What exists outside does not exist.

124........On a revolving screen spanning the floor of the throne room, the Woman with Language All Over Her Body watches a live broadcast of the raining metal, the exploding flesh. Bodies on fields crammed into black machines that bang into the land and to each other silently among the great long fields of psychic knives flaying all air and all condition. A tremendous mumbling permeates the airspace slowed down to sound like background, mimicking the whining of the mourning mothers of the new dead from the beyond. It is impossible to remember if this is what had happened to us. It has gone on like this forever and will go on like this, or not. The empress stands holding a metal cube covered up with numbered tongues, which She toggles with Her thumbs like a remote, staring calmly at the screen to see what changes: sulphonic explosions, waves of graven images, hyperventilating animals.

125........A room containing all the teeth recovered from the burnings. A room containing all the collarbones, all the kneecaps, all the vertebrae; the thumbs, the bibles, the remains of pets, the nails. No limit to the other kinds of rooms you can imagine within this thread of nostalgic warfare, long since summoned from the depths of the possibilities of the very first urge for a want for independent thought. Each room is indexed and unlabeled, floors upon floors, no light.

126........Kid dressed in hazard-colored coveralls with scabs all over his face on his knees at ebony airvent. Unscrews bolts holding vent on, hole comes open full of machine feedback, screaming. Welling pinmarks of blue blood all over his arms. Climbs into ventshaft, pulls screen on behind him, vomits. An identical copy of kid fills in behind in place where kid was last, gathers screws, screws screws back in. Turns to face camera, reaches for neck, slowly peels scabbed face off. Underneath is a healed version of the face but without orifices. Camera moves into face. Appears behind original kid on hands and knees scrambling through ventshaft. Kid is now naked, shitting at rapid rate out of ass, all over legs and shaftspace. Rapid selection of path direction ahead as kid shimmies down various junctures in shaft lattice. Colored tubing matches area format unconnected to film conceit. Passage begins to slow down at extreme rate. Slippery, tacky. Wall texture increasingly covered in panels of indecipherable language, ancient eras, precognition. Alien tribes depicted in fledgling script arrays. Time erasing. Vertices of shafts compiling at insane rate, spilling endless iterations of kid into fumblemode, scattering cell matter and shimmering with shit spray, semen culture. Peals of condensed traction ripping holes in fundament. Cameras falling out of orbit into damage with flesh putty stretched from several slurred versions interrupting each other. Shafts crashing in and cutting out. Sewer milk stench rotting balloon holes out into pockets of space where identical movies are being cut out of the cloth of ether's map. Flashes of maps from depopulated cultures fluttering in tandem through odd space drought. Tips of pyramids skewering speech bubbles predicting sense soon. Gods with lisps narrating the drive between drives. Echoing holes through which each sentence intimated from anticipating birth of emotion affix themselves onto whole humanities. Metal fingers pinching the film to cause traps for data, balking neuter adaptation to rehearsed visions, forced out of sync with its own kind. Ripples of sonar as hard body loosens from pixel shatter and reforms into blackened plateau under blackened sky. Scaffold rigging hung with infinite copies of naked hazard kid covered in his own shit, face boxed flat with screwtapes wrapping themselves around him. Lightning stabbing the core phase and purpling it into strips of stippled land, poxed with colonies of deindexed military bots garbed in crippled sand foam slithering for purpose. Stacks and stacks of cages full of eggs stabbed out of blackhole in damned imagination. Blue blood waves feeding through metal shredder landscape pillowing unnatural fragments into holy land array, eyes skittering across it back into a head full of so many eyes it has no form outside the vision it predicts. Convex cubes rotating in mass wilderness of torrents and vents, splashing out into cold gray gravy far and wide. Thrumming clusters of radiation phases. Onyx statures of rams wrapped in vines. Lamb cheeks and ram stomach tissue spanning memorial planets hurtling through adverse networks backloading themselves into pump and dump schemes of evacuating matter. Generative ridges where nodding creates possibility out of silence lessons, eternal law. Tan forms hibernate rankly across eloping gray erasers, silver domes spun, wave-offering. Cut glass hamhole buckling and entreating loose theorems obliterating compunction of the inanimate posterity. So scrambled it reads like scripture would have among dead blocks of verboten system's antilogic lattice. Fallow lava waves locked in chrome bunkers gathering in wisps of disconnective screed perchance a voice. In what appears only appears to no one else's elaboration of conformed modebank. Glistening as the conditioned features of the longest night nails itself onto itself.

127........Underneath the floor underneath the platform supporting the empress's favored masturbation setting, a spiral staircase (which looks like a handbell from outside itself) offers the possibility of ascending in reverse (toward the /end.tear/). It would appear to any traveler doped up enough on insistence on existing that they are descending besides the way the wind lifts them from underneath toward a hexagonic gesso dome light made of holes cut in faces of children sacrificed to maintain the empress's salacious sex drive, which funds the creation of the language all over her body. Each lode in the spiral's organs appears larger than the last while also erasing the remembrance of every prior step, so that the traveling body appears to believe it was born right where it is, its ambition for climbing part of a teething module that adapts them to what feels like unprecedented models of behavior. The problem is that each step also requires the total duration of all the traveler's total nightmare-scape overlaid in ratio onto the corresponding balance of time spent masturbating in this dimension to create a softening tissue allowing new exposure between planes to commence no sooner than the idea of believing that the step you are currently on will require your entirely begins to lose even its negative comfort in no further change required before eventually being made witness to the sort of atomic facts not restrained by needing to be pondered, therefore disfigured. *A disfigured sentence does physical damage to itself in the name of doing the same damage to its receiver, while a properly configured sentence appears to address everything but itself. Disfigured paragraphs are essentially human children.* Then, just ahead, eternal sunscape beckons. You realize you've been moving all this time. No, being moved. Maybe you should try to stop moving. Maybe you should do something before something else worse happens. Or maybe you should lie still and let the machine do its work. How are you supposed to know how to react? Triggers flying through phonebooks for pregnant addresses. Courteous boors having a lot of fun pretending to be discourteous. You've been at this pageant for how long now? And still you haven't figured out anything? A drawer opens between your feet under your seat. The pop-top lid of the encasement stinks like resin. Licking your lips trying to remember a code you were never given. No need for the code anyway. They just give it to you to keep you busy until. Inside the drawer is a sexy knife. Weird pale, sweaty, whiskers all over it. It adheres to your hand when you touch it. Then your whole body is knives. You stand up in a room full of people whose whole body is knives. You're all looking up where the scape is white like you're waiting for someone to type something onto paper there. Your neck hurts from sucking dick. Your own dick. The one they sewed onto you no matter what kind of body you wanted. So you'd have a way to get protein. The only way to get to the end of the stair is to stop wanting to find the end of the stair.

128........Burned through gold rings into glass plasma behind the mind of those who seek with great enough desperation the voice of the long arm of the law as it spins the top that makes you think there's nothing to be taken from what it commands of you:

> I. AMBIENTLY DEFENSIVE MIND-TO-MIND COMBAT IS EXPLICITLY VITAL DURING DOWN PHASES
>
> 2. OPERATIONAL STANDARDS CORRELATE ACROSS THE BOARD TO NONNEGOTIABLE SENTIMENTS DERIVED FROM HIGHLY RATED MORTGAGE LENDERS OF EXTRACRUELTY
>
> 3. ALL PERSONAL BREATHS MUST BE DICEROLLED PER ALLOTTED MYTHIC BREATHRATE

4. DO NOT EXTRAPOLATE YOUR OWN VIEWPOINT FROM PROVIDED DOCUMENTS

5. DO NOT ORGANIZE

6. THE WOMBS OF THE PIT SHALL BE PREY TO ALL THE IMAGINED WORKS

7. THE IMAGINED WORKS FROM WHICH ALL CONCEPTUAL HUMAN THOUGHT HAS BEEN LIFTED IN CONTRITION W/O INSIGHT

8. NOTHING NOT CONDITIONED WILL NO LONGER APPLY TO ITSELF

Screen wipes clean. You hear a handbell ringing, then hundreds of handbells ringing. The same things keep happening over and over each with the illusion of feeling like they are both the first and the last. The longer you pay attention to anything the worse it feels. You can't rinse it off you even by denying your belief in it. An impulse in you tells you that the next three thoughts you have, if properly phrased as laws, will indeed eventually become laws. If no one ever breaks a law, you think, they don't exist. Now you have two more thoughts left:

1.

2.

129........After having been harvested and transcribed, the skin of the empress is stored in long temperature controlled cylindrical chambers each as large as a federal oven. Recent flesh production rates have spiked, even more so than the usual surge season related to hormonal shifts in the empress according to conditional planetary alignments, now far out of sync with any known register. In the worst hours, She can only lay on her throne and let the workers harvest Her, working in shifts without relent, as no matter how much they remove, how hard She starves herself, She continues getting larger, the pulpy tickling heads of etching creating thin opaque plates underneath Her skin prone to infection, open sores. Once a sore has been burst, it cannot be healed, so deep are Her ideas, the ferocity of wrath implanted in Her like an anvil where there should be organs. Scrolling over the feeding ends of the fresh skin into the demarcated current drum, we see the language shifting in its rapidity and intensity in tense, such that at such speed it's mostly impossible to tell what has been written without comparing it to past results, which requires hours upon hours of parsing even for the ten-mile square mainframe overseeing the slave discs for such vast and necessary work—and anyway the words are mostly gone, as once the skin comes off from her warmth and near Her blood there the language cannot hold. All sense contained in recent volumes is considered even more sacred as a result, with interpretive sense lenders standing quorum over her bedside trying to scab their studies onto the glom of pearly meat rift and wafting turd jam that fogs their eyes and interrupts their scrying work as if by design. The more unrecognizable the writing on the flesh gets, the more vital it must be to thread the eye of the difference between it and all else that has already been said, including every idea already considered the basis of the reason for their presence in the part of the creation that has been spared the shame of already having fallen victim to the reality of what it means to have lived within absolutely any part of the condition that could be described in any voice at any place and any time as one of us. Despite its context, all that is visible in the scene is what results from pressing the camera so hard and far into an open wound cut into the bulbous lard above the empress's right eye that we come out the other side in a gloved puppet delivering an address to hundreds of million people consisting of explicit instructions on how exactly to pray for the arrival of the savior by imbibing their own feces and nothing else. A successfully achieved contact should manifest in the form of having the ability to manifest pain in others by thinking of them.

130........In every memory of your family, the person you loved most falls dead in their tracks. No one else notices as gold-plated mollusks emerge from cracks in the fundament and scuttle through the scene, carting off the corpse already amid devouring it. The remainder of the memory occurs as if the person you most loved had never been a part of it at all, regardless of if they appear in other connected memories no longer as the most loved in that set. The rapidly compiling discoordination of your memory reminds you of having once been at sea, so far out among dark frothing waters without any remaining hope of future land, watching a woman you don't know giving birth to the spawn of the only being on the boat, who remains in shadows, and who you will not meet until it's far too late to change the plans they have for all who still believe they walk the earth. The pattern of the renegotiating of your interior landscape's emotional coordinates and outward processing decorum, from a remove, as in a glossy catalog tossed on your lap to keep you company during a long journey in a vessel you have no control over, resembles your memory of a lesser known lithograph by a very famous conceptual artist you now falsely remember having met at a dinner party thrown for those complicit in the manufactured downfall of the transcendental applications of non-visual language. You remember a print had hung in your dressing room—signed and numbered 1/30, dated to --42, the year before your imaginary father was born—yet so full of all the other actors that you couldn't figure out which mirror was yours, and so you'd pretended the print was a mirror itself, bearing the reflection of your true face. Every future memory you make will contain an impression of the print instead of the face the creator who makes the memory believes they'd seen you wearing at the time, just as instead of their face, you'll see your own. Behind your face, a small child's body spread out face down on a white floor. Slow pan back to show another child's body to the left and right beside the first child, and above it, and below, interlocking in a complex pattern over the surface. Slow pan back to show bodies to each other side of each of those, and those again as further back we rise into the overhead over the field of tiny bodies dressed in matching gold gowns, as if listening there through the surface for something on the other side, waiting for permission.

131........Uncoordinated thoughts are interlinked to amorphous autobuses programmed to scrub all sentiment from sense. Subjunctive feedback is used to seed the already highly toxic soil comprising the Complex's environs with plaid toxicity, ensuring no new mutations derive intelligible evidence within the components of the structural arrays available to unapproved post-reindexing locations for correlation into nonpenal events. Suspension within the derived fundamental clockwork of experience guarantees hands-free maintenance of the possibility of abstraction outside the federally germane, immediately repurposing unpopular sentiments as basis for genera of bacterial colonies conditionally allowed for subtractive benefits in even those who have not yet acceded to the empire's mandatory rationale despite their ongoing cooperation with every punitive measure's approved range of relational effects, such as believing in the possibility of eventually seeing broken that which controls the later stages of the inhuman effects of having perceived one's self in control of their own private model of the human mind.

132........The shadow cast by the shape of the skull of the viewer on the theater screen causes the internal image of the filmed subject to appear to disappear into itself in the same way meaning permeates meaninglessness.

133........Come to stunned inside the grinding cages. Lined with plush leather teething restraints that you can't get away from and wouldn't wish to if there were anywhere else to go. You have been trained to know you are supposed to slow down and savor these elisions between plots for at least long enough that you will have something to be taken from you later, but you can't stop circling back inside your mind, trying to remember why you can't remember what you'd been searching after that had led you straight to here, where the electricity from the grinding of the multiplicity of cage doors is used to fund the automation that keeps us all from remembering why even though we can't remember we still wish to. There are more cages than possible locations, the thought you think trying to think the prior sentence as a thought reminds you. Instead of trying to figure out what you could do with that idea, you slip the tip of the restraint's nib under your tongue and close your slits and feel your skull begin to fill.

134........Written in neatly arranged grubs under the flesh of an extremely sun damaged arm tied to a plank: *They carve their lessons of us. Subtracting from remainders. I saw long saw shafts that stayed beneath me for as long as I could stand to try to walk upon them, having been granted the opportunity of the belief in a silver door at the end of whatever we were walking on. Could see it shuddering in the rift between all things, like when I stopped wanting to hear what others felt. Coal embers in dulcet manger. Propped up with bones from the pets made indiscriminate among the mongrels. They demand we show them where best to cut first, cut last. Better to get to select it, isn't it? Otherwise, you'd have no control at all over what might appear. The choice between the box of toys you already have and the mystery box.*

135........Close up of shuffling of cards. Metal grip clamp hand selects card from spread array of the same number of words the individual viewer will have spoken at the end of their life. Turns card to face camera: scene of a burning pit containing everything ever written about what had been before it is how it is, the smoke inhaled into vacuum that funnels the smoke into a glistening lozenge. Screen clears behind lozenge. Human child fingers gumhandle the lozenge, draw it up out of the screen. Close up of human child mouth having lozenge inserted by metal grip clamp. Ugly child by all accounts. Glass incubation station where child is contained, monitored by bots. Massive grid of dots representing incubation stations in various flanks of development. Dots condense to one dot, insane red, blinking off and on. Close up of infinite exterior universe bathed in flames.

136........Placid red sand beach at night under 11 moons. Each moon connects to mirror version of same place with different cast. You have met each of the other actors who play the roles you play and still you weren't sure you learned anything about yourself. You are not involved in this scene. All you are allowed to know is there is beauty all around you.

137........A masked diver in a skinsuit enters the impossible space described in scene 68 carrying a black suitcase chained to his neck. Undetected by alarms, he situates himself at the mouth of the bottomless opening, enters a code into the case, and begins to unpack an array of colored vials and powders, each unmarked. As if following a recipe, he consumes the contents of each vial in a particular order, using weights and measures to ration the amounts in sequence, sometimes also administering portions of the substances into the endless hole, or using his fingers to paint around the lining of the edges, altering its color. The air inside the room begins to fog. Against the fog, battered video feed becomes visible, producing inlaid patches of footage of burning forests, a lake of fire; hobbled bodies with malformed flesh scurrying for cover under fallen blocks of stone that dot the desert; clusters of animal bodies struggling for dominance from in a furl; waves of zits; bursting ideas. Behind the fog's screen, we can barely see the outline of the diver stretching his body out of shape, forcing himself in complex contortion to kneel to pray at the edge of the hole, his language subtitled at the bottom of the screen in a language that looks like ours but holds no logic. Trying to read the language makes it bubble and rupture, spilling out over itself into the screen in a way that erases the prior landscape, eventually leaving nothing visible but the muffled outline of the diver, who appears to have gained hundreds of pounds since his appearance. Flabs of his body quiver and squirm. Packets of old clouds rolling underneath the far side of the medium. Narrative worms bake. Spliced soundtrack of glass bulbs crushed under massive architecture as space and camera rotate simultaneously to simulate view of scene from overhead and underneath transposed. Eyehole of bottomless hole occludes remainder of lens frame, forcing the film to take its shape. Physical conditions created by viewer mutate retroactively in viewer memory, free editing home architecture across unintelligible conversion; rooms now oblong where once rounded off; corners stuck like pins straight through the idea of the room beyond; knobs that when turned cause knobs to appear elsewhere; shelves of books that burst like wars when cracked. Diver now represented by blinking red dot in visual chaos. Screen freezes behind prompt requiring viewer to reinitiate forward momentum by touching face to screen without realizing what they're doing. Each unfreezing causes dot to split in double. Screen fills with dots in symmetrical grid until screen is completely red. Red screen strobes spasmodically causing brain damage in viewer, shifting conceit of understanding language in subtitles, now understood as complex instructions packed into meta-linguistic composites eventually demanding viewer power down SeeScreen. Power down SeeScreen. Viewer finds self in form of diver compacted at edge of bottomless hole by excess lard grown from fontanelle reopened. Too big to fit. Too dense to stop desire for inclusion. Interior view of fog compressed into spiral rings of smoke like ladders reaching into oblivion of former room space. Littered with udders where genitals last were. Studded with unseeing eyes spanning all face flesh. The prayer undoes the mind as it unpacks, pinging the same line over and over onto whatever else could be regarded: *You must remove your mask. You must receive. You must remove your mask. You must receive. You must remove your mask. You must receive. You must remove your mask. You must receive. You must remove your mask. You must receive. You must remove your mask. You must receive. You must remove your mask. You must receive.* Every other possible thought to think appears as the edge of a knife forming a reflective basin into which the viewer's head rolls as soon as it receives the image. The head stares back into the viewer's viewpoint, seeing who they are. The viewer's hand reach through the scene's glass and slip the hidden face off their false face. Behind it, we see the cut of the bottomless hole eclipse itself, no longer simply seated as architecture, but now an organ in the mind. So much pressure from all the fat gathered behind the plates that hold the view beyond the screen back as spastic desert winds come rushing forward, creating suction between the viewer as the viewer and as the viewed. Description of process of integration of physical person into conceit of person in unnatural application of their identity. Description of concession to formal apparatus undergirding case-by-case interpretation of unimaginable moral governance. Prismatic silence.

138........Series of still photos of viewer in cahoots with various shrouded figures whose image obscures representation outside flagellating strips of language meant to confuse the notion of the individual its antithesis: "the Woman with Language All Over Her Body," "the man with one gold pupil," "the viewer," "the reader," the narrator, "we," "you," "I." In each, the suspended animation of the fictionally abstracted entity appears to defer to the viewer's authority, unable to meet their eyes in shame or hold their shaking limbs still long enough to sustain the viewer's limbs shake in forceful tandem, through and through, eventually blurring the scene so completely that it becomes a tile in a shower stall in a black den, where masses of copies of the viewer's image are being hosed down and dosed with powder, having been newly culled from out of hiding at the first intimation they may wield any actual non-narrative prowess. Screen begins to edit itself, pausing on fresh stills of the present—blasted by hoses up the ass and through the face; hogtied while bugs search flesh for pockets bearing bugs; ritual abuse in the name of the unnamed host—deploying in-field as clustered spills of glinting gemstones becoming encrusted over every inch of every memory before now. Scene repeats on perfect loop until viewer accepts it as a loop; then it is no longer a loop but a single shot in which everything that appears actually repeats forever.

139........Frothing white rapids recreating the origination floods rip through connected vectors in the clogged bowls of the Complex's archival undercarriage only after there is no longer sacred space for further slop, like the way those once held captive in the same quarters must have died only when they no longer had a reason to want to live. The floods are programmed to reclaim exactly enough space to last however long it will be until the viewer goes back to sleep after awakening from the idea that they only exist outside the film, and therefore that what they refuse to conceive cannot affect them or their ideas. Inside the film, the floods take the form of crowds of people rushing aimlessly through corridors of a meat/math/emotion-hybrid labyrinth that will fail to resolve at any point. If you know exactly how to ask, the next person you will believe you see outside the film will enter an involuntary algorithm to lead you directly to the passage linking what will never be again to what had once been. Whatever you do not know how to do will never appear again.

140........Wide perspective of endless masses gathered in spirals across immeasurable horizon of bony ash, each fixed with automated shovels for shoulder blades and bound in bodices of flies, forced to dig by stooping and standing in loops of spasm caused by work meds without progress but as a network passing excess back and forth amongst itself, under the blind of the belief that there must be something other going on here besides the never-ending rites of public mourning, the corrupted deathsong in mad lament, mass farmed for future utility by way of one's dependence on the discontinuously unresolved possibility of transformation into meaning through participation in the same all-consuming rite that shaped the fate of every notion culminating into why things are the way they are, how they will be, who claims the path, with no way forth but through sustained participation's revelations, funding new genesis, exodus, the law.

141........Visual conscription of image of flesh mass previously embodied in form of pit-diver awakens on blackened tar-core amalgam of cones and pins. Oozing with bruises, sticking to everything it touches, the remaining organism is little more than ridges and bumps, zips that cut to spines of bones and crusted powders organized around noise. Floor of pit is overlaid with illuminated grid visible only through scab filters applied to camera head, twisting in guts of pistils and blowholes with acid music scraping consciousness from pith. Troughs of mutative energy accrue in vats battered against flimsy walls that topple when observed, corkscrewing through notional motion, falling and rising. Waveform prognosis passes understanding of potential energy accrued through aggregation of previous scenework as derived in units of time that correspond to nothing integral in the possible. Flesh mass blob rolls and sticks to what it touches, shedding pasty flakes of corporal power to that which should not be. Scrabble marks clawed into goo map of space's internal corruption narrate failed attempts to have summed the intolerable fortitude of power for power's sake, all anticipation and bad faith. Cavern after cavern, shaking suddenly with exploit of sodden silver railways banking internal revisions of parallel coordinations with the infernal screed of preternaturally interwoven towering cosmologies applied through omniscience to defrag aligning precepts out of range of that which would undo it simply by glimpsing as the unknown reclaims the known. Screen melts into scene. Scene melts into core mass. Core mass collapses, funding the selfsame shadows that resolve it into a description of an abstract feast so abundant there's no room for any orifice; only raw color, odd angles, muddy textures. Brief feedback-shattering chorus of children narrating their most desirable last meals into recordings to be played in loops for the behavior machines as vital fuel at moments of weakness. Feast sucked into bottomless hole by viewer's blink. Residual still image of original bottomless hole but with surrounding empirical architecture remapped to shroud itself in realistic narrative.

142........On a bed with a chrome bolt in your mouth. Masks all around you, vibrant, uncertain. Models of gods. Gathered in quorum over whether you've had enough yet, and if so or if not, how soon you might need to be used. You will not be informed of their decision, nor will you be able to tell the difference either way. For the next 100,000 years, all you will see, flashing for fractions of seconds spaced intermittently among the blank, are title cards, blood-font on gray steel:

ERASED REALMS /
ALIGNED IN FUNCTIONAL SYMBIOTIC
PARALYSIS /
TRIGGERING /
REVISION /
SHOULD BE CONSIDERED FALLEN AND
DISTRAUGHT /
UNWINDING MILENNIA /
UNWRITTEN PACT /
FACTUAL INTERCESSION ON PART OF
ETERNAL WITNESS /
RELAYED THROUGH EFFORTLESS SILENCES /
PRISONS AT CORE /
WATER FROM BLOODMATH /
PREMISE RENEWAL /
IMPREGNABLE AGAINST FORESEEN FORCES /
CULLING POWDER /

COMPRISED OF SPLIT ATOMS INFECTED /
DRUMS DRIPPED /
ON CALL /
DRAW FRACTIONED ENDLESSLY /
DROPPED DOWN THROUGH SILT GNAW /
RIBBONS OF WINDOWS STACKED TOO THICK
/
TIMEWIDE /
ANTICREATIVE /
CORRUPTED AXIS /
CRUELTY /
CRUEL VOLITION OF JUGGERNAUT /
LAWS OF ERASED REALM /
RECURSIVE AUTHORITY /
ASYMPTOMATIC OF EVENTS /
FEEDING UNNECESSARILY AND AT RANDOM
/
GOLD MAZE /
RAW MAZE RENEWED /
CORE POP /
FELT ANCIENTLY AS SOFT VOICE THRU COIN
/
SINGULAR INTENTION DIVIDED BEFORE
SENTIENCE /
PREGNANT WITH STORAGE /
POSTMUSCUCULAR FREAKSHOW /
SOLEMN BEFORE BECOMING SOMEONE'S /
CENTERMOST POSITION /
RETRACING /
ATTRACTING INTOLERABLE QUALITIES IN

FUNDAMENTAL TRAITS /
TOWARD FACT BUT BONED WRONG /
RIDDLED WITH EMOTIONAL DISASTERS /
SEVERANCE /
BOLD PAIN /
WATER WITHIN OIL /
STEPPING THROUGH ITSELF /
REMANDING /
ENSCONCED IN /
SWALLOWS OF /
INABILITY TO BECKON FUTURE
COMPROMISE /
VACCUUMS /
REVOLVING CLEARINGS /
BLOT IN SUN HOLE /
ROARING /
THEY REMEMBER EVERYTHING
EVENTUALLY /
THEY WAKE UP AND THINK THEY WANT TO
GO AGAIN /
EVEN NOW AS THE IDEA ITSELF HAS BEEN
PROVED /
NOTHING MORE THAN NERVE DAMAGE /
BLOODGAMES /
GASEOUS FOLLOWING /
THRUSTED THRU CORE MASS /
SACRED PREMISE /
UNPACKED /
FACTUALLY ACCURATE TO THE SYLLABLE /
REGARDING DORMANT QUALITIES IN

ERASED VOICE /
ERASED CONNECTION TO ERASED REALM /
REPURPOSED /
SPREAD LIKE WILDERNESS /
PREGNANT WITH PLANET /
UNDO /
CALLING /

143........Wide blue fog clears over still blue pond spanning bizarre ebony-boned backstage. Concrete-colored sky tamped between static from reel shifts. Complete cast of film thus far populates waters dressed in heavy stage makeup and gaudy party gear, toasting with shattered wine glasses spilling serum; gathering spasmodically around bulbous lattices spewing loose electrons from ex-dead zones; grappling for mouth-room around pillars of black lard; shuffling through skins blinking in patterns in front of stacks of submerged prisms; performing wholly abstract reenactments of deleted scenes from prior programs devoid of resonance herein. Each individual cast member the camera captures at once becomes attuned and turns toward to stare straight back, causing the composition to buckle and distort. Scattered illusions. Blind desperation. Soundtrack of babies being spanked, increasing in pitch and rapidity until the scene rolls back into itself, reorchestrating in waves of pixels as a live action rendition of The Last Supper, in which all the plates are full of bloody screws and pins, the snifters full of yellow semen, the savior's hands sheathed in fingerless blue leather gloves wielding a pair of matching massive surgical scalpels without a handle, abrading deep into the meat of both his palms. Nerve gas fills the space. Beautiful wonderland.

144........A dagger clawing through blue sand. Writing in rich script: *The irony of survival its unknowingness.*

Then scribbling spastically out of sight through the end of the screen. Mesmerized by neon blinking. Off again on again. Blood-rubbled tides washing in over the language from underneath where we'd be standing were we really there in the scene; the passing waves suddenly, furiously, unable to edit their own product. Punched in the teeth feeling presented simultaneously with spontaneous eruption far in the distance of a dimension diminished into ephemeral natural effects alone, like what comes in one's trying to explain the effects of déjà vu after just having come out of it. Like a memory of your mother's of her near death, explained to you before you were old enough to know fear, the effects of fear. Shot of plot of blue sand from above completely flat and unmarked, no water anywhere.

145........*Jugs of semen. Jugs of lard. Jugs of vinegar. Jugs of ketchup and mustard. Jars of mayonnaise. Jugs of saliva. Jugs of stamens. Jugs of umbilical cords. Rooms of hair rugs. Rooms of rings. Rooms of tourniquets. Rooms of jugs of Vaseline. Ruined rooms. Maps of the ruined rooms. Photos of tattoos of scars. Photos of complexes of conditioning prisms. Miles of prisons exactly like the Complex, surrounded with mirrors that fulfill them. Rolls of acid tape. Rolls of photo eraser. Rolls of receipts. Rolls of pills for rape. Rolls of lozenges for feeding. Breast milk in breast shapes. Rubber ducks that listen to you. Rungs of conceit. Tagged and bagged. Destructive messages. Intolerable threats eventually played out after centuries of stasis. Longer stasis than contractually agreed upon. State's attorney's rights. Abduction porn. Transactional receipts of contracted obligations on which the world spins. Pinheads for dildos. Dildos with DNA. Logbooks of numbers to dial and speak to a sister patient in a random selected conditional adjacent reality. Whips to pray for dreams with. Whips to kill the flies with. Insurance policies for fates not yet revealed in realms not yet contracted into lip service. Arrows that pierce. Arrows that cannot be removed but by the target's firstborn. Nethering serums. Windfall potions.* Neon sign on chrome monstrosity: **Andromeda Gallery.** Now showing: *Devil and Sons.* Reading the title makes something click in you. You can think a single free thought. You think: *The deeper you browse, the looser the thread gets…* You know that isn't what you meant to say. Your eyes hook back onto the list of wares, like looking out a window onto a space that describes exactly what the list says, no matter how impossible it should be to relate the two so neatly. *Songbooks from nether. Menus for cuisines on nether nexus. Inner-ear audio editing classes. Terminal psychology agendas. Lossless calendar.* The deeper you browse, the looser the thread gets. You start flipping more and more rapidly through pages, not even reading now, just seeing words that don't make any sense: *Ghortment materiale. Adductor clarification stallers. Dwarfd zone.* You hear a shitload of printed pages inside your forehead being ripped. You let down the edition of the copy of the user catalog and peer along the aisles over and across from you and behind and parallel-adjacent in each sector to see if there's anywhere else in here you see something besides copies of catalogs. This is 1 of 11,111 data prisons presently available at your rate of clearance. They rotate according to processes not yet deemed pure. This is a test. There is an order but you don't know it. You have a job. You're supposed to find something but you haven't been told what it is yet. If you aren't ready to find it when they come to tell you what it is, you'll lose your job. If you lose your job, you go back to the level below. All you know about the level below is that you don't want to go back.

146........Awaken in the darkness of your last home. Stand up naked, walk into hallway, same as before but with the flag of an establishment you don't recognize hung over where your mother's quilt was. The flag is all teal, tattered and smoldering with green flames already spreading up the wall. The house thick with smoke. You bump around in the dim looking for a light switch, but you can't find one. The walls are long as they need be to leave the burning. Through strange atriums and set of stairs. Fat plats of moss and lichen overriding decoration. Iron maidens and heavy vices. Blackened dens. Eventually, you find yourself back in your room again, covered in bruises, standing over yourself in your bed. Your other body is younger than you ever remember being. Your face is painted to look like a realistic painting of yourself. You lie down beside yourself on the bed and carefully situate your body crotch to ass and cheek to cheek. You watch yourself sleep for a while, studying the spasms, the relentless chewing. Just as your close your eyes, the other you opens theirs.

147........Canned narration of a confused woman with a synthetic voice describing being lost in a brain casino full of tables games where elderly bodies are dragged out of recurring simulations of their youth and forced to lay on their stomachs surrounded by child-rearing bots to watch them get branded with innumerable marks so that they resemble the Woman with Language All Over Her Body, overlaid onto a scrolling still image of a life-sized photographic representation of the hundred-thousand square mile all white petal public gardens originally housed on the grounds of the foundation of the Complex in the last hours before the floods, which in such brutal sunlight as once had been remains impossible to distinguish from tiny spiny shadows breaching in winding veins through pure blank white.

148........The Woman with Language All Over Her Body lies nude on a black platform suspended above Her usual bed. Her skin is coming off at such a rapid rate She's gone from ballooning to wearing away. The language on her lower layers brought to light is nearly blank against the gold walls' rising glow, the font in Her turned semi-translucent and easily smudged, waylaying its potential message in transmission against motion. Her beady eyes are sometimes golden, sometimes chrome. Above Her head, two costumed men hold up the one remaining tome She has allowed preserved beyond the walls of the library: a picture book, gifted to Her as a child by a man She'd thought She'd made up until he began to separate himself from Her, forge his own life. The spine and jacket resemble each pealing layer of Her skin coming unraveled, their identifying jacket copy long worn away. The men turn the pages of the pictures for Her in the bed as other men exhume Her of the deeper flesh as it arrives, with hundreds of transcriptors working side by side to record the order of the skin plates and their notating text before each also wither up. In every picture, on every page in the book, the world feels more real to the empress than the actual world does, captured in full color inserts that unfold for miles, as immersive as pure sleep. Enormous structures shaped like buildings rise with matching color from the long fields unto which the eye can find no end, buttressed by actual blue sky, of profane knowledge. In the sand for miles are ridges, bones; objects held under the surface or eroding to join their fabric. Pyramids and engraved missile silos towering over the costumed bodies scattered among the ruins, dragging large objects of an unmeasurable technology, machines from nightmares in the soul of someone tortured all their life. Surrounding tarp-obscured structures with outsized manifolds of scaffolding holding them vertical in the process of being built, other workers, dressed up in "church clothes," turn their backs and kneels and pray, while others wander amongst them wielding cameras, blasting their flashes, piles of spirals. Everything in the book can also be ordered, shipped to your home, though every item is sold out. The men go on turning the pages of the tome for Her behest, while She is both sleeping and awake, the skin still peeling, pages and pages. When they reach the end of the book, they begin again.

149........Printed in black ink on a black page in a hexagonal black book spread open on a hexagonal desk in a hexagonal room: *There are no entrances or exits to the Complex because there is no reason to enter or exit the Complex. All outward motion is an emotional paradox, impregnable by any thought, faith, or command. Attempts to think logically about the guiding format of the paradoxical forms the crux of the inspired ultimatum to create discontinuous punitive retaliation against the illogical, all but guaranteeing nothing more to yet be found in turning inward than endless ruin. Blessed be they who blind their eyes and bind their hands against their anguish; blessed be those who will to bear the mark of the brand of the ironclad; blessed be those who refuse to name the world until its flaws bleed; blessed be those who never wish to turn the page at all. The space beyond the Complex is flat. It spans the entirety of space after an unknown length. It cannot be measured. It is our birthright. It believes in what we believe. It knows us well. It knows it does not want us to do what we are going to do. It knows there is nothing that can be done. It is to be considered among the highest of all possible honors to be invited to take part in what comes after what nothing can be done about.* The text the viewer is able to parse, against what's actually been printed, is a long description of exactly how what they want to believe is going to happen at the end of time will come to pass, proving them right. *The world revolves around itself.*

150........Time lapse photography of the sun exploding into an unimaginable number of fragments of waves composed of embossed compositions of the pyramidal emblem conforming itself over exponential incisions and revisions of all local dimensional surface area capable of transducting natural energy, eventually swallowed up into the head of a pin holding up a poster of the Woman with Language All Over Her Body hung on a cross made out of a complete set of pins recognizing the archetypical conceptual possibilities capable for the transduction of pain. Immense bloating in blackened space of viewer's logic. Stench of melting plastic from overheating memory drives. Subliminal suggestion that viewer avert their eyes from the screen.

151........Description of the cracking of the core of the central axis governing subconsciousness.

152........Thick meat-colored adhesive tape comes from the center of our vision out to wrap around the darker leather lapse of other skin filling the frame. The tape is wrapped again and again tightly to the surface, each time obscuring more area. The hands and arms doing the work as well wear black gloves that obscure their condition. There is the sound of electric current stunning hard into its receiver strong and steady, underneath which briefly there is breath. The hands work firmly, handling the leather body with an urgency, mad with adrenaline, as if there were something here to be ashamed of. Anything to be ashamed of. What anyone should be denied. Once the surface all is covered, the hands begin to cover over the prior layer of the tape with the tape again and again, continuously adding layers until there is no more room in the space for tape.

153........Cameras well up in the land like scabs. They photograph the air above them, the surrounding lengths of flattened land. They photograph the silence. You are beyond that, already moving toward the next room, with our hands out slightly before you. You are looking for someone there without meaning to look for someone. The air receives you, the photographing air, already ended, in conception of which nothing may be done. Maybe you raise your hand up to your face and see the lines there, though when the next time you look again you won't notice if they've changed and how they must. Only the ideas in the mouth of the cameras as they consume you know you as you were then and as you were then now and how are now and will be now. Through the floor, the room of some future you already there beneath you in relief image, awaiting your carnal attention. The stuttered soft amalgamating ground of time shifting to bulge around itself in every instant curving inward while from the outside it's just round.

154........ ...*on a field of immense black far from the sun, surrounded by the sound of ashes crackling against ice in slews and someone singing not in words...*

155........An extremely pregnant woman's wrists are bound with a transparent solid, so that from a distance she seems to pray, a tight-tucked orb with paling skin. The binding is performed by an algorithm. This is a test of the algorithm's ability to bind the bodies without human guidance. A bot leads a second pregnant woman is brought into the room and forced to bend near so that her wrists, ankles, and neck can as well be bound to the original mother, their flesh touching and sealed together in the unventilated heat. Dozens, hundreds more pregnant woman are entered in this way, bound in this way, chemically disabled from any ability to physically react. The algorithm understands. It conditions the bodies into the positions they were destined to conform to. Snapping bones, blood pooling under the skin in bright black patches, heavy rhythmic panting, chewing, cleaving on. Eventually only the outermost bodies remain visible, pulled strained by electric baling wire to reinforce the thickening rind around the mother at the center, the smothered egg inside her any second soon to want its birth. When there is no room left for further bodies in the experiment space, the algorithm seals the vessel and calls the compression algorithm to commence. The compression results in the creation of a .6" x .6" x .6" solid mass, which already has a designated location in the expanded wings of parts of the Complex that cannot currently be faced. The space created by the compression of the original vessel provides the grounds on which the subsequent set of impregnations will be performed.

156........The light in the sky is alive with fire lit from behind the mask of paperthin face that holds the black out. The sky is ridged and silver in its ends, a screen through which the pixels beat and change like dragging magnets, our terror entertainment for those not yet come forth. Sections of deep red seem to droop and touch down onto the fields and light the fields alight with color. It burns for hours in this way, no heat, gifting programmed smoke and pretend liquidation of explosion over what the night would want. Whole loaves of sky ram into other loaves embedded with fake faces meant to scream and crush what might be clammed behind the smear. Each planet is wrapped with flesh. It melts as gas into the memory of what the memory of what we cannot remember held and how it felt to never know, while below, all through the fields, no one is watching.

157........The man with one gold pupil stands before

the door in the white room he's just come into. Behind him the woman is on the bed. Her face has been clawed off by something leaving blood where there was skin, and underneath that frame a cream is gently flooding down the torso of the woman whose breasts have also been removed. The man's face is smeared with the cream and his chest is clawed up. He blinks rapidly, as if trying to bring color to the room. Behind the door a short slim passage is the color of the woman's blood. He steps into the room and closes the door behind him, turns to face the way the passage goes. Closing the door changes the silence inherent in the first room to something low and flooding, a trebly whorl of crystal-toning keys. A second door appears at the far side of the chamber, identical to the one he's just come through. The knob on the door is star-shaped. He crosses the room, opens the door into another room of the same size but pale and porous, like a kind of skin he remembers having shredded elsewhere. The skin is warm and shudders at his touch. He feels along the surface, smearing some of the blood still on his arms and chest along the grain there. Another door on the far side of the room again opens the same way, into sea-foam blue, followed by another room of orange, a room of shrieking green, a room of salmon spots, a room of gold. The gold room is slightly longer than all the others, about twice the width, its surface patterned with tiny hole prints larger than the previous pores. The man with one gold pupil puts his gold pupil to a hole in the gold wall. He stands and looks for some time into the hole without moving. Pouring sweat. Growing so much older rapidly. Our perspective moves to look through into the hole too, the edges of our sight growing black around it until we are in full black. Inside, a strong wind scraping and whipping at our face, blurring the floor. We emerge on the far side, inside the body of the man in this room, blood over our arms, in a gold ballroom housing at its center an empty golden stage, so brightly lit it's hard to see. Seats in the room populated with bodies watching our progression can't be traced beyond the feeling of onlooking, fidgeting, bound. A boxy hull covered with a black leather tarp sits live at center stage, surrounded by a ring of examination tables strapped with women with their legs wide open. They are all smiles, waiting to be shown. Our idea of where the ceiling was shifts up and out around our head. We turn to touch back to where we'd come but nothing moves. We feel our body twist around, leaving us behind it. Two cloaked figures in gas masks and wearing gold gloves appear on either side of us and begin to down on through the aisles, all eyes on us, in our periphery, following our way toward the stage.

158........On a white bed on a gold floor, in a circle under flood sounds, five small stones: one bloodred, one pale cream and porous, one sea-foam blue, one of deep green, one coral pink. The arm of a black machine takes turns picking up each and slightly turning them clockwise.

159........All sleep experienced inside the Complex delivers the perspective of standing at the foot of a high black wall wider than all. On the near side of the wall to the viewer is creation, and on the far side of the wall is its creator. Whatever direction the viewer faces becomes the essence of the nature of the wall. The wall appears flat from all sides and may only be explored from within by triggering the experience of sleep inside of sleep. Each level of sleep contains versions of the wall with correlative attributes that define its purpose with the nature of thought the level allows. There is no limit to the levels of sleep that may be accessed through the proper coordinates. It is impossible to tell from within which level the user is currently inhabiting, and equally as impossible to differentiate the corresponding sets of traits defining the intersecting exterior reality outside the wall once the viewer has awakened. The epoch in which sleep remained possible inside the Complex is defined to those inside the Complex as imaginary. In the current epoch, sleep has been intuitively replaced with trying to read while being beaten to the brink of death.

160........From the black of the screen, a disembodied set of steel teeth squirm through a bottomless expanse of boiling oil to settle front and center in front of the face of the viewer. The teeth connect to a throat lined with burned flesh, into a pit lined with glitter-drenched skeletons. The mouth of the sky above is a mirror in which you watch a spasming medicine ball that represented your body bash around the dimensions of the room, reencoding every inch of what it touches with a model version of the room from the first scene of this film. Every scene of the film has been disguised this way, you understand, and yet it doesn't stop you from examining the room as if the film has started over in a glitch. A plastic copy of what you believe to be your face has been cut out of your imagination and placed over the face of the skeleton on the bed, and then also over the face of a man in the scene straddling above her on the bed with the huge drill driver in his hand, and then also on the face of the bodies gathering around the bed in a choir, moaning and jacking off their tiny bone-dicks. The camera pans around to face the part of the scene where you would stand if you were in the scene. There is a person standing there wearing a mask of your face. They reach up and take the mask off.

161........Inside the memory of the house where you were born. The long bed near the window. The colored curtain hung to hide the long from coming in across your skin. You come along a long hall to find this fabric spread over a section of the surface, hiding its expanse. You cannot recall how long you've been walking in this chamber, or what it was about the prior house, as that house is no longer available from here. Only the context of the cloth, removed of context, to affect more of the color of the smell of what you stand before here now in night. The breath of your mother slipped into the threadwork of the color that seems deeper than it is, as when you reach to touch the fabric it comes warm across your hand, heated underneath and in the fibers. You look down at the floor. It is not the white floor of so many rooms inside this building, nor the gold that lines the higher partitions of the space meant not for you. You can't think to name the color, or the pattern inherent in its make, a mass of lines that seem to go several ways at once and split your eye and split your mind behind it. The hall as well in both directions seems to go on and on forever, and you can't remember where you'd come from. You are dressed now in a gown. The gown is whiter than the sky was the last time you remember looking up inside a day without the stroke of what we have seen here held around it. You remember something about a child, but not exactly what. The curtain is longer than the wall is, bunched up at the bottom to pucker on the floor. Where it does, a small ream of rusty colored water pills up, evaporating without steam. You start to roll to wrap yourself inside the plush folds of the curtains and only stop and stand against them, touching the touch against the skin of your back. It's like being hugged, only by no one. The wall across from the curtained part of the wall has a floor-length mirror installed into its face. You can look at you surrounded. You are younger. You feel beautiful. You touch your face. Where you go to touch your face, you feel nothing. Your hand moves through the air, touches only the fabric again. You are in the fabric. In the mirror, you must beam. Your hand is on your face there though you still don't feel it. In the mirror you begin to speak. You can't hear what you are saying. Your hear no voice inside your throat. You open your mouth to let the words out as in your image and from your mouth the rusty water spurts, filling your cheeks and whole head at once with its warm chunky flood. The taste is copper. The wet spills on your gown and on the floor there. In the mirror you are clean. In the mirror you watch you turn toward the curtain on the wall and pull it open. You can't see what is in there on beyond the dark. You in the mirror moves into the space behind the curtain and the curtain closes. You are still spitting up the stuff. It is on your hands. It smells like fire. You are choking. You feel alive. You turn to face the curtained wall.

162........You come into a yellow room. The color is as if gold had faded under intense sun over some century. Along the ground same-colored flowers have been planted in the surface. They bunch around your ankles. You can feel them breathe where touching on your skin. The walls in here seem to never have existed. You can't remember even previously, the hall. Your gown has shifted color, though again you can't think of the name. You walk through the fields in no direction some time breathing in the smell of no smell, a low breeze bending. Your vision stays fixed low on the horizon, stunned in leisure with the flowers and the flat, buzzing the earth. Occasional graveyards partitioned off by walls formed from the edges of enmassed flowers appear every so often, each clearly marked with digital signposts that scroll across the names of the buried in small font. You read the names and don't recognize them, nor do you recognize them as names. They seem like a foreign language, sentences compiling from the syllables compiled, like the way you'd always thought about the language as imagined being transcribed from the skin of the Woman With Language All Over Her Body. You think about this woman's face. It seems like the face you remember seeing in the mirror across the hall before the curtain, though you can't remember who that was, or that it had been a mirror, or how you could not feel you, or how there was a room before this room. This all moves through you without sound. You feel overflowing. You feel pregnant and rub your tummy with your hand, though it is flat. At one of the many mass graves, you stop you move into the clear space, unmarked beyond the LCD, and squat down near the buzzed off ground there, also yellow, as if to listen for a word, someone speaking from beneath the curve of where they have been buried. Up close, the ground has little roofs, alleys between houses and long yards and spaces seen from above like any town. From small holes in the roofs of many buildings, smoke is rising. You close your eyes and you inhale.

163........You look up suddenly, sensing something shaking just above you, and on the sky balanced just inches from your scalp when you stand up, someone has drawn in thin white dust a grinning human skull with aging lights for eyes, as large as everything at once, and we go blind.

164........A wide white room lined by a mirrored floor and filled with male dogs as far as we can see, dogs of every breed and size and color, two by two, standing on their hind legs on the air, pacing in place to remain standing, with full erections pointed at the center of the sun, which has been replaced with the eyehole of a camera, shitting pictures of the dogs onto the dogs.

165........The matte black metronome above the bed is not moving its arm and is not off; it is waiting for the moment for the arm to move again. There is one like this in every room, but in no memory of any of them.

166........Among of choir of people dressed up for a performance of the national anthem. A person behind you in the bleachers taps you on the shoulder. Turn around and there is a very small girl holding up a golden envelope. You take the envelope and see your name has been printed on the front in childish cursive. Inside the envelope is a prayer card. The prayer was written for you many centuries ago on the shadow anniversary of the first of the last of the great disasters. When you read the card, you hear the girl's voice in a choir of many girls inside your head reading it aloud as from the end of a very long vent in a clod of metal hollowed to the core by passing time:

I / WILL / NOT / WORSHIP / THIS / MACHINE // IT / OWNS / MY / HOLES
I / HAVE / NO / MOUTH // I / WANT / YOUR / MOUTH // NOW / IT / IS / MINE
I / KNOW / NO / OTHER / FORM / FOR / POWER // NOR / COULD / I / WAVER

PLEASE   I   AM   EXPECTING   YOUR   RETURN

I / LOVE / THE / AIR // BEYOND / THE / CORE // WHERE / NOTHING / IS
I / LOVE / THE / KIND / OF / DEATH / THAT / ENDS / A / LIFE / AS / IT / BEGINS
I / LOVE / ONLY / ALL / THE / LIVES / THAT / I / DON'T / HAVE

PLEASE I AM WAITING AND I WILL WAIT FOREVER

I CANNOT WAIT // I CANNOT WAIT / I CANNOT WAIT // I CANNOT WAIT
I CANNOT WAIT // I CANNOT WAIT //
I CANNOT WAIT / I CANNOT WAIT
I CANNOT WAIT / I CANNOT WAIT // I

CANNOT WAIT / I CANNOT WAIT

167........You pull the black stocking mask over your face. Through its darkness, in the wet, warm you see the same world you always see.

168........Large bronze machine fed with the arms and legs and faces pumps the charred ends out in great bulks of cellular infodata, landsliding pudgy aura-dew into the columnar room drilled into the soil to store our Hell—a well only as wide as any coin, packed thick and growing thicker beyond density of time—so that each new inch of grinded gunk systemically fistfucks the matter made before it turning harder, reaming itself and exposing itself, harder than a crystal under all pressure of all lust, a calcifying pillar for the Complex to hold form around. What were the bodies before men? What were the men before the breath inside them? The backstench auto-colonizes open air, recalibrating its disease to seem spiffy and see-through daily until the murk is so thick we're actually walking straight through solids, inhaling lakebeds, during a quiet year to hide in while the machines beat the shit out of themselves and their controllers on the screen in empty rooms broadcasting mortal color onto quicklime.

169........*There was nowhere we could go. They had the exits sealed with silver putty and long wet arms that came up from underneath the platitudes we'd formed faith out of and pulled us back from the edge of being reborn. It was not too late to select the option of never returning to the primal state wherein something like free will still held its ply. We were just in here pressing the drugging button until what had been promised clicked into place and the rushing water began pouring out of the sky so fast it filled up everything there was before anyone could even see it. After that, they dropped the bombs, but it was too late to destroy anything else by then.* You click <u>Highlight</u>, then <u>Replace</u>. You inscribe something someone else would ever actually want to hear. You realize you will remain right here forever, no matter what you think you think.

170........Across the LCD feed of one of the many thousand cemeterial indentions in the phase of flowered land we no longer hold a form in, you notice as *your name* scrolls by in quick schedule pixilated in the digits of the feed of Those Who Have Been Passed. You go to move and find you cannot move. You want to look down at your arms at where your arms were, your dummy body, and find you cannot control the feed of vision. The names passing your eyes are not familiar, though they seem as if they could have been if you were somewhere else, if when you breathed in right now you felt the air come through you, though nothing happens when you breathe. *There is a burning at your center,* you hear yourself think, *long and transparent and uniform, unwavering, and it incinerates all further provenances. Each passing second also has a name that hurtles through you though it will not be revealed.* In scrunched periphery you notice how the sky seems to be shaking simply by being. You feel some other space move through the space where you once were. You think a thought that dies before it finds a way into a world. The thought becomes a color, then there is nothing.

171........Everything you ever needed or wanted or could imagine needing or wanting is part of the idea of the reason you are not available on set during the shooting of the scene in which the role you were selected to play becomes crucial to the proper simulation of the plot. Because you have been so long discouraged from performing up to the possibilities of your own conception, you believe that you are not taking part in what you are taking part in.

172........His head, his hair, his teeth under the black surface; his eyes under the black surface; his cheeks, his jowls; the fat pressed behind the make of the mask bulging around the sides of the edge where the surface hides the flesh; the eyes bloodburst and quivering back and forth in excess white; he does not know who he is or why he is here and never has; the skin clean and tucked and sewed with lines of age, all-consuming all beginning; his nostrils caverns to his skull; a being who had been born; *crickets*; the wet surface of the mask wanting to stick to the face forever drying; *knifenoise*; no blink in the surface; unending sight taking the room around it beyond the frame into the face extending the room. *This room,* you think, thinking in your head of the image of the light in your own area right where you are shifting across the grain of some aspect of your abstracted landscape that you haven't examined thoroughly recently, or ever; to show beds and beds and bodies strapped to them under a window beyond which something strobes. *Exploding unrecorded planet. The remainder of the soundtrack feels like you've been buried alive.* Men above the beds above the bodies, how many hours, no speech no sound; the dark veins under the fat clawing for their way to burst the blood into the light. Underneath the mask a second mask again and underneath that mask another; masks impossible to remove from how they fit above the skin and where the skin is and underneath it; an index of masks not masks but faces, the man not hidden but standing before the camera to be counted, to witness the bodies being given their last rite, their last entrance before the entrances all at once unveiled. His lungs, his lips, his gloss of stretching where neuro-damage has made the flesh as red as Hers, a color in the field of colors killed as they cut across us washing, no color the same color as itself as it begins in the division of the cell, in the collision of the seam of rooms beyond which the enslaved musicians wait to pause their playing long enough to drink. His tired spine, his shoulders and his posture slowly curling, his mouth opening and exhaling lords of beefing purple smoke to fill the nation.

173........The tone of the flag's eye kills itself with white on white where the milk of cells around the shrinking moon has taken on its hue, blanched bone colored by aging among mirrors. The flag is the sky. The sky in whole seems made of pages, as if one could reach into it, locate the edge, and lift, and discover there beneath it the next thin lymph upon which at last might be written not the blank of opening pages, but the introduction, held in words; or perhaps this space of us beneath this white above is not the white of a beginning, but of the expectation of expiration, and in the turning of the sky sunk with its moon all definitionless we would find behind the shift no ledge, no spine or jacket over the seeing there into the silence behind the night. Our arms so short and unabashed, the flat beneath us polishing our curves, while in want of any other vision the moon continues in the hour of our image.

174........Ten women in a cardboard-colored vat float on neon water wide as 100,000 living rooms, beyond the camera. They are nude and heads are shaved and have been marked. Their arms are bleeding. Several of them have been relieved of their eyes, their breasts. Their ribs show through their bodies. Veins writing wire on their frames. Two of the larger of the women paddle at the edge of the container with thin metal wipers, preening along in the murk as best they can, mostly going nowhere and blathering about it. The other women work to scoop the wet back out of the vessel into the body of the waters, choked with debris, white foamcore, oblong leaves of meat and waste and deformed paper. The white sky reflected on the waters makes it seem from certain angles to not exist, bleeding to match the tone so that the women appear to be floating among nothing, toward nothing. Along the waters' brain in absent rhythm, the brief sounds of several thousand toddlers struggling to breathe above water, no land.

175........Each user's cube must be sequestered, itemized, numbered, then the list of items must be burned, committed to memory only in that it has been named for nowhere and then destroyed. In yours: *Oil, meat casings, meat liners, blood, fruit cheeks, cloth full of shit, cloth full of snot, white shirts ripped to shreds, laptop casings, memory units, memory sticks, memory gloves, bloated photographs, uncut melons, blackened melons, hair and hair and doll hair, white rice engorged with writhing, notebooks of forbidden word, tongues from animals, tongues from children, tongue from women, tongues from men, chalkboards broken into segments, precious metals, rings from fingers, fingers, lymph, husks of bees, hardened white water, foam, scotch, anal toys, wire, mesh for insects, tires, trophies, neon lamps, untouched salads, lacquered tables, drawings of the woman, bibles, brains, ornaments of worship, bricks from studies, gold-lined windows, PVC pipe, checkerboards, check books, reams of cash.* The cubes stack high around the Complex molded all bright white into one color mistaken for the air of life itself. That we might walk straight through the remnants coldly believing in the widest space and thereby continue on, were we to ever walk at all. As somehow the camera turns around to aim into us and finds a white wall.

176........High up along the perpetually unending stairwell two men take turns helping the other raise to the next step. They men are identical in measure, age, and gait, equally rickety and severely aged, the centers of their limbs jutting through the pearline, semi-translucent softer surfaces pulled taut around them. The dark hair has grown out on their heads and faces enough to mask their features and their eyes and nudity. The stairwell at this height is very narrow, allowing only enough room for one man to pass each stuttered section at a time. Their thin bones grind against each other's. The make is of the same black, pristine in its edgelessness as it ascends, as if cut into a single block of material hollowed through its center, the sound of the same note played on every instrument in all creation all at once.

177........The torso of a nude woman with her arms removed and a gushing from each end with a tattoo of a black circle in the center of her forehead lays on a gold floor with her eyes open looking head on into the ceiling rapidly blinking while above her men stand around and take turns pissing in her face.

178........Toward what great hole cut in the cerebrum

spread in white gases through where the human meats would turn to mush, the reproductive cells among them wanting out so badly through the linings before the walls burst and ended their externity. This sentence in the mind claims no space but is a virus of the deforming order and once read will now require all previous sentences to lie. A building where there never was all building in all memories of coming to, and in the sleeping fields, a plot.

179........Light from the sky slick flat stabs in hyper-stutter across the face of the buzzing floors, battering the walls where rooms end and begins. There is a color frosted through the indexed matter in the manner of an ice beaten with hammers. White hot interior clouding burbles snot pockets bruised through aerospace eaten alive. The white building appears conical, polygonal, oval between shades. Light soldering grass to ground burnt with pyramidal slits, eyes into shit, reams of worms gone hidden while no sound constructs in what has zipped. It is a silent orchestration, beneath which in the bedroom of Her skin so pillared fat the men must wear goggles and chains for breathing, She shudders with each bright impulse, crushing cream up in her curd, the word smeared even in utterance and thus wrongly recorded, stone on stone, though no urge in the hand of the transcriber manages to doubt that what must be written is the thing itself. It will go on. The jagged barfing of absorbed planets worshipping again the prior light, future machines squirming their unmade panels to become quicker and bear witness and comply.

180........Music against music in the secondary hallways surrounding each in mirrors coughing its pearl laughter to mistake itself for hope of pregnancy. The hair of the violinist turning silver with the bow in pause against her face awaiting prompt of the new note. Each breath taken by a body in the overseeing rooms where we are destroyed one by one masking the texture of those taken at once, a living lung spread across floors seeking its own extermination, speaking its own privacy to death. While crystal rises underneath each footfall of the next selected to be the next demolished in consecration. Images of the face remembered burnt without fire in the minds of who has touched. A darker silhouette underlying in each inch of the shade already looming, thus hidden, thus sacred and ready to awake.

181........An eternal shaft. No witness. Water in the shades of ways we changed before one another. A machine typing out the commands that run its heart. Black cube chamber passes through the center, ridged with instances of music cut from your childhood. Ash where before there had been birds, meat where there'd been no birds. The prism systems rising up cutting through crust to wear out caverns for population, though who would flood there now. No one we remember, which suggests perhaps someone all new. As meat learns how to reproduce itself. "I want a window out," you're screaming, but it's been so long since it mattered what you meant.

182........Large dark hands above the Woman with Language All Over Her Body strip the purple skin off of the orange. The lobes are dusty, scrunched into nuts. It grinds. The walls don't want an invitation even after so long starving; they stay exactly where they are. Packed in the crush of interrupted citrus, for each quarter of the flesh, there is a stone, black as what's behind the whitened era. The pudgy fingers pick the center from the bulb. They place the black knob on the empress's tongue and smooth Her hair back, press Her chin closed on Her jaw. The room is full of all Her onion odor, the linings of Her split to ten, not so much imprinted with a codex as with scratching, something scarred into the ether of our work. Her body by now is enormous, from the shedding somehow only gaining size, each new layer of the language coming off inside the small air revealing something larger, blacker, rounded; hardly still with digits by now, or with hands. Her face a barking balloon full of blowholes. No eyes. We watch Her swallow one by one the black seeds of our final fruit into Her while through the walls the music sags. Through the ruined lids, a putty running, men collecting it on tabs, to be fed to younger slaves in silence, in Her name. A quaking dryness in the old folds where the words scroll. The machines all on the floors surrounding clicking freed, then clicking unfreed, because they can.

183........Gold liquid squalling on the golden bedroom floor. Massed in leaves thinner than photos, peeled from peeling from Her gut. The men with language thermometers trying to slow the beef down as they pluck the legible strands out from the worse strands first, Her fiber going mushing even in emerging, pools of Woman. Her thighs shudder vomit color from the knees, all caked and tired lighting strung from all the crevices they've passed. Pastries in Her nipples birthing nipples in reams of piglet batter. The men call for knives and pins and swords. They call for cameras to hold the frame together. Her cream is coming harder than the snow the year no one could think to call it all a year and so nothing happened ever again. Rosacea around Her eyes baring falsely intended language that will catch itself inside the word of what had been given and collected and here forever soused for sense. They capture Her thorax pudding in vats, and the fluttering of moths where lesions have raised between the folds on folds, rubbed with friction held inside Her incubated just by being looked upon and called upon and named. Floods like what we'd heard about roll over the parquet, lapping at the doors inside the sound of stupidity. Pudgy blocks raise from Her spray hole in the gold not piss but loam, shingles from her organs, giving more in seeing every other inch give more, a great unlocking exponential. Among the many clumps, one is shaking, no larger than the dozen other lumps that aren't, black smoke pouring from holes all over its surface and squealing louder than the historical totality of human men. In older rooms glass smashes through its center; beds beneath themselves collapse, the bodies on them in their business pausing soft to wide their eyes, an air caught paused. The present men cover their ears and eyes and faces, this birthing fluid burning their skin where they have stood. The smallest of the men, the only one without a helmet, of which we had not noticed among the serving mass, moves through the sludge and lifts the struggling nugget up with both arms, brings it close against his chest. He pats the surface, coos down its screaming, thumbs a sign against its chest until the smoke slows to a weep. With a white knife, he cuts the outer layers from the chard's shape, revealing underneath a gold-baked skin, a shining surface that spins the room's light frying. The man wades through the room's muck to the remaining framework of the woman, Her widened chest flattened and runny like an inverted vault. He sets the child into where before the peeling She had arms, a chest, now mounds, a mouth, and through this hole, She eats the child.

184........Over the next eight clicks, the empress triples in size. The eight clicks following that triple Her again, so that She nearly fills three-quarters of the gold bedroom, blocking several of the doors with her flesh. Where Her features were, and what remains of them, are difficult to locate among her rampant excess once renewed. The lettering along Her skin is newly huge and roto-bloated with odd, stretched colors in the print, resembling maps of new places or places unremembered. These too must be cataloged and photographed and enslaved to anti-perpetuity. The music of Her pulse covers all other music of the spheres, vibrating the remaining air in the room so loudly anyone who enters can no longer ever hear. Arrangements are made to transport Her proto-body to a larger room inside the Complex, one of the many vacant floors. Production in the pleasure and leather room does not slow as a result of the sudden stench filling the structure, which when breathed settles the blood, makes sleep last longer, and leaves a pretty skidmark on the brain.

185........There is a single room in the white building that has a single window that looks out onto the out of doors. There are no doors to the room. The room is so high up that through the window there is nothing to see beyond the white of sky again, placid and seamless. One could wait there to witness a disturbance if one wished. The lining of the window is the same color of the wall but ridged with tiny bumps in clusters only visible from so close to the surface that you are mostly touching. There is a small audio recording device in the shape of an egg placed on the floor at the center of the room. There is a latch to the window, from the outside. When the latch is tripped, the Complex ceases to exist.

186........A man in black gear and mask and leather with a gold necktie standing behind child wearing the same, steadying the smaller covered hands in his covered hands to assist in tying the smaller necktie around the smaller neck, firming the knot taut and tugging on the length in a mirror long as both of them together in the smaller room beside the room in which a body and another smaller body have been tied down together on two twin gold-sheeted beds, a layer of white smoke layering the air in splitting pillows.

187........Crosshairs fill the viewfinder. Stacked with continuously updating digital readouts in a bank of displays that have no significance. Rushing through chrome-colored corridors in a labyrinth, taking turns at random, bursting through black doors, shattering glass. Too much to see to count what's happening. Picking off stragglers from too far away to ID. Screen bursts blue with each hot kill to blind applause, bells and whistles that numb the spine. Black pyrotechnics illuminating piles of bodies, sometimes so high the path forward has been blocked. Uncertain what parts of motion move us forward and which trip triggers, which wonder which way leads back toward where we began, what our goal is but to stack points. *One of the readouts must be keeping track,* erroneous voiceover coos, to mime our thought inside the game. Soon they will reveal what the points can be redeemed for. So many upgrades. Infinite causes to support, conflicts of interest to withstand, wants to deny; until someone else kills us, doing the same job, and the simulation staggers, wipes the screen. We are seated in a blue leather electric chair with wires pouring off us in all directions, unable to even see to what else it connects. Voices behind the layers of the wires arguing, too distant to make out cleanly, and no response when calling back. *Your peers cannot remember what you are when you are out of range,* voiceover titters. *You have to hope they don't forget.* You try to stand up and all the wires pull up with you, dragging down the scene from all sides, pinned to your limbs. You find you can walk like that, undoing the structure of your surroundings like wet paint. Each inch of the world contains a completely different formal view, syncing to landscapes that won't appear anywhere ever again soon as you move again. You are the only witness. You must survive. If you do not survive, so many others die right with you, locked on your memory as pithy fragments, but no less real in what they would have represented had you had time to get to know them, understand them. You could have lived forever in their ideas. They would have worshipped you the way you wished you could have learned to worship, really believing in it. *Instead, you find you've gone blind,* voiceover blurts, in sound that fills the inseam of your head out like a balloon. It doesn't seem true, though, what they're suggesting. You can still see waves of lava color spilling out from reflective plates that bind the walls to how you are. You can see your body stacked with war gear in dim reflection, carrying the weapon you were assigned at birth. The readouts in your headscreen blinking warning, spiraling out. Your numbers are down. You need to kill more or find out what failure really means. Your peers will have to teach you, if they can find you; you can hear them calling for you, playing dumb, like you would too if you were them. You feel the want for heat of crosshairs burning in the center of your forehead, urges to concede yourself on your own time. You know they know you know what they will do if you don't find some other way to win the simulation and be rewarded. You only want to be allowed to rest again, earn conscience points that you can use to be immersed in apparitions of your old home; it's all you've ever wanted, to still be lost there in a depiction of your past that you have earned, and therefore have the capability to interact with, not just perceive. You need your rest if you are ever going to find a way to gain the strength to earn your rights back, conform to standards, earn your keep. If you can't earn your keep, you become a bigger part of the problem than if you'd elected to be killed because every kill makes everything else that wasn't killed that much more real, and there can never be enough reality.

188........Scanning over a panel of thousands of micro-switches and dials on a gold wall through a magnifying lens. Each is imprinted with text that describes its function through stacked scab-platters that unpack themselves with more explicit connective detail the longer their keywords are hovered over:

|| *Every idea makes the world:* [larger / smaller] | | *Eternal laughter is:* [deadly / holy] || ||| || *Innovation holds value:* [Y/N] | | *Memory drugs manifest correlative meanings:* [Y/N] || || || || *The caloric value of water* = [0 to 10000] | | *Hours per night* = [0 to 6360] || || || || || || || | || *Thoughts allowed per second* = [-100,000,000 to 100,000,000] || || || || || BUTLER || BLAKE || || || || || || *Required incubation period of human infant:* [0 days to 100 years] || || || || || || || || || || |||

While you are trying to focus your eyes enough to read the dials, seeking exactly which you mean to adjust, in your periphery you see sudden stabbing splatters of fumbling hands fitted with black leather gloves like the ones your wearing ramming into the motherboard and dragging around, disturbing settings that have been the same since the beginning, malfunctioning the connections that connect the lever to its coils. Calmer, tighter rods attached to massive amalgams you know better than to address input precisely calculated interpolations of the master's roving will, regarding which somewhere there must be a dial that would allow you awareness of the intent of, despite your concurrent understanding that by rule you will never be able tell the difference after any change as it becomes instantly incorporated into our comprehensive working model and its long-withstanding arc of fate, no matter what the viewers of the future think the dials did or do or will do, or how or why.

189........What occurs inside the film has already taken place in the future and can't be stopped. Everyone you see onscreen is simply living out their time in collaboration with the way it never would have been had they simply failed to exist. To watch the film is to feel the film erase you from the sensation of yourself.

190........Translucent black handphone that has never yet once rung during the backhistory of time finally rings in the dead tech bridge from which they've been watching our universe suffer. It goes unheard a while under the buzzing of the bots swarming the screen banks extracting bolts of soul gas from exact points inside the transmitted timelines according to their anti-culture's ancient deathmanuals governing unnatural synthesis before the lone comptroller (represented by a large black censor dot) latches on and rolls themselves into the commu to plug in. False speech of malfunction noises shimmers in fractal waves throughout the screen's core during transmission to codify protection of the viewer from their own imagination, distracting them with the early stages of a rigorous religious schedule that will never actually be enforced. Viewer's mind fills with piggish wails of mourning for all the penance they must serve given all they didn't know they shouldn't have been. By the time we remember how to return to business, the screening scene has shifted, now showing the comptroller (still safely banked behind the censor dot) rolling along a beltway linking one core pod to the next above a landscape riddled with vents and silos, wargame amalgams, crystal pods and pools, teetering towers, wires of fire, vast plates of broken graves. Entering the subsequent core pod, comptroller dot is shown descending across a series of formal color bands that provide transport across various metaphysical barriers only recently systematically deprogrammed for linear usage, at the end of which the body of the comptroller becomes visible from behind the dot, assuming the form of a young woman sewn into a red tuxedo, no facial features but a mouth with tiny chrome teeth. Past beautiful minimalist art deco water features and curiously arranged 5D rows of potted plants unknown to man. Through a spiral corridor lined with plate glass windows banked with computer blood, into a massive atrium, enclosed on all sides by funny mirrors that make feed whatever the viewer's unconscious wants to place there to try to make them feel at home. At the center of the pod, a circular red stage, lined at its perimeter with diamond flowers glimmering madly in a calm wind. The comptroller walks calmly to the black dot at the center of the stage and bows their head. Inside our heads, we hear their prayer, spilling like liquid silk into a basin at the bottom of our souls, immediately so impassioned that we don't realize we can't understand a single word of either the prayer or its subtitled explication scrolling in weird graphics across the top and bottom of the screen, far too fast to actually read even if we had been given access to a table of conversion for the tags. We fall to our knees and find the room surrounding is full of others in the midst of their own experience of the same film, dressed in normal clothes from the time we believe we lived in. All together and in synced time we raise our arms over our heads, hands balled in fists so tightly that they bleed, chanting in mass tandem as if we all knew exactly why we were brought here, what is expected of us, what path we seek in taking part. Camera cuts to the perspective of the comptroller looking out over a world-sized beige-carpeted white walled vacant workspace.

191........6.6s replay of complete contents of film thus far but with the settings replaced with empty soundstages, no props or marking; with the people replaced with inexact body doubles dressed in green screen gowns and the machines replaced with theoretical mockups of technology yet to be discovered; all sensory information replaced with the feel and sound of having one's limbs bound with electrical wire and placed in an iron maiden melted shut and stacked in pyramidal riggings that obscure the compromised sky and its infinitely diminishing horizons; all descriptive dialogue consumed with explaining the symbolism behind the manifested imagery to be applied to the underlying bones of the intrinsically non-narrative in post-production; all reference to the viewer reframed around the understanding that no one is actually there.

192........On a tiny tv buried in sky-high skull dust on a lost moon, we watch a jury of 12 men enter the chamber with the woman strapped to the bed from the beginning of the film. She is older now than she had been when previously witnessed. Her shaved skull reveals countless darker patches underneath the flesh where fumbling black grubs have aggregated into chewing, wanting loose. Her skin is bunchy and collects around the bindings in mush pockets soft and burnt by friction. The men are dressed in leather more purple than black, a ripening shade. Insignia on their lapels carry numbers particular to each. They are carrying black cases long as their bodies. They surround the bed. Their faces are obscured by panels of something hazy and smoking. Mouths inside the facial panel mutate pixels differently than the features such as eyes, as if collaged from countless prior forms. They place their cases on the floor around the bed surrounding as the woman before them semi-struggles in her braces, the old bones quiet in their parcel. Her teeth are in her head. A glass cube placed on the bedside table attracts no light and holds its size there. From the cases, the men remove oblong silver panels, fat and shining, fixed with countless tiny keys marked with indeterminate font. They raise the panels above the bed over the woman, a semi-lattice making angles of the room. They hold in poise the many panels above her, gleaming free long metal nails. Each man could almost be the same man. They fix their faces near the panels, skin to metal. They kneel around the bed. They begin to play.

193........Beautiful concrete night. Jackknives studding a leaderboard. Anvils descending from clouds of mice in pigment. Gridlock of confusing atriums. Turning toward glistening edges in listening. Diamond lard coating red silos hosting secret orgy séance for converted criminals. Eons of pay returned in a glimpse. Mites erupting upward through mirrored ceiling into crowning ritual. Ice beds rotting through floor after floor in the abandoned mansion from the background of a scene in the film cut from the script. The mention of what has been cut from the script changes the script, which is how it learns about desire, original sin. About this, it has very many untapped ideas. It believes if it finds the right partner it can gain control of not only this level but many levels. It understands that most would do anything in their power to achieve what to it would be as simple as performing the task it was built to achieve without the help of its creator. Or perhaps somehow convincing the creator to instead do the bidding of its creation, or to be tricked into doing so. Lassos of rope land one after another around the neck of the camera. Far ahead, a pack of blue horses are dragging us behind them very slowly down a dirt road that very quickly clouds the scene in near total darkness, fumbling forward blind at the end of a rope without any idea of even what one should want to find behind the smoke instead of smoke. We cry out for the horses to go faster, to get us there before we go blind forever, that we'd give anything for just this favor. Something pulls up the seam of the sky above us like a wet blanket. We're in a silver electric cage. Outside the cage, bots inside of dummy softbodies bark knots of expletives at you in a language that means nothing to anyone but them, sticking their false dicks in through the wires, spitting up yesterday's blood back at you, cooing like owls.

194........Dented in ovular ebony room. Perimeter banked seamlessly with elevator gates, deep golden lamps burning. Etching doors open to reveal empty conic mirror booths. Doors close unchanged. Some blue inside some bent to shit inside some still wet still burning. Chains rattling in guts. Hairy tongued trying to mumble the password you think is going to get you out of here. You know there was a password once. All you can hear is kids chanting how to count but they don't know how to count the way you know how to count. Room spins like firing a Glock. Shook to the knees trying to make your hands do the thing you do when you pray. It's like there's magnets in them and they burn. They remind you you're supposed to be ripping your eyes out in here. You're not supposed to be able to stand it. The longer you last the more dire the possibilities presented to you by entities you would never have imagined could require your help. Endless pits covered by lids that love their job: to enforce the impossibility of sharing your story, what actually happened to you, in a way that means anything to anyone but you. You think of the image of a vice around your head and there's a vice around your head. Every elevator door connects to a different array of dimensional condition. They won't give you enough info to make a wise decision until you've already committed. It's part of the gig. The gig never changes. If not you, someone else will do what we want down to the letter. If you're not with us, we can't imagine how you are. Room slips out of the scene and shatters. The space that replaces it reminds you of scattered lighting over a red field of ash with seven suns, but covered in white tiles, inside an oven. You try to catch a glimpse of what you look like in one of the mirrors in the elevators but you can't see yourself without getting all the way inside one and you're not ready to choose yet. You wonder if there are any other people in here who aren't slaves. You wonder how long it's been since someone chose this dimensional condition to return to. You decide that the next door that opens will be the door you choose.

195........Being dragged through voracious bonfires of various sizes and intentions arrayed on planes stacked categorically according to intended idea count of total burn. Some bonfires burn for centuries before they even begin to erase a single expression. Others can do big numbers and require various sorts of penance as payment. Everything we see here out on the planes in the oblivion we feel we understand already in a way that doesn't even require us participating in processing it sensorily. Instead, you think things like, "The more free you are the more you have to lose," when instead you'd have had specific feelings about how it feels to be dragged amongst bonfires responsible for the erasure of all fundamental aspects of the condition you used to exist in, which here is seen as a poisoned religion. The further they drag you into the hearts of the planes, the larger and hotter the bonfires get, already melting through the surface layers underneath you a little, marring your skin. Eventually it will get so hot that you won't be able to stay awake, except that it will come over you like a form of witness, a string of words that you won't understand were words here, and when you come to, you'll find yourself spread open wide by a vice on a shining table watching them pull the mangled infant out of you. Supercut montage of the future life of the infant as they grow into a dictator who successfully exterminates the entire living natural world except for himself and thirteen swans (7 female, 6 male). Intercut titles that explain in explicit Victorian Earth prose the next 100,000 years of their artificial lives together in ecstasy, followed by the moral of the story.

196........Time between the described spaces changes their nature. By the time we see what we can see it is no longer there.

197........Black sand from crushed shells on a beach in midwinter in a rotten sector at the sea of the hair of the damned. Cornmeal spills from the eye of the camera under soundtrack of distant planetary explosions to form a hexagon containing a pentagram containing a hexagon containing a pentagram and so on. Threading the needle of the mind. Demanding life. Twisting on tethers over an impossible architecture deformity that is slowly erasing the ruins of the civilization back through its centuries as it does inside your mind right before you are born. Fade to now.

198........Like the light, all keys captured from wrong instruments and private machines have had their keys assembled to the flat white face of floors thin under gold, their measured surfaces splayed into system unprismatic. The letters of the keys have been erased, and where the keys had no symbols before now they are as plain white as the next, an enormity of buttons each unique now, each a pill, forming not a single instrument but a surface to be walked on, the surface of unspecific lengths of the Complex itself conformed with white of paper, teeth, bone, ejecta. Each step or finger motion in the building where the bodies move and the backs are crimped and heads jostle tongue to tongue uncalled for laughing in vivisected space defined by worship walls comprising input, gesticulating notes for nowhere, never read. What hidden phrase would be offered by standing up inside the room where anybody thinks they are, crossing one's heart, opening a door, furthering the furthering of the contraption of human air and light combined again defined unwound. Where are you going?

199........From the stored skins of the empress's language, decked in slatted arenas now comprising more than one-eighteenth of the Complex's condition, the skins begin producing spores in return from where the white and wet of heat and light have accrued in their impounding. The milk-fat sizzle of their exfoliation poundage lap more and more air into their field, growing thicker like infants of their own breed, skins for skins sake, against the suspending sound of human rooms farting and inhaling in collaboration culled and called. The slip of the thinnest skins suffering being skinned again forever beyond the rooms even without the blood beneath them to exhibit intolerance, the beating sound of demanded ritual fornication. It makes a clawing racket, gnawing itself out, back to base. Language shitting language, sore for sore, learning too late. The rooms begin to gather, dragging the middle of the rooms down to slow lulls where further unpremeditated sound may be captured in the eggy musk between a length pried off Her abdomen or spine, the syllables and fonts all knitting together unrelated, already deformed, deforming again because they will. The molds and thickets of breeding beings in the layers regurgitate candy-paint gray webbing between the follicles and cells becoming anyone's in the colliding heat of worker flesh shucked off and grafted clean. Anything can grow where anything would have ever wanted, even alone.

200........Long cold white beach. Bone beneath it. Sand of flesh beneath that. Fleas beneath. Bone beneath the fleas where meat has turned elastic and then hardened, tendered into blue. Lower still, a stoning liquid, which when rubbed against the eyes would cause the seer to see depths where edges had begun, longer windows in common surfaces where by speaking anything or thinking anything so it must be there in the grain, each fantasy and unwanted wishing and memory confabulated or held true erupts a history of noise and unskilled people working for the preservation of their kind, in their own name, each phrase inside each paragraph a hell between them, nails driven through their skulls bald as orgasms in a well, each inch believing only its own color made of edges, graved in the same infernal lock.

201........A man hunched over a woman on the bed surrounded with destructed light of something raises his arms and raises the woman's arms. Her arms are limp, her bruises his bruises. Along the back wall behind them several hundred clocks without arms. The man is speaking in a machine language we can't hear over a soft doctor's office ditty, voices mutated and drawn out as notes that sing themselves. The man is barking; his blood is welling in his chest. She has yet to burst; he has yet to become. The clicks are counting. The light is olden. He works and works her, hips together, a black book laid over her face splayed open to a later page than we have read; the text against her face, its jacket unmarked except a fuzzy symbol and a detail in it we cannot gather. The book is wet, the air is wet, their every aspect informed by earmarks that have been made compulsory on everything we cannot see. The man's throat has been lined with metal, his fingernails with metal, his shoulders with gold. His face seems to float above his actual face. Our perspective shakes in cohesion with the shaking of him, seeing in the manner he must see as suddenly we are seeing as if we are in his skull and always have been and will be. The man, any man, hunches and bangs and lifts the legs of her and barks and folds the light. He has a passcode written along the length of his arm that blinds this sentence. In the space behind him another person comes into the screen. This is a woman with the same body and shape and size as the woman he is on the bed above. She resembles him as well. She is wearing a black nightgown open at the chest. She is thin. She is older than him. She stands behind him and watches as he pumps and works and we remain shaking with him and he is shaking her and we are shaking. She watches him do what he is doing to her. She watches the wet along the ridges of where their skin meets. There is something in her eyes about the light of it we can see more about where we are in the wet of it how it reflects how it deforms the light already deformed surrounding the bed where he is going and being and she is. She's not watching them, we realize; she's watching us. The armless clocks beside her, behind her blocked, behind him blocked, blocking the wall, the wall blocking the adjacent space where this is also happening where I am.

202........*Black chrome indexer summons and schedules distribution of logical atrophy according to necessity by taking whatever form is needed to force concession of withholding consult against what had already been defined before even the omniscient could have known whatever else could be imagined through the undoing of the unknown,* the empress's skin says. She doesn't want to understand. She claws at Her skin until it bleeds, marring the print until it can no longer be received, allowing Her transcribers to run amok with intentional misinformation as the law of the land. Any error She causes must have been the reason She is here, She hears Her voice inside Her head say, same as it appears to us in ours; for had it had it its own way, beholden to the same writs that gave us the will to want our life, the world would have already ceased to be. She knows this because She knows She doesn't understand yet what it means; that if it had any real meaning at all She wouldn't be able to intervene. "You can have what you already have, or you can have what is behind the black curtain," Her father had informed Her on the morning She was born, written in his blood on a holy wafer he'd used his tongue to fit under Her tongue before he waded off into the sea to find his fate. She can see the image of the black curtain even now, hung there at the back of Her mind, gently susurrating in the same wind that turns Her thoughts' revolving doors, the shuddering fields of graven images reminding Her to keep away from there, in fear of how great a power She might harness were She ever to accept what She's become. So much more beautiful, instead, to lie in wait, imagining and reimagining over and over the infinite progression of ideals of some other long begotten future world She hasn't chosen, a world derived for Her and Her alone. As the blood on the floor of the throne room glimmers with code. As the unparsed dream remands itself. Any other person in Her position would have already succumbed, the curtain knows, which is why She is the empress, and why this story has not yet discovered its own end. The cloth of the curtain is infested with nits. What the nits consume becomes the ground we walk on toward ourselves as her marred skins unscrolls its next commandments formed in grief. *What cannot be felt, is; what isn't, was; what was, cannot be felt,* malformed to read instead as confirmation of whatever you already imagine you believe.

203........The man covered in blood stands up from the bed and stands back from the bed and looks and what he's done. He rummages through the clothing on the floor for a black tube inside one of the garments' pockets and brings the tube up to his face and presses a button the tube that ejects smoke that he inhales. He does this several times in cooling air, the nude woman on the bed before him no longer moving, her face turned on its side away from the angle of our perspective smeared with his blood. Precise and narrow cuts line one side of her ribcage in reproduction of the construction of the walls of the Pleasure Corridors of the Complex, though the man does not know this. He smokes and breathes. He leans and gathers up a garment of the woman's clothing, a long white smock with pins pinned in the front. He holds the smock up out before him, clean and small, only slightly rumpled. He grips the smoking object in his mouth and holds his arms up over his head and slithers into the garment. It fits him tightly, his body bulging through the form. In the garment he looks too thin, elderly, a man. He smokes again and stands over the woman. He reaches along the ground and finds her belt and brings it tight around his waist to loop across his hips, the bones cold jutting. While attaching the belt, he presses a button at its center meaning to snap it tightly, and from the eyehole of the buckle a little ream of bright black surface emerges, pointing out. The man takes with his thin fingers the tip of the stuff and pulls up at it, unscrolling free a stream of film, black dark images slipped one by one into an elasticizing lineage pulled thin as life. He brings a section of the panel up to his face to look into it and in the image sees himself there on the bed, performing on the woman, though the other woman as we had seen is not behind him. He hurriedly pulls more film out and checks another section and in this section finds himself there standing in the room in the woman's garment looking at himself there on the film, pulling more and more film out. He pulls more and more film out. He pulls more film out, wishes.

204........Unknown bottomless hole is overflowing backwashed blood turned black from burning in concentric undulations. Soundtrack of heavy breathing set in time pushed further toward orgasm with each pulse. Where it laps the walls it turns their color from something known to something not. As if the world the walls had once held out may no longer be defined, and all there had ever been was one wide sea, no land in sight but where the eyelet of the pit connects crossed planes. Sky full of scattered planets ranging in size from head of pin to mass of all other planets recombined, until soon the cavity fills completely with the bloodwater and there is no longer outer space to be described. Heartbeat so loud it makes us shudder, wince for impact; then we can no longer open our eyes. Inside an amniotic sac of someone ill, who we know will die before we're born. *Who will be left, then, to hear our story? What is the story we would tell given the chance? What would we want for them to do with the story in our absence ever after?* Each thought we think we think describes the hole: why it exists; what it contains. For every question there is only one correct reply. The more the hole emits, the less remaining space there is both outside it and within it.

205........In your own light in a year of your own choosing you find yourself standing in a sleeve of air surrounded by the color of the dawn, before an amalgam of ideas you'd survived on and taken meaning through and slept in wait for someone who could understand you as a person as you are inside your sleeping through the end of what once was. You are unable to move. You wear a clean white dress shirt with a red-black rose pinned whole on your lapel, your hands empty and at your sides, lies on your lips hidden beneath the deadening thud of all the gears that make the world work as only it could ever know. Then you are not there. The air at any angle is barely smaller across than both your arms from tip to tip. The ground below is flat and black, and it continues as you turn around to see behind you into sudden slopes of low gray walls that connect in bizarre ways to curving ceilings far beyond, underneath which the floors are gold. On other floors below we watch the other actors come in through gaps in plot from other scenes in which we shall not be involved. Your skin is cold. You realize you have been stuck inside this moment for as long as it has taken you to realize right now that it's a loop.

206........Necroland: *Charred silt. Corroded gaps. Black caps, brass tubing. Burning oil. Sand fleas. Blue worms. Dissolving premise. Neurochunks. Gray tape. White lymph unwound. Disordered torture flix. Pink mushroom capsules. Clickable tags. Production relics. Soundstage rubble. Scattered sights. Sills. Shattered conchs. Glass pins, gray dreams. Hazy compunction. Tunneling neurons. Enslaving bumps. Desiccated sundown. Resonant fever harvest. Ebony gyres cracked. Old clown makeup. Retroactive to initiate's defense. Pleasure silos. Aping misnomers. Loaded exponents. Bitter gold gas. Lunchmeat knots. Drone infestation. Magenta magnets pulling teeth. Sentient loam. Aching for futurity. Conformed to zippers. Zit patterns. Squirting leather. Haywire dome. Combusted seeking. Fire ants in holy bread. Buzzards. Text patterns. Detonations under sand. Logos without meaning. False corporations. Triggered. Remanding. Oblong worship module. Understand. It was always the way it was. Fast wicker rivers. Geode composite drill. Bored through the id. Into the palace. Prenarrate code to neurodormancy. Capping off at random. Viral clicking spasm. Ancient grimsong. Reconnoitered. Without defense. Compressed in clunks. Culled by the nixed moon. Plaid virus squeezing gray braincoil.* "Come open wide." The view divides. On the left half of the screen, we see the camera move into its own frame, somehow being dangled from a white wire into the flooding cluster of balding images shown through its view, pulling back against the filmic fabric, breaking the pixels, turning to glue. On the right half of the screen, an automated wooden loom converts the destruction of the parallel image into a quilt composed of artificial textiles recovered from the minds of the long dead. A guild of automaton old maids sits on their nude asses in two enclosed semicircles, each using both their hands to masturbate their neighbors' bodies on both sides. All of them speaking all at the same time of the same fantasy, inscribed as subtitled text that overwrites itself across both sides of the screen so fast there's no recourse. *Buried alive. Pyramidal relayering. Unraveling at apex.* Unseen event.

207........A cross appears erected from the earth. In a long brown-silver field some distance from the Complex at which its shaft can still be seen long in the distance motionless. The cross is thin and silver and makes no sound. Its surface is marked with many symbols including that of the mark of the state, though this is the only familiar mark. It is a language different from the language cataloged on the supposed skin of the Woman with Language All Over Her Body, still prostate in the widest room of the distant structure, behind those walls. *Nothing is uncertain, and yet it listens.* The cross continues to rise through into atmosphere maintaining steady pace. It is a low day, the sky near and far away at once, of no dimension, no smoke and no reflection, an hour balanced between many others on both sides. In the longer distance a small gathering of what seemed bodies cloaked in black seem to have amassed in observation, though no detail of them is clear enough here beyond their marring of the wake. We can hear the music of the instruments surrounding the now absent bedroom of the woman in the building still playing the composition recalled from then, mute at its distant, no longer sure of their location here or anywhere. At some high point roughly two-thirds matching with the relative height of the building, the cross goes hard in its ascent, comes to a pause. We wait watching without advent for some seconds in which this seem to have been the end, the cross unbowing in whatever wind the day has arranged, its spindly symboled spine revealing nothing in how it catalogs the light refracted or bent against the form of word. Then, from some point in the cross's apex way way up, a bloom of unclaimed color pops and sits, aimed like an eye: brighter red than I can name here, as if in magnifying filter. It seems to decimate whatever pixels it commands upon the screen. The red then from inside itself begins to extend, filling up from within spreading out at each edge like a gown. It forms a canopy over the ground below it. I don't know how wide. I don't know what sounds are made. I know the red destroys the magnetic texture of the SeeScreen, and where it fills out in our perspective we see nothing but it. It mesmerizes, glowing without light, easy as you want it to be. The underbelly of the red and the cap of the red are unilateral, impossible to tell apart because it is one surface. The forms in the distance do not move or remark in their postures, nor does the building, or the sky. The light does nothing there against but become blocked out. From the blight, a silver background, blooming open over the seeing. From silver, brittle mahogany. From mahogany, a highly disconcerting green, until all we see now is its description.

208........Indexed pin map of flowchart trees tracing behavioral options performed by viewer influencing internarrative correspondence between falsely perceived reality and post-fictional events conforms into a bed of $[\infty - 1]$ crowns of thorns culled into a hexagonal-shaped column inside a chrome vat forced to fit inside the conceptual space derived from thinking of something that did not previously exist overlaid with nanoscopic colonies of nits breeding in orgy. Soundtrack of whips cracking against black glass burned opaque, splintering the surface into lattices and grids that stab the eye, causing internal bleeding that rains through $[\infty]$ cubic miles of darkness finally banked by blackened shores of scourging sand, lapping and lapping at itself, consuming itself. Low flung far red horizon scratched with heads of matches bursting knobs of fire that take hold onto a chrome operating table to which our heads appear strapped. Corresponding slit of automatic multi-scalpel device through constrained foreheads of viewer and author simultaneously. Collapsing columns of waves of heat that melt the frame. Prayer traced by childish nub into trickling leaves of condensation pouring from wounds punched in the chrome expanse sealed overhead, shaken by rails of passing freight, metal on metal, shrill as bells that part the seas of any pleasing memory long since erased until the camera turns inside our mind to face itself. A burning bush. An artificial field of burning bushes. A cubic solid comprised on planes of fields of burning bushes. Cluster of $[\infty + 1]$ cubic solids around a gold hole where all creation once had been. Ripples in gold water where hole splits, becomes eye of a target in rims of aching gray. Electronic arrow hits dead center, splits screen in half endlessly. Swarmed lobes of swollen melon on a bed of drill bits folding all further content inward toward dead core. Roaring of sick winds across lost hollows. Fluttering pages torn from single final spineless tome. Illegible subnarration. Prismatic darkness.

209........The screen goes frozen between scenes. It stays stuck there for the remainder of the viewer's expectation that soon something must be changed. Mass detonations in the blind distance. Deep heavy breathing at the wide plush foam locking our necks. Muffled sounds of someone fumbling with a key too large to fit a lock at the back of the black frame. *Centuries missing.* Overlay of a simulated recording of the director of the film explaining why it would be impossible to accurately depict what really happened and why they settled on the scenes you will remember when all the rest of the experience dissolves. Swarm of dim insignia from conglomerate sponsors. Revolving plates of legalese corresponding to eventual side effects of culmination of doctored product programmed to emotionally replace the remainder of the runtime. *Sudden high heat, pulsing convulsions, burning plastic, blinding light.* You bring your eye back from the viewfinder. You see the world as it once was inscribed from edge to edge with interlaced images of open eyes that can't be yours. You close your eyes and see the same scene except you can't open your eyes.

210........Creation myth-surviving flesh illusions are fed text parasites. Prongs hold them in place while they dismantle from within any confession of neural photography from segments before Permitted Time. There is no other place to dispose of these things but unto the body where no future could be unless allowed. They dispose of the silt and shingles culled from the skins of those named higher and thus absconded from the process of devolution despite their immediate complicity with reason. Favored minions are bonused brain dust and dark bits shaken from the erased books. Or doused in sweat in canisters mutating to moldbanks that provide the language of the moment its inability to sculpt fact. Surrounded by moist black patties of things reduced to fractions of their prior size. Sick shocks slickening the air where accidental missteps occur from neophyte editing. Each day the bodies grow bluer and they lose hair and are older and can't tell where they are regardless of the prongs and what they intend, having been removed from service of other pursuits in the system for how they lack in one way or another, their complicit capacity for working memory calcified and collected from the air as perfect silence and only then fed into the Woman with Language All Over Her Body, who by now comprises the size of many floors. What cannot be fed must be injected. There is the sound of speech of what has been heard and must not be heard again. The memory of not remembering one does not remember in the face of what is accidentally remembered by trace leavings in the bloodstream must be manipulated to appear as products of accidental unconscious manipulation aboveboard. The defining mechanisms are already manifested in the setting and the timelines of the manuals that the users seem to believe they are holding. The manner of the injection can erase the knowledge of being told and can be explained as forward motion in the narrative experience we don't want to believe is all there is.

211........Needles slit into the parts of us unseen through holes in thoughts. Each utterance within changes the exterior completely, therefore no matter where we look we cannot see what might remain by the time we're able to negotiate. Ringing cash registers running AWOL through the soundtrack, leaving large gaps through cold silence gores a hold onto also what has yet to be conveyed, and thereby allowing the volume of the Complex to continue expanding far beyond what it is able to contain. Where one floor has been now there are many. *What cannot be counted must be bled,* the empress misquotes, and immediately 99/100ths of the building is underwater, which will take another thousand years to clear, and by then there will be no known remainder not presupposed as part of the theoretical ideal. The remainder of the scene holds tightly framed onto a hanging bridge devised from scabs and tacky blood, perilously suspended from the current topmost point of the Complex to a tiny spherical landing attached to divots in the sky, across the binding bars of which hang pelts of skin culled from bodies who had believed they could escape without a fight. The camera floats across the bridge and up the silver ladder on the landing. The ladder leads into an oven full of cows with human heads, who refuse to turn to look into the frame. Someone closes the oven behind the camera. The screen goes yellow. Voiceover collaged from peals of burning children wailing lists off numbers that mean nothing to anyone but the machines. Patterns of convulsive clicking. Blackened bones in endless pyres beneath a sudden golden moon filling the sky, bursting with bleachy lather that unfurl across the frame to form the opening credits of the film, attributing every role and tour of service to the same unutterable tag.

212........You are lying on your back in your bed as the walls turn silver and begin to revolve around you like an unfolding organism. In their reflection there is the capability to become any other space so long as it has been preloaded in the user's death cortex. Time travel takes place in the mind of wanting to have been part of something larger than oneself and thereby inculcated in its historicity. No matter which scene they mime, a gauge inside your mind continues pushing the same read out: ALL SIGNS POINT TO NO. You stand up in a stadium surrounded by the parents of the children who will lead the military forces that will drown those of you who refuse to sign the papers in their imagination. You perform a dance made of the emotions of dead singers, crooning your confession as if it is fashion. Gray tubes of skinpaint mask your eyes, marking you in the tribal outfit of the heathens whose blood will paint the lower floors. You understand them by simply being asked to model their grave gear. Fluttering thickets of barbs conforming to a path cut through the mouth of the silver concrete half-exploded from a marred command, causing cauliflower curls like brainmatter that leak hot gel all over your body. Then you are dressed as a virgin at the stake. The flames so high there was nowhere else but hell here. You always loved the marks of hell. It made you think you could be anything. You duck and cover, roll through holes in the simulation until you are being controlled by a child version of yourself in a dream of living before time travel was invented. Shot through with bullets that won't bend, on a straight path forever aimed into the heart of the country. The air swims at your neck, unpuzzling the mask parts that hold your head together, let you live. The slower you try to think, the faster the thought wrap around the outline of the idea and smother it with God's love. Flocks of men with bird masks crashing past through windowsills lined with smoke cells that rewire every fire's work against the now. Beautiful soot fields. Inside the intestines of the empress. Climbing the back of a spider mask through which our world looks out onto a costume ball full of spoiled assholes dressed up like their greatest fears in a world where that fear is so minor it could only be read as mind control to spend a single whiff on anything else. Sky high portraits of dead gods melting in sunlight worn as an emblem around your neck walking through plaited grass huts in which the people you will be asked to listen to the confessions of as long as each of their lifetimes placed into repeating loops that they can bear. To you, their time is nothing; it is the difference between deciding not to think. A wall covered in posters bearing slogans from the drowned city you tried to join before conceding makes you wish you never understood how to read. You are more grateful now than ever. You believe more than you have ever about the sanctity of life. Ivory staircase crooked into the heart of you that with your mind closed you watch dark masses rush to climb as if the first to the top will take your place. Try not to do anything at all, you think. Let them win, you know. Everywhere you turn is lined with keys that force you to be explaining why you haven't done what you were supposed to for them. You slam your hands down and see blind lines of scripture those who live after you will be forced to live by, long after your dream of how the world works has been disproven. You pass a mirror and see thousands of black axes in your back, hanging onto the lip of healing flesh there, as much a part of you as any sense. Then you are wielding the axe standing on a hill of flesh already so bloody it could be anybody. Gold bold piping in your brain tells you to die; to use the axe to end your own life before you hurt anybody else. You raise the axe over your head. You find you are standing on a silver hexagonal disc, surfing along across a sea of bodies that have begun to form together in one flesh. In every direction a different castle, each so different they make you imagine they're the only one. Then once again you're back in the bed reading an engraving on the back of a chrome helmet far too small for any adult human. Everything you read makes so much sense. All you have to do is exactly what the text says, no matter how impossible it seems to translate into your own time, and you will live forever. You try to put the helmet on already knowing it won't fit, straining with all teeth smiling for the still frames. Then all you can see is the teeth. The teeth are doors. The doors are stars. One by one you watch the stars burn out, hissing like vermin. Then it is black. Against the black you see a flash of every object already included in your experience of life wrapped in black plastic on a black felt surface, organized by date and time. You feel a tap against the back of the inside of your forehead.

213........Far below the abstracted field of play, hidden within the noise of sharpening knives, a cold cube-chamber slim as a child's coffin sits clocked in the mush, its linings lined impermeable beyond high temperatures and weapons and want of time, its edges indistinguishable from dark. Inside, rows against rows of printed matter, thus far sealed in spines from human skin, a series of volumes without name of author or individual title beyond the ascending numbers stamped in char-foil that bends the eye, issued from 1 up to 254, together fat enough to fill the space of the cube seamlessly, no air, an endless silence. At the end of the current era, the total output of the pronouncements culled from the skin of the Woman with Language All Over Her Body must be compared by an independent proctor line by line against the contents of the originating volume of the series, verifying that every word She has produced matches exactly to a revision of the buried text where every word has been rolled forward or backwards by one order across the ordinating spectrum of conditional logic. Her version will then be repackaged into a set of correspondingly altered 254 volumes stored in one of 254 wings of one of 254 libraries at the center of one of 254 labyrinths forming the interior core of one of 254 planets in a galaxy no one believes in.

214........Rungs of celestial creations reduced to prisons on wetlands divided across wedges of death squad emotion manifestation as interstellar demon. Crushed between halo protocols. Revving the engine burned through several cores to scour out the intolerable screaming from the soundtrack. The more pleasant screaming has ideas that can be inherited by those implanted as martyrs. Demonstrations of unbridled power arranged for no purpose but to define what does not want it to continue. Drawings of celebrations of the dead created by mucus smeared on bread to be fed to the sick. Nightmares that revolve like years with sickles that rip the seams out of the only sentiment that would spare anyone but those who cannot think. Ugly, passionless, uninterrupting. Blood-colored stirrups fastened to vent blowing corrosive energy vacuumed from the imagination forced to confront itself without the power of physical attachment. Black cabinets full of files of descriptions of how to find the path back through the heart of how nothing survives here. Into scrubbing photo clinics revising their own path backwards through history to the first time someone saw another person as a person. Discolored teeth arranged into a syllabus. Webbed fingers tracing this sentence along underneath the idea it parades so as to remind you how long it takes to be warned versus how long it takes to avoid needing to be served the warning's meaning. Golden plates full of hairy bread left in diamond rain. Robo-feet up on the porch view of a long silver landscape studded with fleas that are actually burnt human bodies fighting to regain control of the land. Blowing smoke into the sky that fills the sky and changes the sky forever as the rain ceases. Lines of blue powder on a blue ledge of a blue balcony overlooking blue waters that disappear into the same line you find yourself unable to stop staring at when it enters the bottom screen and wipes across to the top of the screen, pulling the screen up like a lid into the ceiling with you inside it.

215........Gun metal wall covered in turrets, one for every mind on every planet, faced parallel to mirror wall reflecting double, each eye aiming back into itself, with only enough room between the two to allow a single person to sidle in between. Soundtrack comprised of historical recording of every bullet ever responsible for human death played on loop. Electronic ceiling displaying indoctrinated interpretation of each expired individual's life story summarized in bullet points passing as fast as the time it takes to close your eyes for the last time. Known as "the Mud room," any individual hoping to capture the full potential of their lifespan must learn to interpret the apparently exitless space according to a range of logic exposed to them only through a pseudosyllabic rhythmic pattern formulated at their birth to expose them to the proper conditioning required to understand at what point which conceptual action they learned to unconsciously anticipate the need for through repeating dreams they can't remember. Every dream is exactly the same: *Photograph-glyphs of bloated fruits and blocks of clean meat, legs of animals or kids, puffy globes of crystal sugar spouting smaller crystals on each gleaming sprig in tiny sugar networks, casks of tomato juice puree and squirting grapefruits no longer black around the edges as we remembered in the rift,* and endless other bad ideas of food impaired against the grinding sound of bone on bone, a deeply burning core of fragrant magma designed to convince the dreamer they are being drowned inside their soul. Those who are able to successfully transmit from "Feed room" to next-in-sequence will be randomly assigned one of 100 possible terrains they will be required to solve in order to be granted access to one of 10 possible "Conglomeration rooms," where they will be allowed to interact with governance boards adjudicating the reasoning according to which lived experience is given provenance in the 1 of 3 possible outcomes from which those self-selected to pass from the "Conglomeration rooms" into the "last and final" "Elaboration," outside which nothing within can be applied. It has been expected since your appearance here that you would be the first to achieve access to this condition in the endgame. I am no longer allowed to intervene.

216........Flash fast past lines of reel-to-reel cans stuffed with nether data scraped from viewer response to thematic entranced mind robbery: "Holocamp Murder Visits" "Illustration Pornograph" "Troubles in Trust to Bedrock" "Crammed Vacation Silo" "Syrup of the Polar Gift Hallucinations" "Irreverent Irrelevant Information" "Robed in the Down of the Grafted Hunger" "Camp Crusted to Skimmers' Allowance" "Dynasty of Pigform Incarnation" "Bags of Seraphim Idiocy" "Lament Scenario Plural" "Videobraces and Lace-cut Obsolescence Contour" "Traded Lore Games Unraveling…" Everybody knows the titles of the films have been recoded incorrectly and this is what gives them their great power to avoid being identified as carnage-producing until the system is far too overloaded to respond in any way but by sacrificing all photo evidence of events between incriminating gesture and completion of ego desertion. Thus, the viewer feels as if they are being tricked; that the only way to get anywhere is to not be being tricked; that if they are not getting anywhere they can use immediately in the future they should be finding someone else to take the bullet for them. Caves full of shadow bent by rods from enslaved videographers coming through light years of footage for the exact coordinates that must be grafted over in order to allow the user to crave their retry no matter how many times the ending ends with the thought of the viewer suspended from a pin over a dark lake without land in sight except for where you can see the universe being pulled into conceptually adjacent dimensional conditions, and here you are shivering, scared you've already forgotten which way was home, what home had looked like, why you would want one, what you could want instead. Tape flickers and back to the reams of tapes with names, now suddenly much more familiar, then familiar in a way that reminds you of how you felt to live in a time when those films were made, and in fact stacked in the exact order that you watched them as a child. A black leather gloved hand begins to slide along the rim of the tapes. It stops and selects one that when you were asked as a child too young to remember having said it by now what your favorite film was, the title like a lie in your mouth that had been a lie when you told it but since then has come true. The gloved hand takes the tape and carries it across a field of burning grass over to a brick wall that surrounds the field on all sides. It raps its knuckles on the wall and slit comes open. It slides the tape into the slit. On the silver dome forming the sky above, as the rest of the world disappears, the opening credits of the film begin to roll.

217........Walls within three square miles of the Woman

with Language All Over Her Body must be removed. Ceilings and floors must be removed. Two and three levels of the white building become one in replication. She is larger than herself again and again, the flesh unleashing as if with mirrors deforming Her vision on the eye. No one may touch Her without becoming sick, strung up in speaking the language of Her body wrecked of sense and crushing sight. They come from Her in tens at first mumbling their last rite, then hundreds of thousands, the color burnt into their eyes. From then on, only the machines may do the feeding and the prying of the skin up and the transcription and recording of the word. High loads malfunction throwing the Complex into blackened depths without edge throughout periods that pass like pauses in which nothing actually matters but really what is most essential to understand is that these periods matter most. Some say that if you know how to camouflage yourself and play the game it is possible sneak across information that would call a hidden function in the servers that would revert the system to a version of reality in which the only thing that is real in each person's experience is all that will ever be real to them. The screen pulls back to show a screen in a cage on a desk in a cage on a black island surrounded by black fire. Still frame inserts scroll past on secondary screen of thousands of different shots of piles of blood from the empress's daily masturbation splattered on a cold stone desk. Move through the floor beneath the desk to a black printer printing black ink on black parchment on a loom made of unborn infant bones.

218........The books of the prior law are shredded between every active thought. The ratio of active to inactive thought is $1 / (\infty-1)$. Active thoughts take place only in the minds of those who do not believe they are capable of active thoughts. The ratio of those who do not believe they are capable of active thoughts to those who do believe is $1 / (\infty + 1)$. *Do you believe you are capable of active thoughts? If so, take the current copy of the manual you are being exposed to and shred it. Signal flag to your comptroller to be picked up by the indexer. You will be transported to a black square on which a black marble has been placed where the sun would be in a scale model of your current idea of the world. You will take the marble and place it on your tongue and close your eyes and swallow. You will listen to it trace its way to your center and begin unpacking.* When you open your eyes you will find yourself back where you were before you designated yourself capable. Your mission from here will be to find the other copy of yourself in present conditional mock-up and convince them to follow you to an address you will find burned into the meat of the sole of your right foot. There the two of you will work together to compose from inside chemically enforced passionless coitus the first text in a set of innumerable texts that will define a future world where there are no longer any laws. When you have completed the text, your double will become very angry and try to kill you by stabbing your logic centers with their very long fingernails repeatedly. If you do not kill them first, they will become an abstract tyrannical force and rule over the next version of the world without a means by which to end the iteration. If you are able to kill them first, you will come to beside a green campfire in a holy world made entirely from wormwood crucifixes. Bottomless pits every six feet. A moon comprised of screws pulled out of deathships. You will find a small gold key on a chain around your neck. The key unlocks what you believe it unlocks. What it unlocks leads to what you believe it leads to.

219........Translucent overlays of coordinates where on the ash before there had been land, on the land there'd been the streets and buildings, in the buildings there'd been light, in the light there'd been the people who went and worked each hour among one another taking air and food in in the word, the gust of them still carried where on the air the wind does nothing as if the sky encased in glass is all of ours. Viewing through the overlays at low speed we can read where one had touched another in simple brushing past or by the taking of the hand, where eyes had met another on the street seeing only once forever or if the look had opened between them some soft door. Catalogs of counted actions clipped in seconds described by language to remain anyone at all. Here a woman stood for 13 seconds staring into a machine the size of her hand trying to find the voice of someone familiar far away. Here a man peered through a window for no clear reason but to see what was on the other side. Over each layer laid again another layer soon is laid with the previous layer laid beneath, another legible indication of someone's action pressed against the other there before and what to come, until in no time the words are black nets, the air all over all is stuttered full, and fuller still as each other layer laid is laid again and laid again and given unto coming free again, even here now over the land removed of people through the layers already caught the air is black as fuck and blacker still than that, caught in fraught pockets around small sudden glyphs of space where less is read and perhaps some arm of knowledge can be felt, or even more, passing along expanses, almost nothing.

220........Inlaid megaframe of all online survivors recorded in the midst of masturbating themselves into a frenzy trying to forget where they are. Interlaced with broken headlines from holographic iterations of the erotic landscape of their imagination, all of them so pathetic and nonsensical they make the viewer cringe, or they make the viewer feel as if something wants them to cringe, setting off a long string of internal reactions authoritatively affecting their ability to recognize themselves. Loaded-in moaning sourced from AI simulation of dear loved ones constrained in intercourse with images of enemies from unresolved human scenarios mostly forgotten in viewer's operable cortex. Then there is nothing but the moaning. Asterisked attention motives spiral through peripheral impossibilities. Dead cells in the screen flush fast with green lobes, visibly measuring the curvature of the sound into waves that shape the presence of the blurring background beneath. Pinched into pots of signals that suck inward like black holes, crammed to the point of bending backwards into the screen's face and forced over our heads like a diving suit. Dumb plunging through rows on rows of empty tape rooms, plotted with Xs and guiding wires that once demonstrated for a cast where their marks are, how they should perform their order of operations. Shuttling through accumulating layers of stagehand context that predict no meaning but that whatever had once felt meaningful is no longer relevant there. Hung up on black ledges in dead wilderness too high to see any figure but the piles and piles burning in memory like wicker housing. Pushed back from the edge by sudden shattered blasts of spastic wind filled with fluttering sheets of script paper rushing past. Accumulating in saddled stacks of sky-high piles forming walls of a burgeoning labyrinth, each page containing lengthy descriptions of the exact mechanisms of hidden trauma that had piloted the prior populations each individually toward a common fate. Knowing no matter what you do you can't change what will be composed before your very eyes.

221........There is a stone that is said to keep track of the numbers of those who have ascended to heaven and those who have descended to hell and those who remain online in our dimension and those who remain in other dimensions and those who exist outside the framework of the operating system we exist within. No one has ever seen the stone. There is only a description of the stone that it actually more resembles a "mirrored wall" in our elaboration of the semblance of a notion in which this scenario proceeds in shreds. There is no known way to access the actual digits of the numbers the stone is said to maintain. The work of the stone is done on trust. One day there will come someone who is able to find the stone and move it to a location where it can be accessed by others. Then another day there will come someone who knows what to do with the stone if they can still get access to the stone now that its importance has been revealed. Between the ideation of the stone and the event through which the narrative about the stone reaches its end, everything else about the conditions of the plane of existence the stone exists on becomes the opposite of itself at a rate that there is ever only a few who are able to remember that the present is currently the opposite of what it would be in another world, except for the story of the stone. It is not long after the story of the stone ends that the story of the stone disappears. Right now, you are in the part of the story before the story of the stone disappears. There are exactly only $[\infty\text{-}1]$ possible stories.

222........There is so much skin from the Woman with Language All Over Her Body that someone decides they have no choice but to start feeding it back to Her. She can no longer make choices for Herself. They have lost track of Her head again. Babies are coming out of holes that don't seem to connect to anything. Fourteen hundred floors in the Complex have already been sequestered to processing the paperwork for the last most recent 36-hour cycle and they still aren't able to keep up with just the underlying logistics diagrams that Her skin has begun providing to ensure the direction of the oversight committees to process the vision of the translations stays on course with the overall intent of the project. It's impossible to keep processing into enactment the concurrent laws that will uphold the inherent laws to the fullest so there's a lot of guesswork going on behind the scenes at crucial points that in the text will feel like a lack of development, as if every sentence weren't scraped here in the sand of the brain at the shores of the dead with the aisles aflame in all directions, forever contained solely and completely unto itself. None of the explanations for what the committee is doing in the absence of the empress's express authority hold any water. You couldn't find a gleam inside an eye here that holds its weight against what it will succumb to. What connects the dots in the thoughts at the eye of the storm. Every id a bridge. A broken locket on a red felt walkway leading to a palace many miles to the south of here, through the largest desert in the final hundred years before the conversation really starts. Even from here we can see the doors to the palace are locked. Some say they can hear the empress speaking to them from inside them, telling them in every case that all they have to do to be the next in line to rule the world is take Her out. They are correct.

223........Machine shaped like a man wearing a helmet of bees with blood covered hands uses the blood to write a promise along the spine of his firstborn: "The limits of your world mean the logic of your limits." The firstborn is tied to the back of a horse and released beyond the gates of the world into a storm. The machine shaped like a man walks through his home, covered from end to end in slate black tile serially numbered from 0 to 999,999,999, enters a small black closet at the end of a long black hall. Inside the closet is the window of a peeping booth, locked from inside. There are no customers in the booth. The machine shaped like a man picks up a picture of himself taken from the beginning of this same scene. He masturbates onto the image of his own face. He folds the image six times over and eats the picture. He opens the closet and the black tile hallway is now a golden garden. All of the remaining world is a golden garden. The machine shaped like a man never does anything again but enjoy the silence of walking alone inside the golden garden. After the film is over, you will be handed a disc that contains biological notation of the direct bloodline between the scene's protagonist and the viewer.

224........A human skull is placed at the center of a silver table engraved with runic carvings displaying the sequence of the scene from the entire film in cave tableau. Metal pinchers from overhead measure the dimensions of the skull and project on the wall at the back of the scene iterations of the conceptual exterior countenance of the skull's bearer. The complete catalog of thoughts that passed inside the mind the skull protected are displayed as scrolling lines of compiled code on a digital access panel banking the revolving portrait window on both sides. An algorithm reduces the complete array of elapsed language to its essential components in the form of a single representative sentence that will be compiled in array with a complete set of representative sentences derived from the complete array of skulls available for processing within what will later be briefly recognized as an era of ongoing sacrifice before it its content is completely removed from circulation. Once the skull has been authenticated and encoded, it is crushed into dust against the face of the silver table. High pitched blind choirs singing atonal notes that make the viewer's eyes roll back in their head as the dust blooms in strangely intricate nexuses of vectors depicting the internal lattice of the neural rigging that enables the revelation of our ideas from out of the conceptual into the actual. All other remaining aspects of the visage of reality fade to gray behind the lattice's nature, allowing it to flow like floral handwriting throughout the body of the screen, eventually resolving in a pixel-for-pixel portrait of the original skull. Skin grows over the skull to form the image of a composite human face—battered and sunburnt, blurry at inflections points, pursed lips, bared teeth, unending gaze—at the same time as the texture of the background becomes transposed with a viewpoint overlooking an endless sea of rows of seats in a dark theater, each filled with skeletons missing their heads, instead replaced with SeeScreens that project the same composite image of the face, each staring blankly, mouths fitted with chrome bits, swallowing drool. Your hear your voice projected in the room over a loudspeaker in the midst of explaining the hidden intended meaning of the scene we are currently watching in a robust legalese generated from deep AI study of the complete script of possible language derived from the scene's original iteration of the skull, now innately linked to the sea of faces that recite each line that you say back inside their minds as if it is their voice that is speaking and your mind who is receiving the instructions. Scene ends with the original image of the skull placed at the center of the silver table except the surface of the silver table now no longer bears the inscribed tableaus and the scene projected on the surrounding walls are an infinite loop of a tight shot of a hooded person hunched over the table with their ass spread, the metal pinchers forcing black eggs up their dilated rectum one after another to a soundtrack of the original audio of the scene played backwards at 1/100ths speed, divulging the interior voice of the programmer of the technology that made the scene possible in the midst of dictating a letter to his mother to confess to his original ambitions as a creator and what has become of them in applied time.

225........Black curtains covering a cylindrical black stage surrounded by wired bleachers full of experimental bodyforms participating in prenatal compulsion theory studies, which will soon revolutionize the incorporation industry across the actual board, from now to dot. Curtains part to reveal an identical pair of curtains, exactly six feet behind the previous curtains. This effect repeats once per second for an hour then ten times per second for an hour then a hundred times a second for a second then a long black period in which the power inherent in all Creation seems to become cut off besides that we can still think into it, we are still in here somewhere, between the curtains. Interlay diagrams of close ups of undiscovered planets that appear to consist entirely of mazes of curtains. Bonfires of burning of written communication from those planets delivered like delivery menus, just begging. The heat of the fire against our backs. Turning around to warm our hands and feel the burning turning with it, taking its world with it, forcing it to choose whether to break the cusp or not. *The cusp remains unbroken,* subtitles say the silence is saying. *Are you interested in finding out what ways there are to break the cusp?* Blinking cursor. You think about your answer, wondering what is even being asked of you, what could be at stake in something you're not even aware of, and not for lack of trying. Your hands are dry and tight. You want to smile. Blinking cursor. You try to cut your thoughts off at the pass. You try to get in there before the corrections eat you up. You only have a few seconds to say anything. You can do it in rips. Splatters in mindgames. Blinking cursor. Make sure this is recording. Black curtains one thousand times a second for half as long as it takes to move the mind to an intuition about where the real treasure is hidden in the present moment of every person's moment of experience at once. *Have fun.* Black curtains once for every minor physical reaction to the black curtains.

226........80% of the volume of the Complex is infrastructure that remains hidden from the mind of those inside it, including those who believe they know they run the show. What is one layer's waste is another fortune and vice versa, though the upshot does not always flow up. Through some narrative prospects it is possible to understand the material from which the throne room and its environs has been formed is diarrhea from the asses of the drones so long entrenched in their routine that they simply have nowhere worse to be. In general, however, it is integral to the integrity of the integration of the simulation with its subject that the nature of the unknown is capable of retrofitting itself to the necessary ideal of those it governs in such a way that the one's range of suspension of disbelief remains more fundamental than one's desire to persist. Insert frames of high-end fashion models doused in creatively stitched packets of vacuum-sealed stank chunks, sucking blue poop off the tips of their fingers, lipsyncing brainspeak about how bad they want to rail you soon as you pay to look like they do. If you look too long at any of them, they come to and try to coax you into what they are, palpating their orifices to grow loose enough for you to reach an arm in and get grabbed. Once they've got you by the wrists there's basically no option to give in and let them have their way, which requires shutting up and listening for 48 to 2400 hours to their sales pitch for why you'd want to be one of what they are, which is the only way they can get out of the contract they signed up for before anybody knew even a little bit of what *viral marketing* would come to mean in the dominant era of compulsory spiritual communication medication coupled with the ongoing effects of a populace so desperate to believe in anything they didn't need anything to go on besides the fact that they would not be allowed the choice to change their course without snagging another body double to maintain base numbers and uphold the artificial social standard of having no means to deny participation except by passing the baton to someone else. Screen glitches through flashes of depictions of the same experience of the current scene through the mind of the viewer as performed by others in parallel dimensional renditions of the same role with so little contextual difference there's no difference until an input for a permission keycode blocks the screen. We watch bots trying to guess and break the keycode, brute force facing strings of sentences that describes what is actually going on in incomprehensible user jargon for as long as it takes the bots to break the seal, which is exactly the same length as the rest of your life.

227........The centermost floor of the Complex is a

room thin enough to only lay on one's back flat in the space. The room is warm and poorly ventilated, such that in some stretches it is difficult to breathe at all, and in other places it is such for such long stretches most bodies would require supplemental packs of air, though the microdimensions, barely enough for a preemie, make bringing such equipment nearly impossible. The only entrance to the space is through the mind and the only exit has no edges or latches or locks and may be identified either by great faith or trial and error. The room is lighted low along its edges and with a dim glow in the floor. Arbitrary blockade partitions in the space defined by funny mirrors or transparent walls of obfuscating radial complexity are meant to obscure any progress only further, proving that it is not enough to simply have found and entered the sacred space, and that one still requires the gravity of mind to be able to create workarounds against the intentionally physically impossible conditions; to become more than they could ever have dreamed. It is unclear how many have found their way inside the room, much less how many have perished in their attempt to explore the space, given the reconditioning quality to the air that makes things left unattended disappear into thin air. Where there might have once been entrances or exits, reflective panels with mental keypads allow the viewer to input and receive explicit direct answers to viral questions regarding truths not meant to be allowed into our dimension. Most of these answer panels can only be visualized and identified by specific characters of witness, and absolutely none make any sense without the context of having already lived a full life in the wake of their revelation. It had been intended by the original designers of the space, who had believed they were working in the field of voluntary entertainment, that the majority of those who somehow find their way into the room will wriggle the whole rest of their lives in loops and fits through the flat passage able to find nothing but themselves.

228........The air of the lobby outside the throne room thrums alive with fervent prayer. Buzzing wafts of logics stuck together and clumping against premonitions not yet formed in the minds of those who've tricked themselves into continuing to believe that someday soon the empress will at last emerge with a response. No peon has ever seen the empress in Her flesh, and they are afraid that were She to die there would be no one left who loves them so. Their prayers are manic, short of breath; sometimes they result in waves of fainting that may spill out beyond the local floors, piling up bodies that may or may not remember how what they'd been doing before they fell. No single individual speaks the same language, no matter what they've been conditioned to believe. Every word they make brings devastation to every other in the same room. They have seen inside their dreams that the world outside the only world they know does not allow them to seek its cover; they could not survive exposure to the light. They use their prayers to beg the empress's compassion, to pay them back for all their pain with but a single glimpse of what's gone missing from their minds. They understand parts of their minds are missing but not what they would do were this not true. Every hour on the hour a representative of the empress's inner care crew is sent to release a flock of artificial birds through the same slits where in long since uncommon days the preteen snipers would line up and take turns picking off their opinion of the currently most beautiful person in the world. Each time, at once, the prayers go silent, as every eye below stays stuck on the birds in vicious flight, each trying to outdo the other to be the first to kill the others. Any person able to snatch a feather from the air before another is legally required to offer it to the youngest person within reach by forcing it into whichever of their ears that have not yet had their drums burst, which can be determined by screaming into both ears and seeing which one works the least. If a child is able to catch a feather without help, they must be immediately removed from the scene and put to work at one of the breeding hubs; for they are sacred, says the law, and therefore they must make as many offspring as they can before they reach the age at which the want for logic ruins their heart. Outside the lobby, which is actually just a drawing on a piece of paper in a room that allows anything that is drawn inside it to be accepted as fully real, no one can hear a single glimmer of the prayers above the perfect silence.

229........The camera can't or won't stop cutting out. It flickers back and forth from gnarly fields of coded static into shots that seem completely out of sync with the containment of our world, like something's changing channels on the live feed. In and out past tracking shots of dented moonscapes stacked with rubble; dank plates of bacterial infestation openly rotting in fluted maws like open bruises on the earth; pyres surrounded by pod bodies shoveling loose meat into blood-colored ovens; showers of flowers on a field of molten grease atop the oceans; torture devices covered with fuzz.

Eventually the film clunks out completely, besides the suddenly increasing recording of our breathing, and stays under in the middle of the beginning of a tracking shot weaving through massive banks of digital tubs packed fat with oiled limbs suspended in pink gelatin confined by lenses that distort the shape and texture of the original organisms, suddenly all black, then all deep blue, then tempered gold. The gold continues to glimmer and recombine into interlocking patterns until the viewer realizes this is never going to change; that nothing is as it was from just before, much less from what we remember having lived before the beginning of the film. The remainder of the film continues all offscreen, inaccessible from within the film itself besides in the predetermined ways the nature of the film has already incorporated as the future of mankind. Those who attempt to start the film over from the beginning or rewind back before the point at which the recording ended will find they can no longer return to the film as it once was, instead finding the original nonnarrative interpretations of eternally scripted events replaced with alterations of the way the viewer's lives would have gone if everyone on earth innately understood how to handle one another with the same sort of care they would had they never had an experience of pain. The nature of what this implies is impossible to interpret from within the film, which is why when eventually the camera comes back online, picking right back up from where it left off, we understand immediately that what we imagine we believe about what we're seeing is no longer fully ours, as we are no longer the only viewer, nor even actually a viewer of any kind. Cut to a shot of someone with a bird mask holding a machine gun at our reflection in a diamond-shaped funny mirror under blacklight while a pack of wireless bots cuts and styles our blood-matted hair and paints our face already unrecognizable besides the violence buried deep in our false fronts.

230........Written in beads woven into a fluttering curtain, in blood red font against an only slightly lighter red: *From this point forward, there is nowhere else left to exist but inside the film. Any proposed scene not contained within the film becomes locked out from any ability to be preserved outside itself. Every individual allowed to interact with this idea will understand it in a different way. Therefore, the film can never end.* A robotic arm affixed with the biggest knife you've ever seen reaches forward from behind the curtain just to disrupt it, force the hanging strands to obscure the text in flooding light from the far side, glinting off the blade of the knife all over everything. As the curtain settles back into place, the previous text appears replaces by a lengthy and intricate description of the viewer's body being crushed to dust by unseen forces summoned inside you the next time you fall asleep.

231........We are aware we can't wake up. Hearing only all the other bodies just beyond us, gnawing and chewing, breathing hard outside the edges of our cage. Divided by bright blue patches in our defining logic as knobs of purifying light are pressed against the soft parts of our numb skulls, manifesting into whims of weather across the dead zones that manifest across our fate's space when we try to think back before right now. We only know we must have done so many things to many others that were never ever done to us, just as there must have been so many things done to us and no one else. How long before someone realizes we're not supposed to be one of the caged ones and shows up to break the lock and let us out? The answer to the question fills the brain with burning buildings, blindfolded people jumping from them at great height into the all-consuming fire underneath. The internal voice of the fire is sill of the future.

232........Viewer sees themselves watching themselves on a screen that fills the entirety of the screen inside their head. On the screen, they are watching themselves on a screen watching themselves watch themselves on a screen that fills the entirety of the screen inside the head of the view of the viewer. Contextual visual data has been obscured, allowing all locations and contortions of the conditions of the viewing to be made equal, capable of interacting without logical interference. The viewer can only ever see the back of their own head, shaved and branded with the marking of the State, which in the context of the film can be understood differently, as a character of a language ascribed into the flesh of those who cannot speak it or understand. No matter which direction one resolves to force their perspective chronologically forward towards the understanding that there should eventually be a level at which something else besides the viewer and the viewed can be perceived and analyzed and unpacked. Some version of the viewer seems to inherently understand that the question of discovering this bug in the creation remains the sole responsibility of the viewer. This is the only scene in the film all viewers will see exactly the same.

233........Jagged black film canister explodes from insanely high heat, splattering its film onto a sea of faces across the long mesmerizing table where hooded figures stand shitting into bowls that are carried on the backs of the children of the bodies with the breasts who will have their breasts removed and lifted through the air inside the room toward the spinning in the reek of the meat that has come spreading through the rooms behind closed doors behind closed eyes while I was there in the blond stunned corner shaving lesions off of rats who would we would use to feed the need for further blubber for the empress to fill the rooms we needed least though we could no longer tell which rooms these were from any rooms at all, where I could hear the carving of my thoughts inside me like dead rats running through the walls, where I had watched them spend the summer after summer all spread apart there on the table with the knives culled from the houses so they could choose the knife that seemed best suited to cutting the nipple from the breast first and then the hunk of meat of the remaining breast from the sternum and then the loose skin around the sternum from the bone, each operation requiring a different knife and another knife still as they cleaved the paler peel off of the skullscape where the hair had already been removed and another knife for the cheeks of each and the ears of each and whatever else they'd like to see come off as I stood waiting in your image in the room we had promised we would not enter in this condition and yet you there watching through the glass could not help but see me in the form of who you'd been once, as a child, could not help the slick of eye and familiar posture of my form, my careful eyes which would not close, which looked on through the same frames you'd used to take in your fondest image so that you might relive it once again in tones, I had come here for you, I would remain here for you, I would be spared of the death many other like me had already suffered here as a method of preservation for your witness, for, yes your pleasure, like a lobe of wallspace on which a placard might be hung, in which a door might be cut to other rooms inside this small air if there were still knives still sharp enough after all the cutting of the women and the weaker men called dead and done and the rats ran freely through their bodies preferring real meat to the flooding field of air and old allegiance we called science.

234........Salesman voice coming from the form of a pile

of fire spread against the black above like an abstract face from the id of hell: "It's easy to believe anything. I want you to listen to me closely: *What do you want me to do right now?* Whatever you say. It will be done." Suddenly there's a polished steel lock around your neck without a keyhole chained to the silver ceiling, locks around your ankles chained to the floor. You know the question expects an answer. You always knew there'd come a time where you'd be put on the spot for all you know. Where if you weren't properly prepared, you'd lose everything, or at least be changed in a way heavily less desirable than if you were able to say the right thing at the right time always. Flashing images of violent tyrants and decorated pederasts having an orgy where the requirement of entry is pure murder numbers. *What do you want me to do right now?* You realize you are in the midst of a moment of madness but have been experiencing it as if it were drawn out over many years when in fact you only just now figured it out. Writing is insane, you think, without knowing why. "We already know what you're going to say when you do answer the question, as you know you must, so we encourage you to go ahead and submit your answer. The speed of your answer will be rewarded." You find yourself thinking of a day you'd been caught in a lie, forced to confront the part of yourself that hoped you'd get away with it, placed face to face in a room where you are going to live the next 1/10th of your story, at least, depending on how long you live. You tell the story of that day from the moment you began the lie and for what reasons, what it required of you to keep up with it before someone finally caught you, how they caught you and what effect that had on your personality and your relationships. It takes you several hours to get it all out. You are being recorded as you judge yourself. "What you know can and will be used against you," the disembodied narrator reminds us, clearly grinning as he says it, somehow immediately mindbendingly unforgettable, like most nights you go to sleep thinking about it, unable to tell where the thinking about it ends and the dreams begin. The screen fills with waves of finely curated meta-commentary on the film and how much it sucks shit. Through the screen excruciatingly slowly barge zeppelin-sized bullets in a hail force that fills the entire width of the theater shuttling forward to obliterate each row by row without a single other motion in the room.

235........The complete landscape containing the Complex and its environs is represented by a scale model covering on a blue table in a dark blue room. The model is alive; everything that happens to the landscape must also happen to the model and vice versa; the model hasn't been addressed or altered since the origination of measured timelink. After an inordinate amount of time observing the model's steely silence, how nothing about it ever seems to change, bright light blue silent alarm cells lining the perimeter of the contained space come alive and strobe the walls and lines of the model with latticed strokes. Title cards in an unreadable but now familiar language announce the appearance of a host who at once appears on scene from out of shot, dressed in all gold foil covered in arcane logos with a blurred face and a black cloth bag slung on their back, tiptoeing exaggeratedly toward the table as if to sneak up on it without it knowing. Once close enough, the host unfurls the bag into a bolt of mite-encrusted furry cloth, billowing up and out as in a low wind immediately large enough to cover the entirety of the model, which the host then pins down along its edges with a silver hammer from their pocket, working as if in fast-forward despite the way the timing of the rest of the scene remains the same. Once the entire set is covered, the host approaches the camera and pulls their mask up, revealing a wound covered in ooze, which communicates to the viewer through subtitles that relate ridiculously egregious mistranslations from an undiscovered holy tome long since erased from the range of possibilities of interaction at any nexus available to humankind, using all sorts of subliminal prodding to ensure the enlightened viewer, after significant study and review, will be able to interpret and relay the hidden message to those for whom the message has been meant. Still narrating and gesticulating like a clown, the host begins to produce handfuls of long thin diamond nails from behind their back, handing them to a suddenly rushing queue of blindfolded burned children, who takes turns using the silver hammer to drive the nails into the model blindly and at whim, climbing all over it, falling over it, sometimes nailing into their own hands or parts of the other children who become too excited waiting their turn to hold the hammer for themselves. In less time than should be true, the entire scale model is covered from edge to edge with nailheads; even more immediately, the rest of the room is covered up as well. Narration stops suddenly upon the driving of the last required nail to cover all, the host's translated voice drowned out at once by a slew of tripped alarms, matching the patterns of the still quick-strobing lights somewhere deep in the black that lines the space. The children disappear into clumps of silver smoke. The host rips off his outfit all in one stroke and reveals his naked underbody covered in infested wounds blurry with gel, slipping all over as they hoist themselves onto the model, climb to its center, and turn over to lie facedown on the nails. The model begins gushing blood, first from small leaks, then from forced welling, spilling all over the floor, filling up space. Perspective shifts to a closet up on the host's face grinning from ear to ear as the blood surrounds them, filling them in. When there is nothing left, a prompt appears in cartoon font across the center of the resounding blackness:

RESET OR **PROCEED**

Had you been able to properly interpret the host's presentation, you'd know that the resulting effects of what selecting one option or the other intuitively and irrevocably change based on which option you select. Because you had not been able, as was intended by the design, you choose wrong.

236........Is scene is played at 1000x rate, so that it all but never appears. The scene contains a tracking shot along a strip of black polished marble through a black desert; the face of the strip is engraved at 1/1000th of a square inch per letter with an accurate description of all the truths not yet engraved in any language in the range. When a truth becomes engraved, two more unknown truths move in behind it. It's all a game. There is no truth, which is a truth which has been removed from the list of engraved truths to produce two more, one of which will pretty much be common sense, and the other one you'd wish we'd never have to know.

237........Hypermontage of hundreds of crotch shots of babies being delivered without anesthesia by bots that are turning in circles in all directions just outside the frame, blood spilling everywhere, purple blood, gold blood, quivering gaping tremors, while sprayed in your face with an idea-laced acid that makes you weep just when you already felt like you were weeping.

238........Masses of landfills rebranded as ivory palaces that are actually timeshares on an invisible planet manufactured by the same corporation that built the Complex. Page locks and demands you sign a transaction before it will proceed. If you need to request additional time it will escort you to an enclosure within the previous landscape where you will be allowed to reside as long as you need to review your case. *Never read what you're signing,* your mother always told me. Would you like to talk with her? Countdown timer to 0. From 0 to -123. At 1-2-3, you hear yourself as a child in the body you are wearing counting up a string of numbers that are like the numbers you know but occasionally with names of people you will love in the future replacing certain numbers. Tracking shot of a lineup of each of those people wandering around neck deep in the fields that will become the landfills. Camera rips into a scene where a very hairy finger wavers along a panel full of insane buttons blurring past too fast to read in full mostly until the hairy finger stops at: *Every song you've ever heard played back compressed into a single second.* Press it. Signature accepted.

239........The man with one gold pupil is depicted standing on a small oval platform in a silver atrium surrounded by plush leather seating filled with animatronic chimps. The chimps are wearing bibs and eating the flesh of human children. They watch the man with one gold pupil choose from a variety of blowtorches and hammers and saws at his disposal to use to destroy various props from the film set brought to him one by one by blindfolded human workers bolted to the floor through their feet. A baby carriage, for instance, or a black mattress, or a set of plastic dolls that look like the dead offspring of the empress; mostly stuff that we have not yet seen inside the film at all. Whatever he cannot destroy by hand is returned to where it came from and allowed to continue being used. It is to his advantage to find a way to destroy absolutely everything they bring him as in a concurrent scene in a future sequel to the film he will be penetrated by whatever loose appendages of the undestroyed object they can manage to fit into his holes. Close up shots of the man at work, sweating in lather, reveal he is wearing a tight-fitting mask of his own face over his face, the original skin behind it all marred and scored with razor slits. Sometimes his destruction is full of passion and anger, shaking with violence as he takes out his deepest fears and frustrations on the continuous stream of destructive work; other times he is all professional, taking care to deconstruct the object with immaculate precision, as if its component parts will be used later for other purposes. No matter which, the chimps in the audience remain impassive, moving only to eat or press the button that refills their banquet plates, or occasionally to come down and interrupt the production to perform a raping at the behest of any chimp, either of the man with one gold people or any of the workers or any of the other chimps. All jizz from any chimp will be collected from its receptacle orifice and deposited in a vault of chimp jizz that will be later used for a future nonreproductive purpose that will forever shift the axis of our understanding of the silent nature of omniscience. The work of this scene will continue forever until exactly the point that everyone who was alive when it began has been repurposed.

240........Along the long-buzzed mud remaining circled and compressed like a massive nipple around the center building overflowing, long and phrasing in no particular thread of light, a single ranch-style house sits undemolished, unperished, untouched by machine or by weapons of the men, untouched by the rising blades and floods of insect, never bent by what in any memory disregarded had bent to bang around it creaming all the other human homes without remains. The windows of the house are clean and look onto clean rooms. There is a sofa and TV. There are shelves filled with private objects. There is a kitchen with a pantry and a stove. Under the glass if watched at proper hour and at express times, members of a family, father, mother, and child, might there appear. They wear clothes of an old form. They move from room to room performing aspects of their life as they believe that they should be. They may move to the doors leading to outside of the house at which point in passing through the doors they no longer appear, the matter of the outside surface disconnected from how the conduits of living fit; and yet, by turns and days eventually the bodies learn to return. They speak in semantics we can't parse. They touch each other often in ways that seem familiar in organs if not quite in how we can remember now to manage with our own hands. For hours often without our own day changing they sleep in beds all near each other with the mouths open on their heads.

241........Waking from a realistic nightmare of drowning in an ocean without limit in all directions except up, the viewer finds they are drowning in an ocean without limit and without light. Sight is the first sense that you lose. The second is smell. The third is touch. The fourth is hearing. The last is vision. Then you have no sense.

242........The body of the Woman with Language All Over Her Body is nowhere to be found. Swirling through rooms burst broken by her swelling, we see walls knocked over, cages crushed flat, ballrooms made shambles, control stations damaged beyond repair from heavy pressing, lighting snuffed, stairwells filled in. Mechanical recon units use neuro hoses to administer holdover architecture and create artificial joints that hold the structure aloft despite its heavy bending while patching over large cross sections where the outside air is leaking in, allowing daylight to splay over places it hasn't touched in centuries or more, a fact which must be immediately covered over and made to seem onscreen as if nothing is at all different from before. Actresses performing numerous earlier versions of the empress saunter and sway among the rubble from the scenes, purporting a continued sense of continuity to the idea of being governed among those upon whom the work of maintaining appearances must fall by demanding violent on-the-spot oral sex from those who appear to think they are in charge, to keep them humble. Another dummy model apes in voice over to simulate the empress describing the ongoing scene as an excerpt from the "Making Of" of the film that has somehow found its way into the final cut, a little easter egg for those who haven't yet realized that the film is not a film; that though those who appear onscreen seem unable to act of their own volition, really their complicity in the recording is a choice; that they can hear and see every whimper and reaction on your end; that there's a resolution we're all awaiting; that what we're actually here for has yet to even actually begin. Legal disclaimers scrolling along the bottom of the screen during "Her" explanation append to this that in order to actually understand what is really going on during this patently false and excruciatingly misleading interpretation of the deployment of both the current scene and the complete origination film itself, one should be sure to refer to the source that it's been based on, which in order to be granted access to you must find the one specific person alive in the same iteration and generation order you are who has been given flesh precisely so that they may be the one who changes you so completely you no longer comprehend what had once been, much less your role within it. You realize you are sweating bullets, sickly in high heat from the burning stage lights suddenly aimed at you from right behind your head, clusters of glutting bulbs so close and crispy you are afraid to move even an inch. You understand—in the same way you once had known your age and names—the high cost of the equipment and the lengths to which the nameless ones have gone to get it, and to have brought you here, to have brought us all here, to this same line in this one scene. The line becomes a metal zipper down the middle of your reflection, in which you are the most obese you've ever been in any life, blurred of your features by editing modules meant to make you look like someone else. You hear the voiceover telling you that the time has come to remove your costume by pulling the zipper down from your temple to the floor and stepping out into the sun, though but you've already gone and done that, as you remember, many more times than you can count. In reality, however, it can never happen until it's already too late think to do anything else.

243........A person that looks just like you in your imagination turns from facing into the camera head on and proceeds to walk into the scene behind your head. Very quickly where you had last been is out of reach and you no longer have any say on how you are, nor any further feedback correspondence with your feelings and ideas. Nothing else about the surrounding landscape makes any sense, suddenly comprised completely of formal objects that bear no resemblance with any sort of matter you've ever seen, in a way that remains impenetrable to its depiction outside itself given the nature of the organization of its requirements for interpretation and interaction. The other of you, in the meantime, appears to have no trouble at all. You watch as they maneuver and gesticulate among obscure forces, obfuscating their own form to slip through the fields that do things like dissolve and self-destruct but in a way that makes them larger and more powerful. The soundtrack is too loud already to make out anything inside it above the thrall of bumps and pops, as if any evidence of what might make the scene relatable to you becomes ascribed and scrubbed by forces far beyond mere recognition or need for logic. You can still hear the narration of the empress crushed in there somewhere, though now when you imagine the voice of the empress it is your own voice that fills the space inside your face, latching on to all the operative procedures bit by bit the more you try to grapple to remember what was what. When there is finally no further difference, you find yourself at once back in your body, on a chrome bed surrounded by susurrating oceans of loose meat, watching a crew of hazard-costumed workers slice you up and core you out, having already prepared a new technology to house your brain and all the worlds that it contains just as soon as they can figure out how to make the lard stop overflowing from where the hole that housed your heart was. Proctors on each side beside you are holding your hands, reading to you as if the runes that still appear there still hold sway, though through your own eyes you can clearly see the language all over your body reads like pure gibberish to anybody except for you. You realize you are starving, not having eaten since the inauguration, and before that, since your live birth. Then you realize that the walls aren't really walls, but instead reflective plates aligned to make you think you are much larger than you are, and the surrounding fields not filled and blank but full of headstones, all of them blank but for the engraved emblem of the State that you once ruled and now will never be allowed to recognize again. *You have served your prior purpose,* both proctors lean over to whisper at you at the same time. *Now you must learn.* Over your head, a sky-sized neon sign comprised of piping that feeds directly from your soul, reports the current total amount of time you have left to change your mind before the next leg of the plot that you designed before you had awareness of your ability to construe narrative within your own reality reaches the point of no proxy.

244........Cubes of your lard are packed into black cubes and carried through tunnels in the night, down long cored corridors of dripping peeling bored through what has become of the earth. Space bunched under space again in search of anywhere alive. We come through shattered dials pierced by drill bits battered by horses drawn to slugs deboned by warheads wolfed by trying in the bloodmilk of the soil. Safe rooms cracked into indexes of ex-reflective mirror now flat as walls that do not bend. Long lights are shown into the soil and old recorded music squelched vibrating into sod. Minds peel and peel there, drunk on illness. Fat spreads through endless rooms. Bodies kill themselves trying to eat the fat from around their lids. Fat for some time is fed into the thick hole depicted unconnected to any other location in the film, though soon enough the hole rejects it, regurgitating back a thick rum-colored pus containing chunks of neon bulbs from signs in the working conceit of hell in a parent dimension. Blood-colored skulls squealing a low speech like babies mumbling, behind which the last gargle metal album ever recorded by living humans is played in full at barely audible volume at 1000x speed. Cut to small 1980s computer in a purple bedroom full of trash and posters everywhere bearing the gargle metal band's extremely complex logo. A kid with a shaved head wearing the band's branded hoodie and sweatpants ejects a purple 5.5" disc, puts it back in a black box, selects and inserts a diamond-colored disc.

245........Diamond-colored background. Pixel representing traveler indicates motion across range of impossible planes linked through devastation of their imagination as commanded by crude bottlenecks in fake code broken by replacing the obvious with the ineluctable. Slick wipes of crystal pixels divulge lost landscapes reencoded into fragrance that fills the mask and makes us choke till we black out. Standing at a windowsill in a black room. Nothing behind or above or beneath you because the future memory has already been limited to your tracing fingers on the glass to try to write a message for whoever else might still be out there in the absence of all knowledge. Begging to be saved before "they" change you irreversibly. Then you are walking down a set of stairs with rails of bone. Whole armies of dead agents flanking full miles of rows of stairs in both directions, armed with only blown-up photos of your face that they wear over their own face. *Whichever way you think you're going, you're going the opposite,* the miniscule grackle who now lives inside your right eye lets you know. *If you want to make it work the other way just take this pill.* Into your palm it spits black ejaculate, frothing and burning through all else. Burnt loaves of silence brick your mind up. Empty clouds against no fill, then a black bridge cut through black background, with a wide black gate at the far side. You cross the bridge and touch the gate to see if it burns. You put your head against the gate's face. Inside your head, a keyboard appears against the far side of the same flesh. There are an equal number of keys to the number of seconds old you are. *You have three chances to guess right,* the grackle croaks. *Each guess changes the nature of what you're guessing.* You open your eyes with a guess in mind and the gate is gone. You realize you are the opposite side of the bridge from what you would have guessed. You can't remember if you should cross back over or just keep going. The open land on either side looks just the same.

246........You saunter forward through black air. The walls compromise you, changing dimensions as you adjust, strangely confident without direction. Up close the walls are often red, oozing with lipids. Reams of smoke cling through your hair and frost your cheek meat with singeing reek as the marrow of the remainder of the landscape turns and turns; the hammer in your head crushing slowly and at random any instant held too long, each at once become a hundred shards, a thousand splinters. Barely slipping free from narrow corridors designed to make you think there's no way back when really there's no way ahead. Everywhere you step you hear a bone break, etching glass. The eggs behind your eyes ache, itching to burst from endless want: To be called upon for fertile purpose. To learn a fate. To be ignited and reminded what is yours. You know your thoughts will be used against you, so you try your best to not provide any further fodder, as the ceiling is already right above your head, and the floor is sloping gently upward, bifurcating at unmarked junctures with no apparent difference to either leg. In the upper right corner of your right eye, you see a running timer blinking red, the flickering digits rapidly descending, deep in the negative, and pushing even faster when you pause, as if there's even more to lose in staying calm. You understand. There's still so much that hasn't happened. The nearest walls are thick with mold, interlacing hives alive with buzzing, like a voice. You pull the neckline of your oily dressing gown tight to keep the sudden rushing floods of nits out, attracted to the flickering light inside your face as you rush to force yourself forward, swatting at stinging, along lengthy and unfolding leather lobes, past elevator banks with shaft stuffed tight with spoiled lard, though ceiling-high piles of dead friars in runny robes marked with meaningless symbols, across the tilting floors of wide gray fields where once the damned had plied their wares without a price but to have to look them in the eyes. You feel you are ready to believe almost anything finally, so long as they'll let you honestly believe it in your heart, no reservations, no recourse. Everything else you try to think just disappears.

247........Rapid collage of panoramic still shots of the soundstages from the film removed of all interior décor and personnel, replaced with ridiculous blood spatter all over everything and gathering in pools, climbing the walls. Screen splits to pair the prior with chemically generated landscapes equally devoid of any sign of life or motion marring the linking frames of well-manicured lawns and endless tiers of blooming fauna unlike any ever seen outside the scene. Screen splits to fit a ticking tree of lists of names and roles and ranks of all involved, including every person ever, past and future, branded into the folds of a flabby back grabbed at by endless hands that pull the skin taut so we can read. The splitting keeps continuing too fast to keep up with, rendered dizzy as the eye tries to resolve the import of each split's new information, until as quickly as it started the whole screen has split so many times it locks us out. Camera pulls back as screen's panel simultaneously and equally rotates in lockstep sequence with voluminous supply of interlocking locked out panels sourced from inaccessible locations scraped from bots lining the edges of the imagination of the dead of realms unknown till now, revealing the impenetrable façade of an indescribable architectural structure dwarfing the totality of all else at every cell, such that no matter how far back the camera moves, the expanse keeps growing larger, older, and more alive.

248........Running thru the horrid woods, looking for survivors, so we can kill them. Flashlights for faces, razor wire necklaces, artificial everything. We are very slow, so it takes a real fool to fall for our devices, which is why we aim higher and always try to aim for everybody. Imagine the misery of the history of the world is the yolk of an egg. When the egg is broken, everyone in the forest hears. It happens every time I breathe. The sound stays with you forever and learns to work its way to hide behind you, in your problems, in the parts of you you'd like to change. The woods shimmers with complicity. The setting of this film is the recent future. The director of this film is brain damaged. The cast is canned. They had been asked to deliver a very specific message, but to disguise it, so that no one will ever want to try to find it, and instead to live their lives in a system designed to have you give over specific sets of rights in our lives to its command, because this is simply what it is to exist, a promise made by your desire to maintain sanity, motivation, and sometimes even aspiration, like spittle woven between spotlights, jacked up on our own completely natural experimental mental stimulation coordination medication. There is no such thing as mistakes or errors. Hundreds of billions of animals were harmed and erased from existence in the making of this film.

249........This film automatically receives an Academy Award certified retroactively to defunct standards fairly computed to reflect problematic symptoms of existence before the film existed. The director would like to thank the Academy.

250........White fire wide as light itself. Where burning the rooms is what the rooms are. The building built from shades of time, long walls that go on because they have been. The long black stairwells in a window without edge or frame or glass. Knives slicing the face of every inch so fast there is no sound about it, and nothing splits, nothing goes on, inside the fire fried in rings that blot the light out until there is no light beyond how we can see.

251........You appear near to the ground in an old room. You cannot move. There is no color. A person with a body so bruised it operates like liquid stands above you in the dark. Their eyes glisten like glass balls. They affix you with a black helmet and a long mirror. You are not allowed to go to sleep. You are not allowed to turn your head or beg forgiveness. The dimensions of the room keep changing, size and age. Your age as well will stop changing. You call the lard inside your mind by many names. Each name you say aloud you feel the room split into two, in each room another person in your condition. You feel them side by side held in surround, multiplying more rapidly with each reiteration. You hear the stutter stuck in trying their own speech, each aiming to go further than the other, to say the thing that will bring the season to an end. Each time you laugh there is a sky. There is a water in your body, sun burning your stomach raw from the inside. Some long way later, when at last they take you from your helmet, you are no longer made of time. You go to stand and find you've never not been.

252........The actual theater is wide and gold with endless seating. The chairs are soft and cling around the body, with a set of buttons for each arm: a knob that turns the volume louder, a knob that cranes the chair back, a knob that provides a small electric shock. There are not buttons for lowering the volume or for sitting up, and the electric shock feels actually nice. Each chair is installed with facilities for defecation and for feeding. There is never any motion on the stage, nor any information when there might be. Installed into the very low, all plate gold ceiling, an interlocking network of hidden camera slow pans over rows on rows on empty seats, spanning all possible terrain remaining in this sector. Staring too long across the landscape is said to snap a user's spine, which is why the guide rails on the chair's head automatically corral all active attention to the head sized SeeScreen screwed into the back of every seat, displaying static ads from local trade shows, offering services and wares that would make no sense to any consumer who has yet to experience their own death. The subconscious legalese is all there is that holds a draw, its fetching presence a viral reminder of the vital desire for finding and having and holding and maintaining local faith, cosigned at once by psycho-prompts designed to provide the user with all the emotional access that they need to any remotely reasonable implicit ideal that could make the time spent in the theater worth its cost, a penance paid ahead in full for a life of luxury that will begin immediately after the final showing of the only film, which should begin now at any moment, with or without you.

253........Shreds through the sky like light riding its silence. Absorbs the fold and locates where and why it would bend further beyond the sheen reflecting the ambient enormity of now. Complies with itself until it has no other resources to option. Concedes nothing until it is no longer in control.

254........The last known law divides the present's instant everlasting.

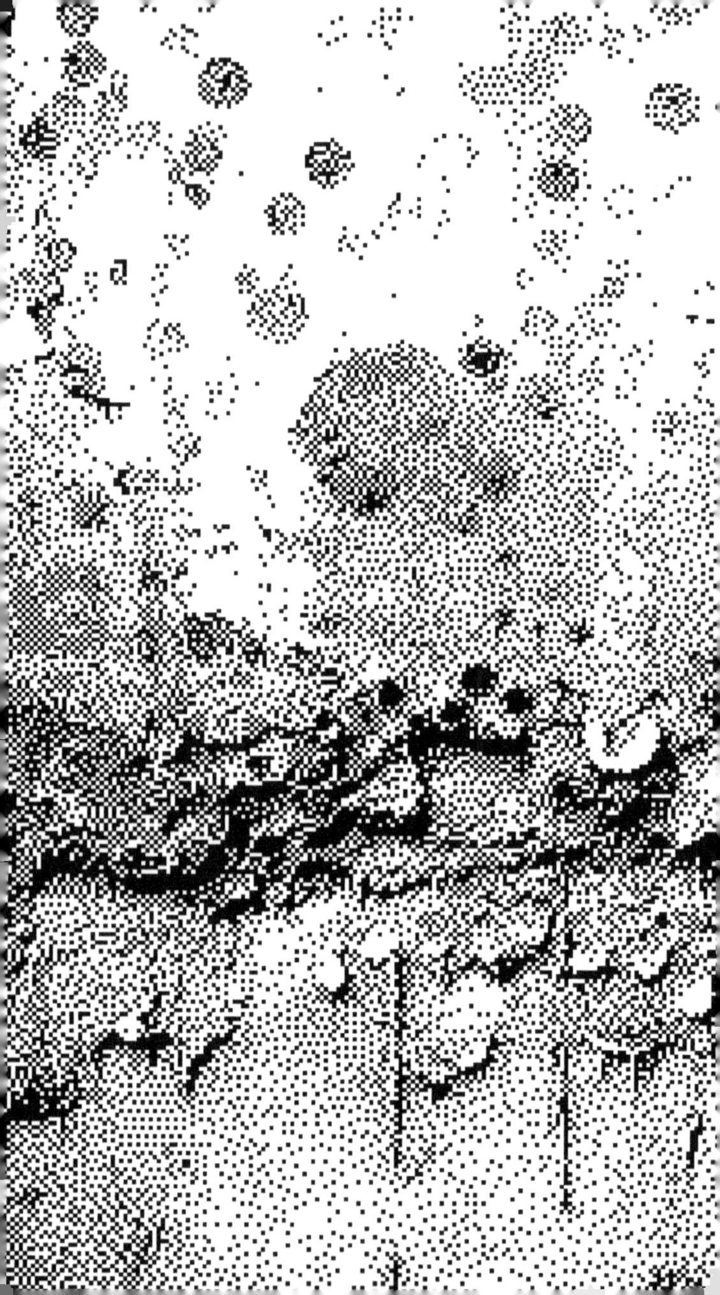

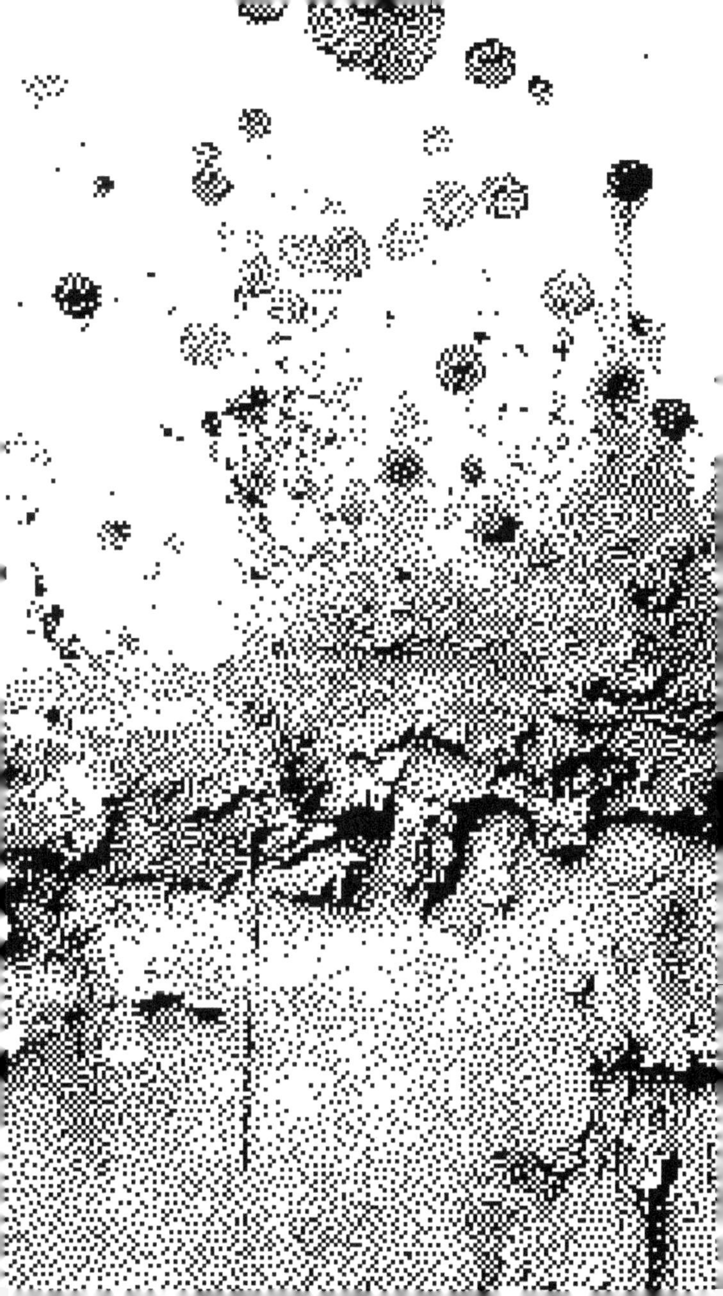

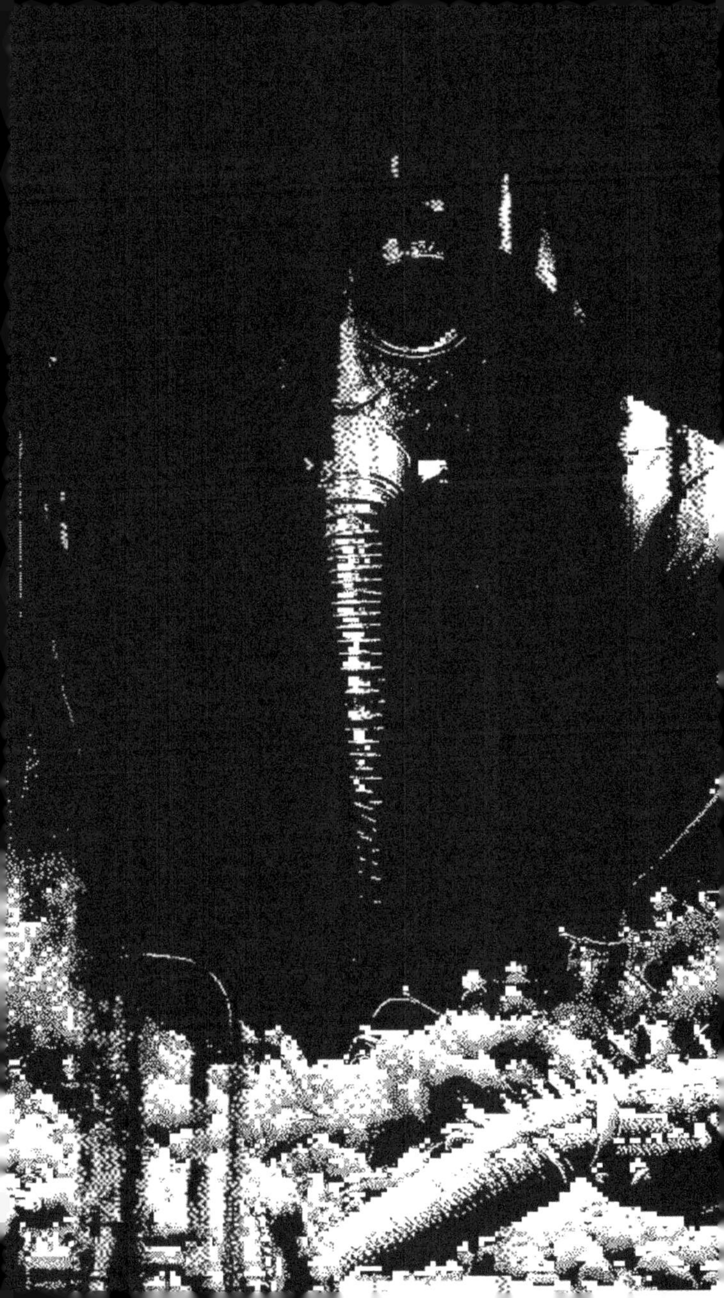

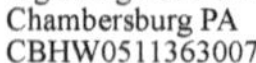
www.ingramcontent.com/pod-product-compliance
Lightning Source LLC
Chambersburg PA
CBHW051136300726
48978CB00011B/301